The Memory of Blood

Book designed and typeset by Victoria Heath Silk
Cover photography by Pony Louder

ISBN 978-1-7396336-0-8 – Ebook
ISBN 978-1-7396336-1-5 – Paperback

www.ponylouder.com

THE MEMORY OF BLOOD

PONY LOUDER

Louder books

'The way we view our past affects how we see our present and shapes our future'

Dr Janina Ramirez, University of Oxford

For Chel
With love, and a boat

GREY

It's always different, and it always feels the same.
From the darkness comes the light.

Dawn is a sharp blade, cutting right to the heart of my aloneness.
From the rich inkiness comes a tender smudge of blue.
So sure of itself.
Like it had never seen a war. Like all the blood had never flowed.
Like everything that comes together doesn't fall apart.
And, like any drab-winged insect, I'm irresistibly drawn back to
the shining.

Where a story starts isn't easy to pinpoint. Beginnings tangle,
wrapping like vines, and everything is connected.
Nothing exists in isolation.

What I do remember watching was a young girl...

MINA

Late September 1811, England,
Home

Shoes are an odd thing. There's a lot to be said for having the world under your feet rather than a piece of old leather. It was a long time before I could decide whether shoes were help or hindrance. Maybe I came to them too late. I'd had eleven winters before I could wear the pair they'd taken from Mama after she passed. Even then I needed to fill the toes with twisted hay and wrap rags around my heels to keep them from sliding loose. They flapped about my feet like a pair of chained crows. Noisy and blister-making whenever I walked with any sense of purpose, but I persisted, out of respect for our dear mother, and in the hope that one day I might fill them.

I was in Mama's shoes when they came for me. The milking shed door flung open, hands on me, tearing my dress. Like a bad wind roaring in, it happened so fast. There was no time for goodbye, no chance to comfort Billy.

In one cold rush, the whole world I knew, all that I loved, all that I understood, was gone.

Only it wasn't a wind, and it wasn't the farm being dragged away. It was me.

We had woken that morning to frosty half-circles on the window panes. Winter's bony fingers inching across the skies a good month earlier than usual. I'd dressed Billy quickly, hurrying to keep the bed warmth on his body before seeing to the fire.

Next there was the cow to see. She didn't take long to milk so I'd not bothered with my own coat. Stepping outside, the sweet peatiness of fallen leaves wound out from the woods. Dew shone across the grass, making gems of a spider's web strung across the porch. Billy swished his feet across the silvery lawn, giggling and puffing tiny clouds as we made our way to the cowshed.

I knew to listen for the sounds of change, and I'd noticed the hushed birdsong. But instead of early warning, I'd taken the stillness around us as more sign the year was turning: the last of summer's swallows on the wing.

There had been talk of missing children. Some months before, word had trickled through. No child we knew. No families from the village. It was a shadowy thing: the taking of children, something spoken of in hushed tones. Fireside tales told long after dark. It was not something that happened to us. Not something that happened in daylight.

But whether the danger felt real, Papa's instructions were.

'Listen out, keep Billy close,' he'd told me clear enough. 'Be ready to run. Into the forest, you'll have a chance there. If they come and I'm not here, run for the trees and hide.'

In the cowshed Billy had been talking about blackberries.

Before they came, he'd been standing neatly beside the cow, and always in her view, like I'd taught him. His small hand absently patting her neck, as he explained why we needed to go and pick berries. His thinking was that he liked eating them and if we didn't go soon, right after breakfast, the birds would finish them off – and we'd be left with none. He'd mimed this last point with solemn empty hands and I'd been trying not to laugh, hiding my face behind the cow as I milked her.

I remember thinking it would be good to take a pot to the blackberries too. Mama used to send me to pick them so she could keepsake summer's sweetness in a tidy row of jars. Billy and I had been wolfing them straight from the bushes – our hands, and Billy's face, still stained a tell-tale, greedy red hours later. I wasn't sure how to make jam, but getting the berries home would be a decent start. Billy would be as pleased with a spoon of jam in his winter oats as I used to be with mine, and it was only fair my brother had the same treats.

It had rained in the night, so going out to the brambles could also be the chance to pick mushrooms. I was teaching Billy which ones were safe to eat, and now was the time to start hanging them from the rafters above the fire, so we'd have smoky dried mushrooms in our winter stews.

These were my thoughts that morning.

Before they came, this was the weight of my head.

The crack of cart wheels on the hardened earth road, the horses' hooves. I should have heard them coming some way off. Not been startled by the sight of two heavy-footed men already inside with their hands out. Landowner Ruthers and his great bulk of a man, Locke, blotting out the light. I should've heard him coming weeks before he was taking up the doorway.

'Don't let them close enough to lay a hand on you. Kick and bite if it comes to it,' Papa told me. 'Whatever it takes. Throw what you can reach, even if it's animal shit. They won't want you if they think you're touched.'

'Yes, Papa,' I'd promised him.

But I'd let them drag me from the shed, hoisting me up into the cart as easily as they would a cowering animal. Billy left alone, wide-eyed and crying. The pail of warm milk knocked over and steaming into the dirt floor. The cow only half milked.

Instead of holding my little brother, close and tight in the safety of the woods, I could only watch him from the back of Landowner Ruthers' cart. Billy's face becoming smaller with each turn of the wheels, until he was a lonely blur against the wall of the shed.

If I knew an inch of what lay ahead, I would not have gone so easy.

Timid as a field mouse, I wasn't used to strangers then. We lived in a three-room cottage on the edge of a forest, the door of our nearest neighbour half an hour's walk. Months could come before we'd greet another person, and grown men were to be obeyed. I was a simple girl. It was a simple life. Papa worked the fields until sundown, Billy and I saw to the chores. Our horizons stretched little further than what we could see, or what our hands could hold.

If I knew what was to come, I'd have fought like a cornered rat that morning, but we don't get to do things over. None of us can look back and pick the bad pieces out.

There were other children in the cart with me. Another girl and three boys. Landowner Ruthers and Locke rode up front and we were in the back, pressed up together against bundles of hay and close enough to whisper without the men hearing. None of the other children knew where they were taking us or when we might be coming back. No one had been allowed to bring belongings.

Harry was the youngest. Just turned six.

'What if no one lets her out?' he whispered.

He was talking about a cow. It was his job to take her out in the mornings. No food in his own belly, the little boy fretted Brownie would be left hungry in the dark of her shed. I looked at his hands as he steadied himself against the cart, still pudgy and soft like Billy's hands. He was so little. Whatever the men intended for us, surely Harry was too young?

He sat between Ty and Calumn, the two older boys. Cal's coat had been ripped, threads swung down from a wide tear at his shoulder. Ty must have put up even more of a fight. He had a cut lip that was bruising to purple and he flinched each time the cart jarred his shoulder. I knew Cal and Ty were friends. I'd often seen them laughing together at the harvest gatherings. Of the two Ty spoke the least, although it didn't seem from shyness. With his long legs folded up in front of him, he must have been the most uncomfortable of the five of us in the small space.

Next to me was Helen. Sweet, pretty Helen, who I'd never known to be unkind to anyone. I saw one of her long braids, usually so neatly plaited, had been yanked loose.

———

The men drove the horses hard and we rattled along at an uneasy pace, our fears a metal tang clattering along with us. We were heading south, but that was a meaningless detail to me then. Reaching up around us, the trees were turning gold and red, as though their leaves had caught a slow, deep fire. But there was no warmth here. The day was grey and damp, and we shivered as the wind rushed through the slats in the cart.

I knew we had to keep track of our journey. I'd begun counting the groves of trees and stretches of open fields, keeping measure of how long it would take to walk back. But as we travelled on, my grasp of the land's patterns loosened. The tighter I gripped, the more it unravelled.

I started counting the forks in the road we passed instead. Soon, even those became too many, over-stacking and jumbling in my head.

It was a desperate twisty thing. If we couldn't remember the path away from our home, how could we find our way back?

I looked down at my hands. A splinter from the cart was caught in the skin of my palm. Pulling it free brought a bead of bright red. Frantic as I was, terror sloshing inside me, I couldn't think of another way to mark the journey.

Up ahead, another crossroad was fast approaching.

I pulled up a larger splinter from the cart beneath me and dug it sharply into my finger.

As we swung left, I drew a small mark with the blood on the inside skirt of my dress.

I would do a dash for every left turn the cart made, and a cross for every right.

Pressing my finger into the splinter each time we came to a split in the road, I made sure the marks were soaked deep enough into the cloth that they'd stay fast. Moving to another fingertip when the cut on the first became too ragged to press a clear mark, I kept them in a neat line. Circling the inside of my hem, just high enough to be clear of any mud.

The crosses and dashes lined up. Inching around my skirt as the day wore on.

My fingers ached, but having something to focus on kept fear from taking hold. I told myself the blood I was drawing would keep us tethered to our home. The blood that ran under my skin was made of this place: it would bring us back.

By afternoon we had travelled further than I'd ever been. Farther than Mama or Pa had gone. The familiar was running to wide, unfarmed lands. Strange rocks jutted from the ground.

We came across an iron cage. Swinging from a post and cross beam. We didn't know what it was at first. Until the crows lifted, shrieking and calling, their black wings beating angrily, and the smell reached us. The unmistakable animal sweetness of death. It was a person, a body that had once been someone. Bound in chains, locked in a cage barely bigger than itself. As we passed, the crows closed back around the wretched thing.

The men stopped regularly to rest the horses and let the animals relieve themselves. I badly needed to go too but we weren't allowed to get out of the cart. Ty asked to stretch his legs. In answer he got the side of the crop and a stinging red line across his face to match his bruised lip.

We kept quiet after that, even when it started to rain. Stony drops that fell heavy to our bones. Landowner Ruthers pulled the cart to a halt, Locke jumped down to check that the bundles of hay were still covered in their tarred sheet, and the men urged the horses onwards.

Shivering, we huddled together in the back.

I knew my brother would be cold and hungry too. The kitchen fire would have died after an hour, two at the most. Billy would know not to go into the woods alone, but would he think to pull the blankets from our beds to keep himself warm until Papa got home?

I looked down at Mama's shoes on my feet, shamed all the more for letting myself be taken. Mama had trusted me with Billy's care.

Keeping him warm was the smallest that I could do. It had been barely a year since she died and here I was, already failing her.

He had grown so much. Mama would smile to see how much of himself he had become, a proper little person. How he talked now. His chatter keeping up with his little feet as he followed me about, trying to help with the chores. But still only three years old. We'd never left Billy alone before, not even for a few minutes.

Night came and with it a deeper chill. But the storm of dangers I'd imagined Billy facing alone calmed.

I knew Papa would be home and the fire would be lit. There would be a different storm now: Papa raging against what had happened. Slamming the chairs; yelling, throwing his tin mug across the kitchen. But what could he do? Even if Papa were able to come this far after me, what could he be against the reach of Landowner Ruthers? The man who owned our farms, and held our lives to his whims.

Hollowness twined and twisted my stomach as I pictured my brother and father together, rosy in the warmth of being indoors, my chair empty across the table. I didn't know what they would do tomorrow. Pa was needed in the fields and Billy would have to go with him, but what of the chores? Winter's survival was as dependent on the wood being chopped and cow being milked as anything else. No days could be missed. I looked at the children with me in the cart. They would be needed at home too. Especially Helen – she and her mother lived alone.

The rain had eased but it was too cold for our clothes to dry. All of us were shivering. None of us had eaten today. No one had spoken for some miles: not wanting to risk Mr Ruther's crop, nor was there much to say to each other. Why had we been taken? What would happen to us? There were no good answers.

Where we come from, the world is small. Some people might laugh at how small our lives were, but even now, with all I've seen, I wouldn't trade my beginning. Large isn't everything, and I've yet to see the sheer weight of numbers make anything right.

On the farm, the world felt possible to understand. Everything had its rhythm and its way, and if you leaned in close and watched carefully, you could learn the world and how to be in it. The forest roots that were good eating, which grains to feed hens for eggs with yolks the colour of golden sunrise. How to raise a fire from wet wood; which leaves to pick for the fastest-healing poultices. The sounds an untethered horse will listen to.

The world didn't feel small then; it felt big as a clear horizon and full as the day. I was just a farm girl but I didn't feel simple then, I felt part of the world and in tune with its melody. Everything had a reason and a sense to it, and I was a piece of that. I didn't think to question whether it was a fair world or if I had my rightful share of it. There were simply rhythms that I could rely on, and a place for me among them.

But that was before I'd seen a machine.

The night whistled on past our ears, and through our wet clothes. My bones ached from the cold; all the water inside me turning to ice. The others had fallen into a juddery sleep but I was afraid to let my eyes close. If I missed even one turn in the road, all the marks inside my skirt would mean nothing. Curled up and shivering against the cart's side, the warmth of morning seemed unreachable as we rattled deeper into the night.

Then, out of the darkness came a strange noise.

At first, I took it to come from the cart. But as the sound grew louder, it was clear it ran separate to the drum of the horses' hooves, and was coming from some distance away.

Soon the noise was loud enough to wake the other children; startling them from sleep and swallowing the sounds of the horses and the cart altogether. A fearsome, repeating hammer, it was unlike anything we'd ever heard.

'Is it thunder?' whispered Harry. 'Maybe hitting the same spot?'

'Thunder won't do that,' Ty answered softly. 'And look, the sky's cleared.'

'What is it then?' asked Cal.

Ty just shook his head, not knowing.

We knew no good could come from such a noise. No human hand could create such a hammering. Surely no right mind would want any part of it? And yet it seemed the sound pulled us forward, drawing us ever closer. Each crash now timing with the circles of the cart's wheels.

In horror, we realised the horses were quickening their pace towards the hammering.

The woods we rode through were thinning. The road beneath us becoming smoother and faster. Everything rushing to bring us to it.

As the last of the trees cleared, a monstrous building rose ahead. A vast, shadowy bulk that dwarfed the landscape around it. Larger than twenty of our cottages piled together, it was a house built for giants. From ground to gable, five storeys of windows punctured its walls. A towering chimney, tall enough for twenty fireplaces, stretched up into the night skies.

Helen pressed closer into my side. I reached for her hand and looked over for Harry, Ty had put his arm protectively across the little boy.

This was surely the source of the noise, and as we got closer, the monster did nothing to dispel our fear. The thunder coming from it was evenly spaced; a pulse almost, as though the building lived. I didn't understand how Landowner Ruthers was able to drive the horses so close, but as the cart came to a halt outside it, I saw the horses were familiar with the crashing. They had the witless indifference of animals who had never faced down the cause of a thing. As Locke fastened their bridles to a post right out front, the beasts practically nickered. For them it must mean rest and a feed. It was unlikely to mean the same for us. Landowner Ruthers would not have put himself through the trouble of bringing us this far for anything so pleasant.

We watched him walk to the doorway of the monstrous building. For a moment, before the door swung shut behind him, yellow light spilled out, cutting a sharp triangle that raced across the grass towards us.

I thought about running. My legs were cramped and shaking, would they get me to the cover of trees before Locke caught up? Could I leave the other children alone here to face Ruther's wrath? Were they thinking the same thoughts?

Ty must have been. Of the five of us, he had by far the strongest chance. But Ty stood fast, his hand resting on Harry's shoulder. Maybe I wasn't brave enough, or just too tired and cold, for I stood with him.

Ruthers came back with a bony, odd-looking man. Half the width of Ruthers, taller by a good few inches. The man's hair was dark, but the long lines of his face were sliced crossways by a fat hedge of moustache red enough to glow like embers in the lamplight. His trousers and jacket had been cut from the same dark blue cloth. I now know to call this a suit, but it looked particular to me then, gleaming silkily from his neck to his heels.

The two men spoke heartily, clapping each other's shoulders, leaning in to hear each other over the roaring house. At one point the thin man stepped closer, his lamp casting deep hollows across his face. His eyes had the same look Mama used to have when she was buying supplies at the market. There was a distinct sensation we were being measured for quality and freshness as he swung the light at each of us. After a second look at Ty's bruises, he said something to Ruthers who laughed. The matter completed, the men bid each other well.

Locke prodded us. We were to follow the thin man down a path into the darkness. It was a great relief to be walking away from the hideous building. I looked over my shoulder to see Ruthers climb up to his seat. He didn't trouble himself with so much as a glance back at the children he'd had in his cart.

The path curved past a throng of trees and down to another building. Smaller than the one at our backs, it was still far larger than any house I'd ever seen before. Instead of going to its doorway, the thin man left the path, the circle of his lamp swinging across the grass, and walked to a small shed built against the back of the building.

He unlocked it. We were herded inside and the bolt slid back into place behind us.

The lamplight shone briefly under the door. I saw a stack of split wood before the light swung away with the men's steps, leaving us in pitch black. Reaching my hands out, I felt for the stacks of wood. The shed smelt musty and cobwebby. Chopped wood that had sat undisturbed for some time.

Outside, past the second building and up along the path, the hammering suddenly stopped.

For a moment the air hung empty, then I heard the other children's breathing. The scraping of wood being leaned against. Our feet shuffling on the dirt floor. Simple, normal sounds that were a comfort to hear in the darkness of this place.

Little Harry was the first to speak, 'What are they keeping in there? In that massive house?' His voice was quivery with fear. 'What creature could make that noise?'

'It's got to be a city noise Harry. We're probably not far from the city.'

Calumn was trying to comfort Harry, but this idea only increased the child's fear. His voice rising higher. 'The *city*! Why would they want us in the city? What are they going to do with us?'

I heard the rustling of a body moving, Ty stepping closer to reassure him. 'Just think Harry, how good this story will be to tell everyone when we get home.'

'Whoever nailed this wall together wasn't too fussed about it staying up,' Cal's voice was now coming from somewhere near the ground. 'Won't take long to get these planks loose.'

We could hear him pushing against the wall, feeling for weakness in the wood.

Ty sighed. 'They know where we live Cal.'

'What are you saying?' asked Cal. 'Ruthers will come, get us again?'

'Or take one of your brothers instead. Would you want Eddie or Jon here?'

As Ty's words sunk in, the creaking stopped. I thought of Billy. There was no way I wanted him here in my place.

'I can't hold it much longer.' Harry voiced a concern I had too.

'Hang on. There's a bucket or something here,' said Cal.

We took turns, Helen and I squatting over the bucket with our skirts covering everything but the sounds. It was too dark to see anything, even after our eyes had adjusted, but it still took me ages to be able to go, knowing everyone couldn't help but listen. Ty went last and when he was done, he carried the bucket to the door. We heard him feeling for the gap between the ground and the door, then slowly emptying the bucket. The shed was on a slight incline, but to be sure he laid a few pieces of wood down by the wall so no one would have to sit on wet ground.

'We should try and get some sleep,' he said.

'I'm too thirsty,' Harry's voice was now beside me.

'Here Harry, let's get a button to fix that.'

'A button? What can that do?'

'It's magic,' I smiled at him in the dark.

I pulled a button free from the bottom of his shirt and slid it into his mouth. I could hear him clicking it around his teeth, then a surprised intake of breath. 'It works!'

Mama taught me this. I did it with Billy sometimes when we were out in the forest. It couldn't properly cure a thirst, but something hard like a small pebble or a button could wet your mouth and keep you going until home. After that, the sound of buttons clicking against teeth filled the shed.

The ground was cold but dry. There was space for two to sleep comfortably. We slept folded up and curved around each other, the heat from our bodies drying off our clothes and keeping the shed warm enough.

As I drifted off, I could feel the juddery rhythm of the cart still. I knew it was just my body reliving the day's dealings, muscles remembering the cart's unfamiliar motion, but I pulled my skirt around me tighter all the same. My fingers sore and bloodied from the splinters.

Slipping in and out of fitful sleep, I dreamt of Billy. Dreams that he was calling me, that I was trying to find him, protect him from a fierce storm coming. Then he was with me and the feeling of him in my arms drew me from sleep. But when I woke, it was Harry's head heavy and warm on my lap.

I lay awake and stared into the blackness. At some point the walls began to take shape. The sleeping bodies of the other children slowly emerging from the gloom as dawn trickled through the cracks in the wallboards and up from the gap under the door. The only one of us small enough to stretch out, Harry had spread out sweetly across everyone, his arms and legs flung trustingly wide.

I saw Ty in the opposite corner, propped up against the wood stack, and realised he was awake too, and had been watching me.

He smiled, a sideways crescent moon in the murkiness. 'I liked your trick with the buttons.'

With Helen asleep on his shoulder, his legs tangled with Cal's, and Harry's feet across his lap, Ty reminded me of the raggedy king of the harvest scarecrows. We had not spoken much before. I'd seen him plenty of times at village gatherings but something about Ty always made me feel shy. He seemed so easy in his measure of things.

'Did you mean what you said?' I asked him. 'About having a good story when we get home?'

It was light enough now to see the doubt in his eyes, 'Harry needed to get some sleep. We all did.'

A little later, the hammering started again. Rumbling through the dirt and taking over the air so thoroughly it was a wonder there was still space for the sky itself.

Whatever was making the noise, it was as angry this morning as it had been last night.

The thin man with the moustache came to unbolt the door not long after that. He told us to get up and hurry after him. Blinking in the light, we untangled ourselves and, as instructed, followed him back up the path we'd come down the night before. Back towards the terrible noise.

EVERY

Present day, London, Friday,
4.55am

I'm running and everything is white. Everything is shuddering and coming apart. Powdery feathers float through the air. The only way out is through a tunnel of collapsing buildings. The air is chalky with debris and hard to breathe.

I must keep running. Chest heaving, feet pounding.

Towering high-rise blocks tumble and fall around me.

A shard of metal slices through the air, barely missing my head. The shaking comes again.

I look down. Under my feet, the concrete cracks open and gives way. I reach out, trying to keep my balance, but there is nothing to hold on to. The road beneath me falls away.

I fall with it, instead of down, I'm being pulled upwards.

Up through feathery layers of quilt and sleep, to where my phone is ringing.

It takes a moment to understand the cool blue familiarity of my bedroom, that I am safe, that the phone has been ringing for some time. Vibrating and rattling against a glass of water, sending tiny earthquakes across the bedside table. Book by book, my pile of reading has been sliding to the floor.

I stare at the phone dumb. Catching my breath as another book tumbles to the floor.

The number calling is a long string of digits my mobile phone doesn't recognise. I know the voice instantly. We haven't spoken for the best part of a decade, but the precisely clipped vowels are as familiar as family. I realise she's crying, and all sleep flaps away as I listen to my father's assistant describe the situation unfolding ten-and-a-half-thousand miles away.

Details arrive in a breathless rush. Dad collapsed a few hours ago. He's in hospital. His doctors have ruled out the possibility of recovery.

'We don't know how much time he has,' Janelle says. 'You need to come now Evie.'

The numbers on the digital clock beside my bed flicker from 4.55am to 4.56am. Janelle pauses, waiting for my reaction. It's late afternoon where they are. Summertime in Sydney. I picture the wide, blue-rinsed skies and imagine him on his balcony, majestically gazing out to sea. Respectful breezes gently ruffling his hair. A tumbler of scotch and soda leaving a wet ring on a pile of scripts. I blink that away. He couldn't be on his balcony now.

Down the line Janelle exhales. It's my turn to say something.

'Thanks for letting me know,' the words bubble up in my mouth. Janelle and I listen to them together. They're not the right words; there are far better words.

'Shall I book your flight Every?'

'I can do it from here.'

'I'll tell him you're on your way?'

'Yes.'

Outside I hear the deep purr of a black cab pulling up in the street. I listen to the click of its passenger light going on, a girl laughing and two car doors clunk shut. She's wearing heels. Her footsteps teeter and echo away. There's a throaty acceleration as the cab makes its way back up the narrow street past the tightly packed houses.

Inside my head is an empty vacuum, the expanding hollow before an explosion.

I can't remember ever hearing Janelle cry before. I put the phone back on the bedside table next to my clock. Seeing the time,

I register there's still two hours before my alarm goes off and I'll need to get up.

Then the screen on my phone flicks off. The room goes dark and the explosion hits.

My father is in hospital. Right now, on the other side of the world.

Even if I left within this moment. Even if I could walk directly out of my bedroom, onto the tarmac and up the steps of a waiting plane, Dad is still a 22-hour flight away.

There *is* no time.

I jump out of bed and switch on my laptop.

Pulling my suitcase from the back of the wardrobe as the computer whirs into life. It's hard to focus on what I should be packing. What things I'll need. It will be hot in Sydney but holiday clothes feel wrong. I start throwing things into the open lids of my case. T-shirts, jeans, underwear. When I get to a black dress, I stop. What am I packing for?

Twenty minutes later I'm in the backseat of a cab, asking the driver to get us to the airport as quickly as he can. As we power up the hill away from my flat, I remember I've forgotten to water the plants. The airline ticket I bought was an open return. I don't know how long I'll be gone. I don't know if I should hope it's for a long time. I haven't emptied the fridge or locked the windows either.

I text Janelle the flight details, tell Dad I'll be there as soon as I can.

It's night still. The sky inky and low. It must have snowed earlier: the sleeping streets we skim through are lace-edged in white. Rather than around, the driver's sat nav takes us through the city. With few other cars on the road, we thread smoothly through the labyrinthine turns forged by two thousand years of human life. Roman walls up against curved glass towers. Open-all-night, deep-fried-chicken shops operating out of Victorian terraces. London is a maze I can still lose myself in. Usually I love this. Right now I'm watching the sat nav closely.

Forty-two minutes until destination.

The driver flicks on the windscreen wipers and I see it's snowing again. A ballet of flakes twirling and falling through the headlights.

The streets widen, we speed up and onto the motorway, reflections wrapping faster across the windscreen. A pale face whips past on the glass, for a second I see my mother's eyes but it's just me. Tired and dark-eyed.

Twelve minutes to destination.

Beyond the rhythmic swish of wipers, signs for the airport become more frequent. The driver asks if I want Arrivals or Departures. It seems obvious until I remember the two half-shells of suitcase left stretched across my bed. The black dress swaying on its hanger in the wardrobe.

Even at 6.45am Heathrow is crowded and aggressively bright. The check-in line is a long shuffling snake twice-doubling back on itself.

On the flight information board my flight is listed as Go to gate.

The queues drag through to security. People fussing with their shoes, belts, loose coins.

My flight is now boarding at a gate on the far side of the airport.

I start running. Down the long, rubber-stretched walkways. Chest heaving, feet pounding again. This time I'm awake but it feels more dream-like. Where I am, where I'm going. What is happening. None of this feels real. I run past hyper-bright duty-free stands. Through unhurried clumps of people, laughing, waving cups of coffee and melted-cheese paninis at each other. There's a sensation of moving through a film shot in slow-motion. I want to keep running, harder and faster, until all of this sharpens back to normal.

Back at my flat, my alarm will be beeping for me to get out of bed.

When I get to the gate, sweaty and shaking, it's not boarding at all. Just people sardined together in a glass room, waiting. I lean against the wall until we're called to board.

On the plane I sit, seatbelt buckled, watching the other passengers find their seats. Each person dawdling down the aisle. Chatting, fumbling, dropping their boarding passes; stuffing the overhead lockers.

My hands are two white starfishes gripping the armrests.

Outside support vehicles make circling tracks in the snow. A swab of grey morning skulks up the runway. I wonder if Dad is awake. It will be 6pm in Sydney now. Two hours before sunset. *We don't know how much time he has.* That's what Janelle said. But what does that mean? That Dad's future no longer stretches to years and months? That his time can now only be measured in days or hours? My wanting to live on the opposite side of the world from him suddenly feels petty. A leaf fighting with the wind.

The stewards thump shut the lockers, the plane accelerates towards take-off and we are finally airborne. There are safety announcements, the yellow life-vest that must not be inflated on board. A drinks trolley clatters up the aisle. I surprise myself by ordering scotch. The flight attendants were offering tea and coffee but don't seem inconvenienced by a passenger wanting liquor at 8.40am. I fiddle with the foil-wrapped peanuts, ignoring the man next to me winking conspiratorially.

Taking a sip, I look out the window and down on the wintery greys of Europe crosshatched neatly below. I'm still not keen on the taste of scotch. Turns out, it was the smoky wood smell that I was craving.

Twenty-one hours before we land in Sydney. A full day and night. *We don't know how much time he has.* I picture a large hourglass, each grain of sand slipping through its narrow funnel for the last time. I ask for another scotch and keep looking out the window.

Marshy aromas swamp the cabin. Food trays are handed out and collected again. Window blinds are pulled down. Lights go out. Six different movies flicker across the backs of seats around me. The films finish, then skip seats, playing out in staggered formation across the rows for different people. I try to watch them too, but can't seem to hold the threads of a plot together. Even the films I've already seen need too much concentration. I find myself staring at back-to-back episodes of *Friends* without my headphones plugged in. The old sets familiar and soothing. I wonder what made the designer think of putting a gold frame around the peephole of a purple door. I read a feature in the inflight magazine about the drawbacks of vintage motorcycle ownership.

Eighteen hours to Sydney. We rumble on.

We don't know how much time he has. I try to picture Dad in a hospital bed. The references I have of what this might look like are from TV and films. Wired to monitors, an oxygen mask on his face, sterile tubes running across the sheets and into his veins. But I know life is never as clean, and it doesn't feel real to imagine him like that.

It's been almost 10 years since Dad and I were in the same room. Obviously I've *seen* him since. I see him most days. My father is hard to miss. Magazine covers, chat shows, red carpets – photoshopped, charismatic, beloved, a beautiful actress usually sparkling off his arm. Once I caught a number 38 bus with his face wrapped large as the moon across its side. I sat upstairs, just between his left eyebrow and a Mont Blanc pen, all the way up Rosebery Avenue into Islington.

I do not know the shape of life without him in it. The thought of life without him is unreachable.

It's 3pm, but not here. I slide up the window shade and peer out into the darkness. Nothing below and nothing above. Whatever time we are flying over, the density of night outside is so complete, so solid, that if I were able to open the window, my fingers might sink into the sky like soft velvet.

Gravity always seemed to have a lighter grip on Dad's shoulders. Even as a little kid, it was clear to me that he was the golden centre of every room he walked into. Everyone – even other stars – leaned forward to bathe in the warmth of his presence. The comfort he had in his own skin made him seem somehow otherworldly. He was not like other daddies. But nor were we like other families.

My mother once bought him a silver flask. A beautifully slim bottle to slide gently inside his jacket pocket. He complained the metal made his scotch taste tinny and overheated, but he still carried it with him whenever he left the house for any significant time. Mum just laughed at his grumbles. On the side of the flask, in old-fashioned swirling script she'd had a message engraved, *'A lion is not concerned by the opinions of sheep'.*

I knew it was intended as encouragement against the critics and unappreciative studio execs and I liked the sound of the words, but it felt unnecessary advice for Dad. He never seemed the least bit concerned by anyone's opinions, sheep or otherwise. He did what he wanted, when he wanted. Not in a cruel way, Dad was simply unweighted by other people's expectations. It was the same with his fame. For him, the attention wasn't something to pander to, or be troubled by. Like the weather, it simply rolled past his windows, inevitable but unrelated to what was going on inside.

Even after it happened, after the world was ripped open and carved apart. When life was reset red and ruined. When the adoration turned to hostility – people screaming horrible things from the crowd: murderer, wife-killer. Even then, other people's assessments weren't relevant to him. The Hollywood specials, the around-the-clock news reports: they did not describe his situation. It all seemed to slide off my father as though water from a fish. His gleam uncut.

And it didn't take long for the swing of public opinion to soften, circling back around. There was no arrest, no official suggestion of criminal involvement. The general consensus became that the poor man had suffered enough. It had been an accident. A terrible, tragic accident.

It was different for me. I was just a kid. I've never had my father's immunity to judgement. Not now, certainly not then. What these strangers, these people who had never even been in the same room as my parents, said about Mum and Dad, pierced me.

The press camped outside our home, my school. Swooping, squabbling pigeons, stopping my classmates for quotes. Springing from bushes like demented jack-in-the-boxes. Chasing us down the street. Scary and devious. Their flashes designed to blind. The sickening questions they yelled out.

I don't recommend any of it.

The idea that anyone would actively seek out this kind of scrutiny is horrifying. All those eyes constantly watching you, that's not love. People seem confused about this – the people who think they want to be famous; for the galaxy to chorus their name. They have no idea what they're wishing for. Take it from me: standing out from the crowd, there's little advantage to this. Attention is not love. They are nothing like each other. Not even close.

I kept reading about what sad timing it was, with Mum's soon-to-be-Oscar-winning performance in *Foreign Tides* only just out in the cinemas. And her being so beautiful. As though it was her beauty or work schedule which made her death tragic. They always mentioned the blood too. So awful, so shocking. *All that blood.*

But that was seventeen years ago. I left home; grew up. I use Mum's maiden name, and stick to Evie. I'm normal now. Far from the line of fire. I am not my father's daughter.

I avoid conversations about my family. I don't tell people who I am. Why would I? I know exactly what they're going to ask. It's the same questions every time. People want to talk about that night. What I saw; what really happened. If I saw it.

The world may have felt she belonged to them, that they knew her. That paying for a movie ticket also bought a piece of the actor. They have a right to feel they lost something precious that night. But Therese Mitchell wasn't just an actor. She was a person. A person with dreams and plans; she had a husband and a daughter, and so much more life to live. She was my mum.

I understand the curiosity, of course I do. I understand why they feel they need to know. But I don't want to talk about it. It happened; it was terrible. It was a long time ago. We've all faced monsters, lost who we love. Dark beasts stalk all our nights.

We've been in the air for eleven hours. Singapore is two hours away. At Changi there will be an hour's wait for refuel, then another day of flying onwards to Sydney. How many falling grains of sand will that amount to? I look through the seat pocket again. I read the flight safety card: the cartoon families adjusting their air-masks, happily preparing for impact.

I see a lot of Mum too. In re-runs. She still catches my breath if I'm caught off guard. She *was* beautiful. I have all her movies. Once

I watched Mum dying on loop for hours. I don't know why. I just sat there crying and rewinding and crying again. The one where she has cancer. I know she was pregnant with me when she filmed it, but she looks so young. Too young for babies and marriage. For me and my father.

Even though she's meant to be dying in half the film, she's glowing. No amount of make-up can dull the happiness shining in her eyes. She told me she was so in love with Dad, and excited about having me that she hardly needed to eat or sleep. That each moment felt too full and precious to waste on such things. She said that at the time all she truly needed was the air that she breathed, and to love us. Like the Hollies song they play at the end of the movie.

She used to sing the song to me when she told me this story. When I was very young and still imagined everything revolved around me, I asked to hear this story a lot. Mum had a very sweet voice; I always thought they should have got her to sing it in the film.

If I was the one handing out Oscars, this is the film I would have given Mum hers for. I think she would have enjoyed wedging her own little gold man into Dad's congregation of them at home. I think she would have laughed at that. What was the point of giving her one after she died? Just a spite of timing.

The captain announces we're descending into Singapore. He breezily adds that the scheduled hour's refuel will now be two and a half. More than twice the time it should be. Panic flutters up, coiling around my shoulders.

Landing takes longer than expected; our designated gate is not ready. We circle above Changi Airport. Taxiing into the parking bay 54 minutes later. All passengers are required to disembark.

I rush to call Sydney. Dialling the number as I bolt down the airbridge. Janelle isn't answering her own or Dad's phone. I send texts to both numbers. Neither of them has their answerphone messages switched on. I don't know what that means, if it means anything. It's possible the number I have for Dad isn't even his anymore. They have to change it regularly.

I call the hospital. They won't let me through to Dad's room. I ask to speak with the person in charge. Minutes grind by as I listen to static, hoping I haven't been cut off. An exasperated voice eventually comes on the line. I can't prove I'm Ford Mitchell's daughter. The hospital's phones have been ringing off the hook with journalists and distraught fans claiming to be next of kin. These people knew his date and place of birth too. There's really nothing they can do for me at this stage, says the hospital supervisor. Perhaps try contacting Mr Mitchell's management team. In the morning, he adds snootily. The line's dead before I can reply.

Across the departure lounge is a newsagent kiosk. Two walls of glossy magazines. From where I'm standing, I can see three-quarters of Dad's face in replica on a neat stack of *Vanity Fairs*.

I go online and type in Dad's name. According to the headlines, the legendary actor-director has been hospitalised. There's vague insinuation it's a drug overdose. One 'showbiz' reporter demands to know if it's plastic surgery. The relief buckles me. If the pigeons are scratching up dirt and hazarding guesses, it means no official statement has been issued yet. Which means he must be okay. Death in a hospital is not something even Janelle could keep quiet.

The information boards are flashing an alert. I rush over, hoping our flight is boarding early. It's a further delay. A four-hour wait is now listed for the Sydney flight. My stomach drops. This has to be a mistake. I feel lightheaded, blanched with fear. I can't process how this can be happening, to *this* flight. There is not a flight I've ever taken where time mattered more.

People are crowded in front of the airline information stand. Staff behind the counter are handing out vouchers for meals and drinks. A man in a tight-fitting mauve uniform walks up to me, nudging my arm with the offer of boiled lollies from a small woven basket.

The airline doesn't have any other flights departing earlier to Sydney. I run back to the departures board to see if any other airlines do. A flight to Brisbane left two minutes ago. The next plane to Australia is the one I'm on. I try Janelle and Dad again. Still no answer. I don't know who else to call. What else to do. It's the middle of the night in Sydney. I scroll through my contacts. The number I have for Lenny, Dad's manager, rings out. My father is one of the most well-known people on the planet but I have no one else I can call to find out if he is alive.

I slump down next to a large display of potted orchids. Their fleshy little faces bobbing impassively at my drama. I count up the hours again. Three-and-a-half before we get back on the plane. Another eight flying. Immigration. The drive from the airport to the hospital will take at least an hour.

We don't know how much time he has. I feel sick.

In the bathroom I throw up, just making it to the toilet in time. On my knees on the white tiles retching slimy water until my stomach cramps. I wash my face at the sink without looking in the mirror.

Pacing the airport terminal, too jittery to sit, I find myself back at the newsagent, staring at the stack of magazines with Dad on the cover. Maybe a hundred Dads. He looks good. Healthy. His gaze direct to the camera. He looks like a man who has all the time in the world.

With magazine lead times, I know this photograph would be at least a few months old. I buy a copy. Dad's been busy; filming in London, judging at Cannes. A bear-watching trek through Jasper National Park with his Canadian girlfriend, Kara Lonsdale, the statuesque and accomplished thirty-two-year-old star of *Primrose Park.* There's a red-carpet snap of them together in evening dress. Sleek, blonde and six-foot tall: she looks like a beautiful praying mantis.

It's strange to think Dad and I were in the same city and didn't speak, although I realise his schedule must bring him to London often. I wonder how long he's known he was sick.

The boarding call for Sydney comes at last. I refresh the internet pages until final call. The websites don't have any updates. Standing by the gate, I keep trying Dad and Janelle's numbers, sending one last text message as I walk through the accordion folds of the air-bridge.

A different seat. Eight more hours belted in, lost to the roaring skies. Another round of drinks trolley, food smells, lights out, back-of-seat movies as the flight path crawls sluggishly towards Sydney. A whole day and most of a night has passed since I spoke to Janelle. We're flying towards the sun, the plane's red wing-light blinking through powdery blue clouds. The man next to me turns in his sleep; his arm flops into my lap. I look across the cabin of sleeping people, messily folded into their seats and breathe down a wave of claustrophobia. Lifting the man's arm back into his own seat, I climb over him into the aisle.

The face in the toilet mirror looks tired. My eyes are sore and red. My jaw aches. Getting some sleep would be smart. I know I'm too wired. I think about asking the flight assistants for a sleeping tablet to knock me out. That's so far from safety protocol I imagine they'd just stare at me. I ask for a glass of water instead and make my way back to my seat.

Four more swollen, pointless hours.

Below, we've reached Australia. I watch the plane's tiny shadow skimming along the red Martian landscapes thirty thousand feet beneath us. Green tuffs begin to sprout in the dust, and gradually it becomes bushland that we're flying over. There's the odd sign of human habitation, which multiples and spreads until the green gives way to grey suburban sprawl.

As we sight the long, southern coastline Sydney sits on, the captain announces we're ready for landing at Kingsford Smith Airport. There are whoops and claps in the cabin, everyone craning to peer down at the shoreline. Waves wash against cliffs, then beaches, until we're low enough for the wheels to thump down.

We glide over Botany Bay, hitting the runway in a lurch of deceleration.

I'm home. It's been a long time.

In the queue for passport check, I try Janelle's number again. No answer. I try Dad's. It's 5pm local time; their time. My time. We're finally on the same time. Janelle should be answering. A security officer waves at me, pointing to the signs showing a mobile phone behind a crossed-out red circle. I pretend to look at my passport and send a text to let Janelle know I'm here.

Through immigration, I run past the baggage carousels and out towards the Arrivals hall.

I see my name, my birth name in thick, black letters held high on a card.

Then I see the wall of flashing cameras.

The scrabbling pigeons.

GREY

A kidnapped farm girl, unwilling witness to the dawn of machines. More than two centuries later, the daughter of the world's most celebrated film director. What thread could link the two?

We, all of us, are stories to tell.

Blue and green that runs to red.

I've seen a lot of stories. It's one of the perks. I get to watch. I get to notice the patterns. To see the themes emerging as the great tapestry is strung. It hasn't always felt like a reward.

Something I've noticed: History isn't always made by the loudest voices.

But let's not spoil endings. First a little scene-setting.

Did you know blood is made in the bones? Those rivers which run through you furious and deep, washing each last twist of you – even as you read these words – in sweet crimson currents. They spring from your marrow. Just like longings and dreams, you make your own blood.

Every drop is a story in itself. A single cup can hold a life. At first it did. Roughly a teacup of blood is all you were born with. You probably knew this; it's basic biology, but it's interesting to remember, isn't it? There's no other source. Blood cannot be made any other way. People have tried. The wheels of human enterprise ever-spinning. No one has come close.

Cells can be created. New skin can be sprayed from a can. Very existence can be paused and reanimated. But what once seemed the simplest thing – the mere oil greasing your machine – remains an impenetrable mystery. A code that won't be cracked. There's no recipe for blood. To make something, you have to understand it.

Another smudge of background to consider:

You were formed at the heart of a star. Oxygen, carbon, hydrogen, nitrogen, iron… Like almost every element on Earth, you are literally made of night sky.

Where am I going with this? Stay with me. *Rush* with me.

Let me show you a story.

MINA

The Mill

Rising up towards the clouds, in daylight the building somehow hulked larger. This was where the hammering was coming from, echoing now inside our ribs, and not one of us wanted to know the cause of it. As though alive and watchful, its windows looked down on us with little pity.

It was a dark invention we farm children had no frame of reference to understand, but whatever was waiting for us inside. Whatever they kept in there, I knew we had a chance of coming back out if we kept breathing. Papa had taught me this. Life has movement he said. He'd put my hand on soft, still-warm fur, told me to feel for the rise and fall. But there was none. I remembered the feeling of still bones beneath the warmth. The life had gone. Man or beast, we're the same, he'd said. Knives and sickness are only details. What kills us is the stillness. Fight that, Papa told me. Whatever this life shows you daughter keep breathing, keep moving, and you'll stay alive.

As we reached the building's door, I stepped to shelter Harry. 'Stay behind me', I whispered. 'And breathe. No matter what happens Harry, don't stop breathing.'

He nodded, his eyes shining with fear.

The thin man pushed open the door and jabbed his crop at Ty, 'Quickly then. In you get.'

It took a moment for my eyes to adjust to the gloom after I'd followed Ty through the doorway. Then I couldn't believe what I saw.

The roaring enormity of what we stood in front of was unlike anything we could have dreamed possible. There were more people here, under this one roof, than we'd seen in the entirety of our lives. Hundreds of men, women and children. All of them working together in long rows; each with their eyes fixed to where their hands were moving furiously. A scene of unimaginable industry.

But it was what they were working *with*, that was most terrifying. A metal beast that coiled around the people, snaking up from the floor to high up into the rafters. Thousands of parts stretching out from it, and each one of them moved separately. Huge metal wheels, far bigger than any cart could use, spun down from the ceiling. Everything clattered and whirled. I couldn't tell where it started or ended. Where its head or tail was, nor what its desire or purpose might be. All I could be sure of was that this was the heart of the thunder.

The heat rolling off it was stifling. A grainy fatness that pushed up against our faces.

High above our heads a man walked a railed walkway. He was watching the workers below with an intent that was clear, even from where we stood. This was a place people didn't want to be.

We shouldn't be here either. Every bone, every string in my body told me to pick up my skirts and run. Fast and far from this place, not looking back.

But instead, with the other children, I followed the thin man to a stairwell, up four flights of stairs. Then down a long, wood-panelled corridor, and into a room.

The door closed behind us with a weighty thud, muffling the noise from below.

The room we now found ourselves in was almost as extraordinary as the one we'd just walked from. It was a room of books.

I'd once seen a book. I knew that inside each of the leather boundings were papers filled with black symbols: a code that some could understand. I knew that books were where rules were kept; the laws set down by powerful men in cities. There must have been hundreds of books in this room. A table was piled with them, two walls shelved floor to ceiling with them.

It was hard to understand how so many rules could ever be needed.

Behind a desk, a man was writing in one of the books.

He continued writing as we stood there. His clothes were very fine, even without the books we would have known his importance. There was a weary air about him, perhaps the weight of all those rules. We straightened up, tidying ourselves into a row as we waited for him to finish.

The thin man eventually cleared his throat. 'Pardon Mr Coleman. Not to disturb sir, only the new apprentices have arrived. Were you wanting to view them?'

The great man looked up at last. He took a deep breath and leaned back in his seat, his gaze sweeping the line of us. He did not seem pleased with what he saw.

'You missed the bell?'

The question was directed at us, but the thin man answered. 'They arrived later than expected last night sir. Thought best to keep them in a shed overnight.'

'A shed, Wilks?'

'Yes, sir, one of the woodsheds. No point wasting good fo—'

Mr Coleman raised a dismissive hand at Wilks and turned back to us, 'You'll not want to miss a bell again.'

He spoke decisively, in a voice long-accustomed to being heard. 'There's a bright future for Mercer Mill. Work hard and you apprentices can be part of it.'

He paused to frown at Harry shuffling his feet. 'But we do not suffer laziness here. Mr Wilks will acquaint you with our rules.'

Mr Coleman then wrote our names, ages and fathers' names in a book he pulled from a shelf behind him. One by one we stepped forward to commit our mark against the little black symbols Mr Coleman indicated were our details. Four shaky Xs and an awkward line of symbols Ty was able to sign for his mark. Mr Coleman sighed watching him struggle with the writing quill, visibly drained by the incompetence as Ty shaped out his name.

It was an odd thing to know we were in a book. Marked there for ever for anyone with understanding to see. We were told it formed a contract to labour at the mill on behalf of our families. What we earned would go to Landowner Ruthers to pay the debts on our farms.

'Be proud of that,' said Mr Coleman. 'The cotton you work here keeps a roof over your families.'

As we followed Wilks back down the stairs, he listed out the mill rules.

We were to start work each morning after breakfast, being at our posts before the third bell rang just after dawn. There was no leaving the post without express and prior permission, which could only come from our supervisor or Wilks himself. The post must be immaculate at all times. No talking. No whistling. No looking out the window. The more cotton we produced, the sooner we could go home. Naturally, he said, today's pay would be docked owing to our late start.

At the foot of the stairs Wilks unlocked a small door. A gust of air hit our faces as the door opened out to the other side of the mill. There was a river just a few yards away. Strong and fast-flowing, it was strange to have been so close and not heard the rushing water. More incredibly, some of the river was being funnelled off to run inside the mill. Why would anyone want water flowing *inside* a building?

Wilks pointed to a pump drawing up from the river, 'Scrub. Rid yourselves of as much natural filth as can be done before you touch the cotton.'

Remembering how thirsty we were, we rushed to the trough. Scooping up as much water as we could before Wilks got impatient. The splinter cuts I'd made in the cart stung in the water, but I was able to wash most of the dried blood off my hands without Wilks noticing.

Going back into the mill was no less overwhelming a second time. The air as furnace-fierce and scratchy with fibres. The hammering just as loud.

We saw now that most of the workers were children, with some women and only a few men. All of them pale and thin. Their shoulders stooped low towards their tasks, faces slicked with sweat. No one looked up from their work as we walked past. I wondered if this came from fear or simple lack of interest.

The first post we came to was mine. Wilks pushed me into a gap between two girls a year or so older than myself. I looked back to my friends. Harry risked a little wave behind Wilks' back before the four of them followed him away.

Up close, the metal beast was horrific. Dozens of metal spindles whirled and rattled. Each one on a metal arm that shot towards me, whipping downwards, then shuddered back into place and started again.

Every bit of sense in me screamed not to touch any of it. But watching the other girls, I saw I would need to do more than just touch it. The task was to thread the thick cotton yarns through the eyes of spindles, pulling the thread through with lightning speed before the metal arm jerked away. The yarn was then spun and tightened on the spindle, until it had formed a reel that could be eased off and placed in a wooden crate at my feet.

This was some kind of colossal loom.

Without taking her eyes off her own spindles, one of the girls showed me how to slow the metal arms down enough so I could thread my spindles.

The work was simple but hard. You had to concentrate, not looking away for a second, and the repetition was dizzying. I understood now why no one had looked up as we followed Wilks down the rows.

To see the spindle holes well enough to thread them, I had to lean down. After a few hours standing curved like this my legs shook and my back ached. My forehead throbbed from the roar of all the spindles shuddering out across the mill.

But far, far worse were the long red smears I was leaving on the cotton.

The splinter cuts on my fingers were bleeding again.

The bleeding wouldn't stop no matter what I tried. I pinched my fingertips together to apply pressure, and blotted them on my sleeves quickly before casting off.

But each time the yarn ran under my fingers, it pulled the skin afresh, dragging red lines down the reel. I didn't have time to stop and rip a bandage from my skirts. I was already in trouble for being too slow. Three times the man on the walkway overhead had needed to come down and shout at my idleness. He was now standing directly above me. I could feel his eyes on my back.

He hadn't seen the red marks on the cotton, but each time he leaned over to check how many reels I'd put in my crate, he got angrier. There would be punishment for wasting mill time he said.

The hours lurched on, stretched with panic, my fingers raw and useless.

I could only hope my reels would be swept up and lost in the hundreds of crates piling up across the mill floor. The windows were at my back. I didn't dare look behind to see how far into the day we were, but this felt the longest I'd seen. I wondered how the other children were doing. *Please don't let Harry have been set any task like this one.*

Finally, a whistle rang out.

The workers stepped back, and the pieces of machinery clunked to a halt. The sudden absence of noise made my ears ring.

Outside, the sky was black and well into night. Slowly everyone straightened up, unfolding back to themselves. Having stood shoulder to shoulder all day, I saw my neighbours' faces properly, in full circle for the first time. I thanked the girl who had helped me with my spindles.

'Don't worry,' she smiled. 'You'll get faster.'

'She'd better,' snapped the other girl, turning on her heel. 'She'll be answering to me if she doesn't.'

The girl on my right had clearly taken a measure of me and found me lacking. I couldn't blame her: both my neighbours had stacked their crates twice over with neat white reels of cotton. My crate wasn't even half full.

'Margery will come around. Bite isn't half the bark with that one,' said the first girl. 'Doesn't like the supervisors being so close, that's all.'

I realised having the man watching me all day meant my neighbours had also been under close inspection. 'I'm sorry. I'll be better tomorrow.'

'Ssh, none of us started on two crates. Not even Margery.'

Her name was Clarice but she said to call her Clary. Together we joined the mass of people filing out the mill doors and into the cool night air.

I passed the post that the cart and horses had brought us to. Where Harry, Ty, Cal, Helen and myself had first stood in Wilks' lamplight. It was just last night, but it felt another lifetime ago. Time felt wrong. All that had happened since I woke up in my bed and dressed Billy had stretched time out of shape.

That cart would be back home now. It was lonely to think of it having returned empty to where we belonged.

Some of the older workers were heading out, down the road that the horses had taken, but Clary told me that apprentices did not leave the mill. There was a special house here for us. We would eat on the ground floor of it and sleep in the two floors above.

The house for apprentices turned out to be the building next to the woodshed we'd slept in. Inside, long rows of tables and benches stretched its length. Tea was a hunk of bread and a ladle of soup, drawn from a dirty-looking cauldron. The soup was watery and unseasoned but the smell of food almost made me cry. I was so grateful to take the warm bowl, my hands were shaking. It had been two full days since we'd eaten.

I found Helen and the boys in the line for food. Seeing their faces in the sea of strangers almost made me cry again.

The five of us sat together in a tight cluster. They looked as tired as I felt. Ty and Cal had been set to lifting and packing carts, Harry said he'd been told to sweep and clean. For Helen and me, it was a task that required only our hands, we stood in one place, yet my body ached as though I'd ploughed a dozen fields.

We were used to working. Farm chores kept us busy morning til sundown most days, but this felt different. It was strange indoor labour.

'It's an unnatural place they've brought us to,' said Cal. 'Those hellish machines. The way everyone is.' He clunked down his spoon. 'This food!'

'Everything's so fast,' said Harry.

'And so loud,' whispered Helen.

'Not the people. No one spoke a word to me,' said Cal, leaning in and looking around suspiciously at the rows of apprentices now chattering around us. 'Not a word all day. Like working with a herd of cattle.'

'Hey. Brownie would've said hello.'

Cal laughed, 'Not all the cows in England are as fine as your Brownie, Harry.'

Scraping up the last of his soup Cal got to his feet, 'This pebble-broth hasn't touched the sides. Might as well go for seconds.'

Ty shook his head. 'No one else has gone for more.'

'So? I'll lead the charge.'

Ty set his spoon beside his own empty bowl, 'Cal, this can't be filling anyone.'

Cal sat back down.

'We should keep our heads down in the mill too,' said Ty, his voice quiet. 'That Wilks has a mean set to him. Let's not give him the chance to prove it.'

I looked down at my hands, worried I might already have.

Helen leaned over to see what I was looking at under the table. 'Oh Mina, your hands! Your poor hands. They're shredded. How did you work like this?'

That night I fell into bed. The hard mattress welcome as the kindest pillow. In the dormitory there was no nightwear to change into. We slept in our clothes. The girls on the second floor, the boys up another flight of stairs on the top floor. The door behind us was locked and the lamplight taken away for fear of fire.

Helen crept into my bed. Together we looked down the long lines of bunkbeds. Each bed with another two built over the top of it, none with any room to sit. Each row indistinguishable from the last. Hundreds of bodies, all of us layered on top of each other as though we were no more than simple insects. I'd always imagined the insides of a beehive to be cheerful: the bees all working together to one purpose. This couldn't be lonelier.

When I look back on our first day at the mill, besides the fear, what I remember most clearly is the size and noise. These were measurements that had to be relearned. Everything here swelled and boiled over, pushing too hard, roaring too loudly, and leaving no room for us.

Mr Coleman's bright future was a frightening new world.

We woke to see a woman swinging a big brass bell by the door. She looked frail but swung the heavy bell with a formidable sturdiness. We learned later she was our dormitory superintendent, Mrs Hoyle.

How long we'd slept was hard to tell. It was dark out and seemed just minutes since I'd closed my eyes, but the girls around us were all tumbling from their beds. Tidying their hair and lacing up their shoes in a shared reflex motion. Whatever time it was, the day had begun.

Downstairs the lamplights were blazing high and everyone was loud and rowdy. At home it was the shortest of exchanges in the softest of voices that broke the day's dawning. Here, children were calling out, yelling to each other. I wasn't sure if it was to make up for the lack of conversation later on the mill floor, or just that everyone had grown used to the short nights here.

Blurry-eyed, Helen and I joined the line for breakfast. The boys, all three with their hair still sticking up in sleepy peaks, found us as we looked for a place to sit.

Breakfast was a faintly savoury gruel doled from the same grimy pot as last night's soup. But seeing the children around us gulping theirs down, we did the same.

As we scraped the last of the gruel from our bowls, a hush ran down the tables.

Wilks and one of his men had entered the hall.

Everyone sunk low into their benches.

The men walked up the first row, each taking a side.

No one was eating now, all eyes following the two men. The only sound in the hall was the clicking of their shoes on the wood floor.

Wilks was making some of the girls stand, turning their faces towards him before dismissing them and continuing on. He clearly wasn't looking to reward anyone: each of the girls slumped back on their benches loose-boned with relief.

The men were now halfway through the second row, one row away from us. I saw Wilks was only pulling up dark-haired girls. Helen realised this too; we looked at each other frightened. I felt for her hand under the table, gripping it tightly.

Wilks was at the beginning of our row, making another girl stand.

She wasn't the one he was after, her spoon clattered on the table as she sank back, released, to her seat. Whoever Wilks wanted and whatever she had done. However wicked it was, I hoped he didn't find her. I pictured a girl with dark hair running through the woods, free and far from him.

Six feet away now, the air seemed to chill as the men approached, cruel shadows drawing near. Helen and I looked forward, rigid with fear.

The footsteps slowed behind us.

I stared at the bowl in front of me. My heart pounding, the blood rushing in my ears. I focussed on a greasy drop of porridge sliding down the bowl's curved side.

Wilks' hand on my shoulder made me jump. Gripping the edge of the table to steady myself, I turned to face him. His narrow expression brightened with recognition as he saw me. He called to the other man as he yanked me to my feet. 'Over here Greaves.'

'Sir, this can't be the girl you're after.' Ty had stood too, his hand on my other arm, pulling me back towards the table. 'We just got here yesterday. She's done nothing wrong.'

For a moment Wilks stared at Ty. Then he stepped forward and stabbed the wooden handle of his crop into Ty's stomach. So hard and fast I'd barely registered what had happened as Ty doubled over, choking to the floor.

'You'll not speak to me like that again boy. Not if you want that face to ever heal.'

To drive his point home, Wilks delivered four more bone-crunching whacks across Ty's head and shoulders.

Everyone watched as they marched me out. Wilks a step ahead. The other man, Greaves, half dragging me. I could feel hundreds of eyes on me but none of them could help, or stop whatever was going to happen to me.

Outside the day was dawning. The sky a smudgy blue behind the black outlines of the trees. A blackbird trilled from the branches above our heads.

The men were taking me up the path towards the mill. After the lights and noise of the kitchen hall, the way ahead was desolate.

My heart was hammering so hard in my chest that it spangled my vision. Any thought in my head now no better-formed than gulps of white panic.

They led me to a wooden crate and when I looked down, I knew they had the right girl. It was the cotton I'd worked yesterday. Even in the dim early light, I could see rust-coloured trails along the reels of yarn. I buried my hands in my skirt.

Wilks kicked the crate, 'What do you see?'

I opened my mouth to reply but only a raspy sound came out.

'Answer me.'

The other man shook my arm.

'Sir, my crate of cotton?'

'With filth all over it. This cotton's likely worthless.'

He kicked the crate again, the thud making me flinch. 'We can't have this.'

They took me to a tall fence running down from the back of the mill. As we got closer, I saw a part where the wood was scratched and worn: circling lines etched into the wide planks. A leather strap had been looped around the top of one of the planks. A thick cuff hanging down from each of its ends. I didn't understand what I was looking at, but knew it was a sight of dread. Of something terrible.

Greaves pushed me into the fence, the wood rough against my face. So stupid: even as he buckled my wrists into the cuffs, I didn't guess what lay ahead. The straps weren't quite long enough to reach me. I had to balance on the edges of my toes, arms stretched up over my head to stop myself hanging from my wrists.

I tried to look behind to see what the men were doing. Wilks had gone to get something from inside the mill. Were they going to leave me swinging from the fence? Would it be for long? My arms were already hurting, the cuffs cutting into my hands.

Then the lash hit me. First the crack in the air, a cold flash and then a deep, streaking burn. Like slices of fire opening up across my back. I couldn't believe what was happening. Couldn't believe it was possible. Papa never raised his hand to me; we never even whipped the horse. I didn't know pain could be so sharp. Or that a body could hold so much of it.

Again, and again the whip whistled towards me. Wrapping itself across my back. Curling down to my legs and up along my arms. Each lash a shock of pain as it ripped through cotton and skin. Someone was crying, begging for it to please stop, and I realised the crying was coming from me. Still the whip came down. After a while I couldn't tell where it was landing, my whole body a pulpy mess of scream.

When they finally unbuckled the cuffs, I fell to my knees, shaking and wet, vomiting on the grass. They dragged me back to the woodshed we'd spent our first night in, and threw me on the floor.

I lay there for a long time, my face on the cool dirt. My back and shoulders throbbing, the tracks of the whip burning into my skin. The pain was unbelievable still. Even a small movement meant excruciating waves of nausea, so I lay very still. Trying to breathe in only the air I had to. The back of my dress felt wet and sticky. I was scared to think what my skin looked like underneath it.

I must have passed out. When I woke, I could tell from the gap under the door that the sun was high in the sky. I was very thirsty. I couldn't swallow properly and my mouth felt like drying mud.

I watched the square of sunlight on the dirt floor. As the sun arced the sky above, the square stretched into a rectangle. I wondered if it would get long enough to reach my face but it didn't seem to. I tried to lift my head and fainted again.

The sound of the bolt sliding across jolted me awake. A lamp shining in my eyes. It was night time again. Expecting Wilks, I flinched at the touch of a hand, but it was two women. Mrs Hoyle and another, younger superintendent. The women peered down at me.

'C'mon dear, let's get you cleaned up.'

Moving sent fire-hot lightning across my back. I couldn't walk by myself, I couldn't even stand. With one on either side of me, the women half-carried me back to the hall and up the stairs to the girls' floor. Each step was a slow, painful process. A two-minute journey that took eight times longer.

With the mill thundering in the distance, the three of us were alone in the dormitory. In the lamplight they examined my back.

The younger woman inhaled sharply as they shone the light over me.

'Yes, when it comes to discipline, Wilks prides himself on a thorough job,' Mrs Hoyle told her. 'Now, fetch us a bowl of hot water and my basket of dressings. We'll need to be just as thorough, won't we?'

'Yes Mrs.'

'The ointment will be there too, on the shelf next to the basket. And bring clean rags. Quick as you can now, Sadie.'

Mrs Hoyle asked my name. 'Right Mina, we'll give you something to bite and get this done best we can.'

I gripped the bedpost as she unbuttoned my dress. It came off in a blanket of searing pain, ripping skin with it. My legs gave out and I fell forward against the bed.

Gentle though she was, each dab of the cloth was like the whip again. It took a long time to clean off the dried blood. There was a feeling as though Mrs Hoyle was sewing my skin close and I realised that's exactly what she was doing. It felt strange being pulled together. I hoped her stitches were as neat as Mama's. I pictured Mama's embroidery on my coat at home: a pretty black-threaded robin on its lapel. I wondered if I'd have a bird on my back.

The ointment felt cool then burned hot. Finally, they wrapped bandages around me. There must have been blood on my face too because Mrs Hoyle dressed that as well, smearing ointment over my cheek first. She also put ointment on my fingers; bandaging up each hand.

Before they let me sleep, she made me drink something from a tin cup she left on the floor beside my bed. It tasted earthy and metallic like the blood I'd smelt and tasted all day.

Deep darkness filled my head.

EVERY

Sydney, Saturday, 5.09pm

People ask how it feels.

If you're the object of a paparazzi scrum, first thing you do is look for cover. For where you can find shelter. You calculate how many steps away from you that shelter is. Shelter. Cover. These words don't feel melodramatic. Not while the pigeons are coming at you.

The architects of Kingsford Smith International airport probably weren't considering paparazzi when they were drawing up their plans. Once past immigration, arriving passengers are funnelled out into the public hall via a narrow, elevated catwalk. Separated from the crowd by thin silver railings, these passengers are displayed to the entire Arrivals hall. It was probably designed this way so that anyone coming to collect newly deplaned friends and relatives could easily spot them in the crowd. But, for 207 long steps, you are very exposed.

Sydney airport is as savagely bright as most other airports. The pigeons don't need their flashes, but they're not using them to light their pictures.

You think you're walking normally. You won't be. Your head will be down. In front of the cameras your body will betray you in strange ways. In the photographs you'll look angry, drunk, confused, overweight. Your hands will be up near your face, instinctively trying to protect your eyes. The flashes are bright enough to momentarily blind you, even if you're wearing sunglasses. At night the intensity is so disorientating it can make you stumble. All you see are blinking squares.

These pigeons have been waiting all bunched up along the railing. Shouting and pushing each other to get the clearest view for their lenses.

In the rush of flashes you might recall odd details. Things you don't remember forgetting. I remember how I used to carry dark sunglasses everywhere with me as a little kid. I had a round purse with a unicorn on the front of it. Suddenly I see the candy pink strap that looped over my shoulder. The hard, shiny case. Mostly, all I kept inside the purse was my lucky four-leaf clover keyring and my sunglasses.

They like it if you cower. It makes a better shot. Crying, flinching. Looking angry or upset. It's more money for them. That's why they yell what they do. It's a simple equation: the more emotion you show, the more their photographs will be worth and the wider they will be circulated. A picture where you look upset and out of control will be picked up by websites and magazines across the world. Pictures of me have been published in places I may never travel to in person.

How it feels is a wet grip of panic, a sweaty clench rising up from your stomach.

There's an aluminium swell in your mouth, and you rush and swallow for air.

It's a very specific sensation. Like you're prey.

I keep walking towards the sign with my name on it, past the pigeons and their wall of cameras. I hold myself together and fight down the panic. I remember to keep breathing, and try to ignore what they're saying about my father. What they are shouting about my dead mother.

The man holding the sign with my name must be used to dealing with paparazzi. Most of the people in the airport are transfixed by the flashes and yelling, but he stands tall and indifferent.

'Is he still alive? My father?'

For a moment the man looks surprised that I don't know. Then in one smooth motion he's nodded yes, checked I have no luggage, and is steering me to the exit doors. The way he shields me from the swarm tells me he's a bodyguard. Together, we are bundled and pushed. He pushes them back. Someone grabs my arm and catches my hair in their watch, yanking my head backwards.

The electronic doors slide open and I take a deep breath of outside air. Fumy from car exhaust and the smokers clustered around the door, but already so different from London.

The bodyguard opens my car door first, before moving quickly to the front seat. There's another man behind the wheel, the engine's already on. Camera lenses rattle and clink against the glass, someone's hand splayed out across the tinted black window. Black leather seats, black carpet, all of it lit up like x-rays from the flashes. Just glass separates me from the swarming pigeons. I tell myself not to cower. To keep breathing. They can't hurt me, not really.

That is how it feels.

The driver pulls away from the kerb. My chest is beating like I've been running. Out of the airport laneway, the car enters into the flow of traffic on the expressway.

The pigeon network is as fast and wide as the internet: already photo editors will be pouring over the photos. My face on screens, magnified and distorted.

When I was little, I thought the words they wrote to go with their photographs had to be true. I didn't understand back then that what I read about Mum and Dad in newspapers and magazines could have just been made up. That what they reported, might never have happened.

The bodyguard turns around in his seat. He's sorry for the welcome. They weren't expecting paparazzi. He can't tell me anything about Dad except that he was alive two hours ago. If traffic stays clear, the bodyguard says we'll be at the hospital within the hour.

Janelle is still not answering her phone.

I force myself to focus on the road ahead, reading the street signs to quieten my dread. The driver keeps the needle just above the speed limits, weaving cleanly through traffic. The M1 expressway merges into Southern Cross Drive, before fusing into the Eastern Distributor. Roads stretch out wide, footpaths look positively wasteful. Billboards are showing the same brands they advertise in London but the faces and slogans seem strange and foreign.

I open the window: paper-dry wind roars in. Warm and textured with sun and wide-open spaces. Coming from an English winter, the colour is surreal, almost violent. The rowdy spill of bougainvillea pouring down over the sound barrier wall; a pineapple fringe of palm trees. Wild lantana, red and orange as traffic lights, punching up from the gutter.

The expressway curves around, skirting the city's edges. Each skyscraper taller, shinier than the next. Every surface mirrored and glinting as hard as it can. Up onto the Cahill and – *whoosh* – Sydney harbour herself. The art deco arch of the bridge, the jaunty Opera House seashells, and the sapphire sea, sparkling with yachts and ferries. Showy as a supermodel. Even unfiltered she's a mega-budget film set.

I catch a glimpse of the jagged teeth of the Luna Park clown along the north shoreline as we flow across the bridge, over the water and past the aqua rectangle of the Milsons Point pool. Then we're fast-tracking up the hill to Bradfield Highway and into the northern suburbs.

A few pigeons are half-heartedly smoking next to a landscaped strip as we pull into the hospital's driveway. They scuttle into action when they see the car but we sail straight past. There's another entrance in the basement. At the boom-gate the driver pulls his pass from the glovebox. Waved through by security, we glide down into the dimness.

We sit for a moment, the bodyguard scanning the carpark. He looks back at me in his mirror.

'You ready Ms Mitchell?'

—

The lift doors slide open to the airport-grade brightness of the hospital's fifth floor. I say who I am at the nurses' station. And there's the look, the one I get whenever I say who I really am. When people realise who my parents are. You see them trying to find Mum and Dad on my face. They don't at first, as they reflexively lean in, searching out confirmation. I don't have the looks of my parents – their features weren't quite so striking combined – but people usually find something when they know what to look for. The set of Dad's jaw, Mum's eyes. You can tell when they do, there's a satisfied straightening up, sometimes even a little hum. I don't think they realise they're doing it. Even in poor reproduction, it must be pleasing to recognise features they know so well.

The nurse directs me down the white corridor to Dad's door. There's the smell of hospital: antiseptic and suffering. But expensive suffering, like its pretending to be a day-spa. There are pots of aspidistras, a slight sweetness of Diptyque blackcurrant. I walk past open doorways. Breezy white rooms, airy with afternoon sunshine. The beds are bare. The whole wing appears empty, but I imagine they've just kept the surrounding rooms free.

There's no answer at the door, I turn the handle and step in.

It's dark inside. Blackout curtains are drawn and it takes my eyes a second to adjust.

He's there. Lying on the bed. His eyes are closed but I can see he's okay. His chest is moving up and down. Long, slow breaths that are being tracked by the monitors around him.

Standing next to him, I realise I was expecting him to look thinner, frail… He doesn't. There are shadows around his eyes. A tube runs across the sheet and into the back of his right hand. A purple bruise spreads out from the crook of his elbow on his other arm. A fold of gauze has been taped there, a rose of blood blooming in its centre.

But underneath all of this, he looks like Dad. Just a little older.

The relief almost makes me laugh out loud. This isn't a dying man. Dad doesn't even look sick. There's been a mistake. Some kind of horrendous misdiagnosis. Dad's probably just overworked. Stress can cause all sorts of symptoms. I remember an article I read about it causing heart attacks. Maybe I just misunderstood Janelle when she rang. I was half asleep.

Even the way he's sleeping looks healthy. His face is calm. *He's tanned.*

'They've given him something to sleep.'

The voice makes me jump. I hadn't realised anyone else was in the room. Peering into the corner I see a woman sitting in a chair against the wall. I can't make her face properly but I feel I've seen her before. She sits straighter, moving into the light of the machines and I realise she's the woman from the *Vanity Fair* piece. The Canadian actor Dad's been seeing.

'Is it Kara?'

She sniffs in agreement, not looking up from her mobile phone. 'Aavaree. Janelle was worried you weren't coming.' She drags my name out so hard, it takes me a few seconds to recognise it.

'Where is Janelle?'

'I sent her home to get some sleep.'

Her voice is loud, a declaration of territory in the quiet room. It never occurred to me that one of Dad's girlfriends would be here. I wonder how serious he is about this woman. Whether he'd want her to be here. I can't imagine Janelle would want to be sent home.

'How is he?'

Kara's reply is a long sigh, 'It's not been easy.'

I suddenly feel very tired. The monitor by Dad's bed says 6.17pm. I haven't slept since Friday morning London time. I'm not sure how many hours ago that was.

'Do you mind if I sit down?'

Kara shakes her sleek bob. There are several shopping bags on the spare chair, I try not to rustle them too loudly lifting them out of the way. The leather seat creaks as I sit.

I'm too wired for small talk and Kara seems to feel the same way. We sit together in the darkness in companionable silence, her face lit up from her phone.

Then she starts typing. Her keypad volume turned up loud, each letter Casio-tone theatrical as she stabs the tiny screen. But Dad seems undisturbed, his chest still rising and falling peacefully.

I lean back into the chair, looking past her to Dad's profile. I wonder if he'll be pleased to see me when he wakes up. Did he even know I was coming? Never mind Kara, would Dad want *me* here? Then I remember Janelle wouldn't have called without his permission.

I watch the monitor tracking his heartbeat. One beat falling steady and solid behind the next. The unhurried breathing of a heart with decades ahead of it.

Now that I'm here, now that I see him, I feel sheepish about getting so hysterical. There will be pills. Perhaps treatment in a far-flung clinic. A time of healing and recuperation, of special diets and wheatgrass shots, but Dad is clearly going to be fine. The whole world knows he's invincible. Every inch a living legend. He will grow old. And maybe there's a positive from this. Maybe it is this scare that will bring us back together as a family.

After so much travel, the rush of the past two days, the room feels warm and hypnotic. Kara's text messages continue to be chirped out. Past that, there's the music of monitors. I focus on the even, measured sigh tracing Dad's heartbeat and let my eyes close.

When I wake up Kara and the bags have gone. The monitors breathe heavily through the room. Dad's heart steady as before. I get up to check what time it is and see Dad's eyes are open. He smiles groggily.

'You're awake?'

'Hey sweetheart.'

'How you feeling Dad?'

'Tired mostly. How are you?'

'The same.'

We look at each other for a beat, then both smile.

'Can I get you something Dad? Do you need anything? Some more water?'

'I just want out of here.'

Janelle is at the nurses' station. A knot of medical staff gathered around her. Before I'm close enough to hear what's being discussed, I can see the doctors are putting up a fight. One is actually waving his hands in protest. I almost feel sorry for them. I can vouch for the pointlessness of arguing with Janelle.

Indispensable, immaculately monochromed Janelle. The neat, ballerina bun is now more white than grey, but her frame is trim and upright as ever.

Like a drop of bleach stirred into a glass of inky water, Janelle gets things done. From that first morning when she went from being Dad's PA to something more resolute. Handling the police, the ambulance, the studio, getting the blood cleaned away. Taking care of me.

I stand there, waiting for her to see me. When she does, she steps back to give me a quick, efficient hug. 'Evie! It's good you're here.'

'I've been trying to get through on the phone. Didn't you see the missed calls?'

She looks confused. 'Missed calls? No… Oh, we swapped over to new numbers yesterday. Too many calls were coming through. We have to do it every few months now.'

'I was worried. You could have let me know.'

'I'm sorry, you're right. But we knew you were on the plane, safely on your wa—'

'The flight was delayed. The hospital wouldn't tell me anything when I rang. Dad wasn't answering his phone. It was irresponsible Janelle.'

She pulls herself up, taken aback at my anger. I am too. I'm about to apologise when, ever the professional, Janelle rises above it, calmly changing the subject.

'Every, I understand there was no time to pack. Shall we get a few things picked up for you? You'll need fresh clothes.'

I take a deep breath and rub my eyes. I was the one being irresponsible. Some poor assistant would soon be rushing out to buy their boss's spoilt daughter underwear.

'Thank you, if that's okay? And thanks for sending the car Janelle.'

She smiles, 'It's been a long time Evie.'

I nod to the gathered doctors. 'What can I help with?'

'Go sit with your father. I'm sure he'll be wanting you close. We're just finishing the paperwork for him to come home.'

Halfway along the corridor to Dad's room, I remember I need to use the bathroom and turn around. Janelle has her back to me, signing the discharge papers laid across the counter. Two doctors are unhappily overseeing the process.

'I'm concerned about how long he's been sleeping,' says Janelle.

'Yes, that's to be expected,' says one of the doctors. 'It's quite normal.'

'Not for him. Could this be another symptom?'

'Possibly,' interjects the second doctor. 'Mr Mitchell was also given medication to sleep.'

Janelle's shoulders stiffen, 'On whose request? If there's as little time as you say, Mr Mitchell will not want to spend it sleeping.'

The doctors exchange a look. One of them clears his throat theatrically. 'Ms Richards, at this point Mr Mitchell really may be more comfortable remaining here.'

'I don't see why. Mr Mitchell hasn't been comfortable in hospitals at any other point in his life.'

I feel lightheaded. 'Janelle, should Dad be leaving the hospital?'

She turns, surprised to see me standing there, 'He's been here long enough. He wants to go home.' She lowers her voice, 'They can't help him. All they're doing here is pumping him with drugs.'

'Is it safe though? What if he needs something... an operation or something?'

Janelle pauses, softening her voice, 'There won't be any operations Evie.'

I stare at her blankly.

'Your father has a brain tumour. He won't be getting better.'

'Can't they take it out? People survive cancer all the time. What about chemo?'

She shakes her head. 'The tumour is too big, and where it is too important. It's inoperable.'

We look at each other.

'What will...?

'What will happen?'

I nod.

'We don't know. So far, he's been tired, and the headaches of course, but he's been fully coherent.' Janelle's tone is sympathetic but the emotion I heard when she rang has been tidied away; enough shock has leeched from the details she's telling me for her to be able to resume her job.

'He must have been in terrible pain. They've had him on morphine here and he'll have that option at home. But you know how your father is. Being stuck in a bed is the last thing he wants.'

'How long?'

'They don't know that either. It could be today. We could have months. The specialist this morning felt it would be a matter of days. A week at the most.'

Janelle reaches out to touch my arm. 'I'm so sorry Evie, but you need to know. The next few days will be so important.'

GREY

There are points in time. Little knots that pull shift, turning everything in a different direction.

Let's call them moments of significance.

Sometimes there are losses. Sometimes it's a song being written; a different road being taken. Always there are decisions. Always there are options. Paths not followed. They might seem unimportant, too minor to note, but one thing leads to another.

That's how life is. One thing shuffling gently, quietly, to the next.

Small moments: colossal effects.

Even the smallest of movements can create ripples that become towering waves.

MINA

Mr Coleman

They gave me a new dress. A design of strange blue flowers entwined on coarse white cloth. From now on it was what I was to wear.

My own dress, the one Mama had sewn for me, was ruined. Its seams had been ripped apart, and the back of it was in tatters. Wilks' whip had cut through the cotton as though it were paper. Loops of bloodstain ran from the back to its front.

'Good sturdy cotton this, outlast the both of us,' said Mrs Hoyle dropping the new dress on the bed beside me. 'You'll be wanting to grow into it a bit of course...'

Lying there, shaking and feverish with pain, the cotton of it seemed far from what mattered. Until Mrs Hoyle reached for my own dress.

'Fire's the best thing for this one now.'

It had been made by the fire. Unfolded out across our kitchen table. A week's worth of Mama's sewing. I remembered the soft weight of her hands on me. Turning me, measuring my lengths and widths as I stood still and straight as I could. I'd watched her stitches gradually draw the cloth up into the shape of me.

Mrs Hoyle couldn't understand the fuss I made. If she were here with us now, Mama would have probably agreed: the bloodied mess in Mrs Hoyle's hands little resembled what she had buttoned me into. But it wasn't just memories. The dress was also our way back to that fireplace.

Mrs Hoyle held out the blue-patterned dress for me to see. It was enormous. 'Look, it's hardly been worn. Just two small patches, here and here. You can't wear your old one Mina. It's not decent.'

In the end Mrs Hoyle let me keep both dresses. Personal items were frowned on at the mill so I promised to keep mine hidden in my bedding. After she left, I looked for the crosses and dashes I'd made in the cart. They were still there. Smudged and browning as though their edges were rusting into the cloth, but low enough from Wilk's whip that they could still show us the way home.

There was not much to remember of the following days. They passed in sticky shadow. I lay on my front. Moving hurt, so I kept still. Mostly I slept. Slipping in and out of blackness. At some point I must have bundled my dress into a pillow. I woke with my face buried deep into it and didn't think to move. Breathing in its smell of forest and burning firewood, the dark loam of blood and mud. Mrs Hoyle came and changed my wraps each evening. I held tight to my bundle as she did. Biting into it to stop from crying out as the bandages took skin with them.

The girls around me rose for work in a flurry of voices and lamplight, and returned again in the evening, but they were separate to me and I felt no connection to them. I lay still and hid my head against their light and chatter. Helen cried when she saw my bloodied wraps but I felt no part of her crying either. What could I say to make her feel better? There were no words to explain what had happened. To me. To all of us. This was a terrible place. None of us should be here.

When they were gone, the dormitory was dark. The three small windows on the far side of the room didn't let much light in. I knew it was wrong, but I longed for the shadows to come and cover me completely. The red places inside me, down past the stitches, were broken.

I knew my skin would heal, already I could feel it tightening and itching. But underneath my skin, where it should feel red and fresh, had turned black and rotten. Dark thoughts I couldn't control or push away took over as I lay there, and all that I had lost ached inside me.

It wasn't just Billy and his sweet roundness. His chubby little arms around my neck. I mourned the smallest of things. The feathery heartbeat of the hens in my hands as we collected eggs. Bluebells across the forest floor. Wind rushing through trees in full summer. I'd thought nothing of these things when I had them. Now I remembered each leaf rustling as part of a great chorus; the very sound of the freedom we had lost.

By the fourth day I could stand on my own. The stitches had held and Mrs Hoyle was pleased with the healing. She told me I must get up and eat properly. She'd brought me broth in a tin cup when she changed my wraps each night (although she called it medicine; at the mill you only ate if you worked). I knew Mrs Hoyle was right, I was hungry and a fifth day without food could leave me too weak, but the thought of going back into Wilks' view filled me with cold dread.

The next morning Helen helped me into the new dress. The stiff cotton made me wince as it was fastened over my back but we both giggled once it was on. The dress was loose enough for us to both fit inside, with fabric spare for a shawl each.

I held the skirts out wide to make Helen laugh more, instead she looked worried.

'Mina, you must eat today.'

Downstairs, once we had our bowls of porridge, I headed straight for the table furthermost from the door. Putting my back to the wall. Helen didn't ask why, perhaps it was obvious. Walking into the hall, I knew I had to sit where we could best see Wilks coming. The boys found us there a few minutes later. I saw Ty exchange a look with Helen as he sat down, but no one said anything. From that day onwards it was where the five of us always ate, and we never spoke of why.

When the bell rang to call us to work, I stumbled getting up from the table. It was just a wave of dizziness but scared of tearing the stitches, I'd flinched righting myself.

Ty's arm caught me, steadying me before I had the chance to fall.

Up close I saw the faint yellowing around his eye left from the bruises he'd got in the cart. I thought of the horrible dark marks that would be inside his shirt from the beating Wilks gave him when he'd tried to help me.

'You okay Mina?'

'Just need to watch where I step.'

'I meant your back. Helen told us how bad it was. I'm so sorry Mina, I should've done something.'

I didn't know what to say. What could he have done? Already he had done too much, and been punished harshly for it. We were lucky he hadn't been whipped with me.

Ty's worried eyes felt too close. I pushed his arm away.

'We need to go Ty.'

He looked hurt, confused. 'You sure you're alright to work?'

On the path up to the mill, the porridge churned queasily in my stomach. The thought of facing Wilks made me lightheaded. I turned to run back to the dark of my bed. It would be a simple thing to bury my face in my dress. To close my eyes and let my chest go still, my breath slowly empty out.

As I hesitated, falling behind the others, the wind tugged at me. Billowing my skirt like it wanted to play, then puffing through the trees, pulling a handful of leaves free from the branches.

For a moment everything seemed hazy: shuffled out of time.

I looked up at the leaves spiralling high into the sky and watched one leaf floating up with the wind, twirling far into the blue.

I knew Mama would not want me thinking this way. I was alive. The breath in my lungs was not a gift I should take for granted.

Coming through the mill door, the first thing I saw was Wilks' whip coiled around a hook by the doorway. Kept there as clear warning: ready and gleaming as a snake. Twice a day, every day, everyone who worked in the mill filed through the door. No matter how many days followed, I was never able to walk past that whip again without a shiver hissing down my back to see it there.

Back at the machines I was still hopelessly slow. By noon the crates around me had filled and been replaced. The reels of cotton in my crate barely covered its wooden base.

On both sides Clary and Margery reached and wound in a nimble blur. Their reels piling up neat and even. Skilfully threading, the girls never missed their mark. My reels looked clumsy. No matter how closely I concentrated, my threading was messy. If I went faster, I missed the loop, my arms always a good beat behind the machine.

I didn't know why I was so slow. The whip marks still hurt. A sharp, pulling ache from my neck to my legs. Each time I twisted to reach for a new yarn, it pulled sharper. I could feel a warm trickle along my stitches. I couldn't tell if it was sweat or blood, and dared not stop to check. But the stitches couldn't explain my slowness entirely. Nor was it my hands. The skin there had healed, and the cotton had run clean and white under my fingers all day. The other girls were spinning off three reels for every one of mine. It was clear I was just idle.

Every click or shuffle behind me I took for Wilks.

I imagined him leaning over to inspect my crate.

Seeing how slow I was, and dragging me back to that wall.

I thought I felt his breath on the back of my neck a hundred times. Jumping dozens of times as I pictured him strapping my wrists into the cuffs.

When Wilks did come for me, I didn't hear him until he was already far too close, his voice next to my ear, distinct even over the roar of the machines.

'You better not be soiling the cotton. We don't want that again, do we?'

He was so close the hair of his moustache raked against my cheek.

'No.'

'No who?'

'No Mr Wilks, sir.'

I tried to turn my head to see him, but his crop caught the side of my face.

'Eyes don't leave the cotton.'

He leaned across me to look into the crate, shaking his head disappointedly at what he saw. 'Slow. Far too slow. These crates won't make the ledgers until you're twice as fast. At least.'

I felt his crop drag down my spine, his voice back at my ear, 'Mrs Hoyle tells me those lashes will last for good. No better reminder, eh? Keep your eyes on the cotton.'

It took a moment to realise he was gone. Then tears blurred the spindles. Spilling down my cheeks as though I was a helpless baby.

I blinked furiously at the cotton until it was in focus again. A simpleton could see what lay ahead. I had to improve myself. Billy home alone and I was the one wetting my face. There was no time to waste cowering at the machines, frightened by the noise. I'd been at the mill almost a week, but if no crates were added to the ledger against my family's debt, not an hour of that time counted.

If I didn't work better, I could be here a hundred more weeks and still not be a halfpenny closer to home.

Up and across the spindle flew and I locked my eyes to it. Narrowing my world down to its movement. As the yarn tightened and thinned, I let the roar of the machines push out all other thoughts. Limp and then taut, through my hands, limp then tight.

Eyes on the cotton, eyes always on the cotton.

It took me longer than I hoped. But every day I was a little quicker, a little surer. My arms becoming stronger as the muscles remembered the machine's patterns. My hands learning where to be.

After three weeks I was almost keeping time with Clary and Margery: my crate filling within minutes of theirs. A month in, one of the men told me my crates had begun to count and were being noted down with everyone else's. By twelve weeks I was one of the fastest on the floor. Some days half a crate faster than even Margery.

At the mill we knew time from the bells, one to get out of bed, to start work, to go to bed. Up with the first bell, we woke up in the line for breakfast, adjusting our aprons, pulling ourselves together. By the last bell we were to be back in our bunks.

Breakfast was always a thin porridge. Sometimes a little savoury, mostly not. No one left a scrape of it behind because there was no chance of food or water again until night. The evening meal was soup or stew; sometimes with a hunk of bread.

As with everything at the mill, food had become uniform. Each bowl a bland sameness with the sole purpose of producing cotton. Food was no longer a reward, it was simply fuel to run the people who worked the machines.

Sun-warmed apples, bread fresh from the oven, window-steaming roasts, even something as simple as carrots, bitey and sweet from being washed in the stream. At first, I'd thought a lot about the food I missed. The blackberries Billy and I were going to pick. But even comparing mill porridge to the oats we ate at home became too sharp. Like thoughts of Billy and Papa, these were dangerous memories I had to hide away with my dress. Precious things to be carefully wrapped together, hidden safe until our families' debts were paid.

We got used to being hungry, the constant gnawing in our stomachs. We weren't starving; it was just never enough food. The thirst was harder to ignore, by mid-afternoon the factory had warmed to a thick, gummy heat that glued clothes and hair to skin. Most days our throats were sore and our heads pounded.

I would often imagine sinking into the stream that ran in the woods behind our farm. Drinking the cool water. Tasting forest, the flinty sweetness of fallen leaves and creek-bed pebbles, in each mouthful. I imagined holding myself under the water until it had washed me clean. Until every bit of the mill had crumbled and swirled away from my skin.

I pushed those thoughts down too. They took me from the path ahead.

The white cotton path, where each crate was a step towards home.

At the end of the day's shift, the whistle would blow and piece-by-piece the metal beasts juddered to a stop. One of the foremen would fling open the door and we were free to the cold night air. A cask of water was kept in the hall. Warm and woody, it was the sweetest drink I'd ever tasted.

Unless the mill ran late, there was usually an hour or so before we had to go upstairs to bed. Leaving the mill's grounds was forbidden. For an apprentice, even being caught near the boundary fence was a lashable offence. Also strictly out of bounds were Mr Coleman and the foremen's cottages. We were allowed outside – as far as the river and to the edge of the woods – but it was usually dark when we finished work, so everyone stayed where we ate, on the benches in the kitchen hall. It was an indoor life at Mercer Mill.

Sundays were different. We were given another two, sometimes three hours. I always went to the line of trees at the edge of the woods, even if it was raining. Just to breathe the outside air.

Sunday was also wash day. A bucket of cold water allotted to every apprentice to use how we chose. Not everyone took their bucket but with the mill's grime and sweat, there was no way I was missing any of mine. It felt good to scrub the week off my skin. Helen, Cal and Ty felt the same. But, as it had been with my little brother, Harry usually needed convincing.

'Minaaa, I don't need to wash, I'm fine, really.'

'Harry, won't it feel nice to be clean? Go with Ty and Cal, they'll help you.'

'I *am* clean,' he'd say, holding out filthy little hands. 'Look, hardly any dirt at all.'

Sundays went by. This pattern became our lives. We told ourselves that each day was a step towards home, and we thought we had the measure of the mill.

We were nowhere near.

The whistle blew early one day. It was a Wednesday and still light outside, yet above us the wheels were juddering to a halt.

Confused, I stepped back from the cotton and looked at Clary, who shook her head.

'Someone's been hurt.'

Greaves hurried past, returning with a wheelbarrow. He was flanked by Mrs Hoyle and Wilks when he pushed the barrow by again. I caught a glimpse of a small body flopped inside. There was something wrong with the child's arm, even against the awkward angle of the barrow it was twisted wrong. Blood was running down his hand and had splattered his trousers and soaked his shirt. I couldn't see the little boy's face but from the way he lay not moving, it was clear he was badly hurt.

The looms cranked up again and Wilks rapped his crop against one of the bars. 'Right, back to work. No point everyone missing their quota.'

'Clary, what's happened, will that boy be alright?'

'I don't know. The little ones don't often come back.'

'Come back from where? What hurt him?'

Accidents were common at the mill. There were broken bones, cuts and scalding most weeks. That night Clary explained there were also more serious injuries. She said we'd been lucky to be at the mill this long without seeing anyone else wheelbarrowed to Mrs Hoyle's room.

The little ones – who the foremen called scavengers – were the ones most often hurt. Wilks kept a measuring mark on the wall by the mill stairs. Once a child reached their ninth birthday, they were free from the line-up. But until then, any child small enough to fit under the fifty-inch mark worked as a scavenger. A scavenger's job was to crawl under the machines collecting bobbins and scraps of cotton that had fallen. They had to move quickly and keep very low to the floor. Lifting their heads an inch too high could mean being caught by one of the spinning parts or rotating belts.

It took minutes, sometimes several, for the alarm to be raised and the engines stopped. Getting caught under the machines meant terrible injuries. This is what had happened to the little boy in the wheelbarrow.

Harry's job was a scavenger. It was shameful I'd not understood what this meant before. He'd told me that he swept and cleaned. I had been so consumed with filling my crates I'd not questioned him much about it. The boys worked on different floors and it had never occurred to me that the youngest of us would be in the greatest danger.

We found out the next morning that Jack, the little boy in the wheelbarrow, had not lasted the night. His injuries were beyond Mrs Hoyle's reach; there was nothing she could do but sit with him and give him something for the pain. He came to only briefly she said, calling for his mother.

They wrapped Jack's eight-year-old body in a grey blanket and set it in a cart back to his mother. Bundled and still, he was not much bigger than a sack of wheat lying there. There would be no happy homecoming. Not for his family, certainly not for him. We watched the cart leave with its sad cargo, as we walked up towards the bell ringing us to our stations.

Clary had been right, by the year's end we saw the wheelbarrow come another three times. Small arms flopped over the edge. Two boys and a girl, all three children under nine years old. Mrs Hoyle stitched up one of the boys, resetting his bone with posts from the garden. He was back sweeping floors after a few weeks, his arm in a sling.

The other two did not come back. Crippled and broken, unable to work, they were both sent home to their mothers. They were considered lucky: free from the mill, not making the trip wrapped in blankets on the cart floor. But with Mrs Hoyle's bandages barely holding their small bodies together, and fit for neither factory nor field. What kind of life lay ahead for them?

Any hour it wasn't expected, the shriek of the whistle sent ice down your spine. *This time let it be a mistake. Let it not be too terrible. Never let it be for someone we knew.*

I looked for Harry first at the end of every day. Waiting for him outside the mill door, watching until he came into view, weaving his way through the crowd, his blond hair fluffed and spiked with cotton pieces. His grease-marked little face grinning widely as soon as he saw me.

He promised me he was careful. That he always kept much lower than he needed. He showed me how nimble he was, 'Look Mina, see how fast I can sweep! Like a squirrel! Pdarr, pdarr!'

Up against furious metal, our bodies were more vulnerable than we'd ever imagined possible. Machines showed us ways of breaking bones and tearing skin that our grisliest nightmares could not have formed. They could rip limbs from sockets, trapping and tearing a body as easily as our hands could pull apart a tomato.

Different areas of the mill had different dangers. Those working with the vats of boiling water were often scalded. Steam in the pipes could cook a person where they stood. If the pressure built up unchecked it could crack the metal, shooting steam jets at anyone with the misfortune to be standing nearby. Once I saw a piece of skin hanging off a woman's back as though it was a thick sheet of paper. Boiled and pale, it was no living thing anymore.

These horrors circled us, always in the back of mind. But strange as it might sound, it was Wilks we feared the most. Like dread itself, he stalked the mill. Demanding faster work, more cotton. The whip he kept hanging by the door wasn't in the habit of gathering dust, and his voice was always there. Behind you the moment your mind wandered. He noticed every ragged edge, every imperfect reel.

Maybe it was just easier to focus on Wilks and the whip. We were powerless against the mill's dangers, but Wilks was something our hard work could ward us from. To be able to walk onto the mill floor each morning, maybe we had to believe it was only Wilks waiting there for us.

I was heading for the line of woods one Sunday when Harry ran by. I saw a flash of blood smeared across his forehead as he bolted past.

He circled back reluctantly, only after I'd called after him several times.

'What's this?'

'Oh Minaaa, you're always fussing, it's a tiny scratch. C'mon I'll be late.'

'Late for what? How did you do this?'

'Late for the fishes Mina! We're catching a fish. Kitchen says if we catch one, they'll cook it.'

Harry had made fast friends with three of the other scavengers. The four of them ran together, tumbling and bouncing off each other like puppies.

'Harry, this is a nasty scratch, we should see Mrs Hoyle.'

'Ssh, if I didn't have time for sweeping, I *really* don't have time for Mrs Hoyle.'

'What do you mean you didn't have time for sweeping? Harry!'

But he had wriggled free and was sprinting off in the direction of the river. Yelling over his shoulder as he disappeared behind the trees. 'Fish for tea tonight Mina-Meens!'

I stood on the path. If Harry had left cotton pieces on the floor again Wilks would be told. Twice already Harry had left his area littered with bits of cotton. He was on his last warning with Greaves for forgetting his pan and brush, last week he'd even answered back. We'd seen apprentices lashed for all of these offences. Everyone liked Harry, even the supervisors chuckled at his cheekiness as he danced about, but that would make no difference to Wilks.

The mill would be empty now. Entering it alone was forbidden but no one, not even the foremen stayed longer than needed. Sunday afternoons Wilks spent in his cottage.

I didn't see how else Harry could escape punishment.

Walking up towards the mill, I kept checking over my shoulder. The path was empty but I knew anyone could be watching from the trees, or looking down from the mill's windows.

There was no reason for the door to be locked, but how easily it swung open when I turned the handle made my stomach lurch.

Inside dust motes and cotton fibres floated in the air. It was eerie to be here alone. I looked back to the doorway where Wilks' whip was coiled and waiting on its hook.

The machines sat tense and watchful as I crept past our stations. Our crates still neatly packed with cotton reels. Each footstep I took creaked the wooden floorboards.

I'd never heard the floorboards in the mill before. It had never been quiet enough.

The scavengers' brushes and pans were on the second floor. I found a tidy stack of them together on a shelf along the back wall. It didn't take me long to find the area that must be Harry's. At least a pan of cotton twists were scattered across the floor.

To reach them I had to crawl flat on my stomach under the pipes, then squeeze around a huge engine. The metal was still warm. How much hotter and more cramped would it be to work here while the machines were running? The heat and noise coming off them would be terrifying.

On my hands and knees, I swept together the bits. Twice banging my head on the belt above, something that would have meant a terrible injury for Harry if he'd done this while the machines were on. It made me feel sick.

Harry was seven. Unless he grew taller than Wilks' fifty-inch mark he would be working under here for another two years. But none of us seemed to have grown since we'd arrived at the mill. We didn't know if it was the lack of food or the work. It didn't really matter for most of us. Not getting taller was only dangerous for the scavengers. From now on, I'd make sure Harry ate some of my food too.

I was putting the brush and pan back on the shelf when I heard footsteps.

I scrambled behind a pillar.

The footsteps were heavy. Too heavy for Wilks, and too slow. Maybe Greaves? Whoever it was, the rules were clear: if they saw me here, it would mean the whip.

The lash marks across my back had faded, but Mrs Hoyle had been right when she said some were cut too deep into the skin to ever come out. There were two pale half-circles curving from shoulder to waist and three lines down the centre of my back that I'd always wear.

Reminder enough not to get myself caught here now.

Heart pounding, I peered out from the pillar.

The figure down the other end of the room was making his way towards the stairs. I saw it was the great man we had met in the room of books on our first morning at the mill. Mr Coleman.

Something looked wrong with the way he was walking, even from where I was hiding, I could see he was moving strangely. His pace was lopsided and his head was down.

As I watched, he tilted and keeled to one side. The papers and books he was carrying slipped from under his arm. He lunged for them, staggering forward, his hands grabbing air.

Somehow, he then tripped, fell against the wall, and slid downwards to the floor.

He landed in a sitting position, swayed to-and-fro, then slumped sideways where he lay on his back surrounded by the scattered books and papers.

Crouched behind the pillar I held my breath. Sprawled across the corridor, Mr Coleman was blocking the only way out. I waited for him to get up, but he didn't stir.

Long minutes dragged by. As far as I could tell, he was sleeping.

I thought desperately of escape options. I could hide here until work started in the morning but any empty bunk would be seen long before then. Already my absence might be noticed. Most of the apprentices would be back in the kitchen hall by now.

The only way out was to get past Mr Coleman.

Holding my skirt tight to keep from rustling, I tiptoed towards him, keeping to the edges of the floorboards so they wouldn't creak. Pressing my back against the wall, I edged past the rise and fall of his stomach, carefully stepping between the papers and books.

Finally, I reached the door. I gently turned the handle downwards and slowly, slowly, inched the door open. Afternoon sunshine was just yards away.

As I tiptoed into the doorway, a shriek of cooling metal from one of the machines behind me pierced the air.

Mr Coleman mumbled and opened his eyes, staring straight at me.

We looked at each other. My eyes wide with horror, his blurry and indignant.

'You there, help me up.'

Frozen to the floorboards, my hand still on the door handle, I looked at the empty staircase in front of me. Freedom just a few steps beyond that.

'Hurry now girl!'

Even with the wall to lean against, Mr Coleman swayed slightly after I helped him up. A strong smell of liquor was coming off him. I'd seen men drunk before. Too much mead and ale at harvest gatherings put fires inside them. Then it made them either too loud or too slow. Too merry, or too melancholy.

Mr Coleman waved his arm at the floor, 'Those books need taking back to the office.' His voice was slurred: he was one of the slow ones.

I knelt to collect his papers and books and followed him up the stairs and into his office. He landed heavily in his chair. None of us had been back to this room since we first came to the mill. We'd rarely seen Mr Coleman. Only once had he joined Wilks on a mill floor inspection.

The office was fuller than I remembered. The piles of books had grown. Stacks of papers covered both tables; some had fallen on the floor. Two of the books were face-down in the corner, as if they'd been tossed angrily. The room smelt stale. I put the books I'd carried for Mr Coleman on the desk in front of him.

'Pour some water, will you', he waved vaguely to a white jug balanced on a heap of books. There was an empty glass on the desk beside him. I filled it for him and waited. He gulped the water down, then gestured impatiently for more. I refilled his glass and stood back, watching him fearfully.

He sat still, his eyes closed as though he'd forgotten me. I waited, edging backwards towards the door. Sometimes drunken men didn't remember what they'd done when they woke the next morning. Was it possible Mr Coleman might forget he'd seen me? Perhaps if I left quick enough.

'Sir, shall I leave you now?'

He opened his eyes slowly. Regarding me hazily. He looked down at the neat stack I'd laid in front of him, and then around the room. 'No. I may need you to fetch more water. Make yourself useful in the meantime girl. You can see the office needs straightening.'

I set to tidying. Quick as I could. I started with the papers on the floor. Not being able to decipher the tiny symbols on them, I couldn't tell which papers went together or how to best arrange them, so I collected them into one pile. The books I put together according to their colour and size. The brown ones on one shelf, the thin little ones together on another. It was easy to make the even shapes of the books look nice; if I wasn't so scared, it would have been an enjoyable task. Every so often Mr Coleman blinked open his eyes and nodded in my direction. When I was done the room looked better. The books in rows along the shelves. A tall stack of papers in front of Mr Coleman.

I stood there, waiting. 'Mr Coleman sir, would you like anything else?'

He looked at me properly. 'What's your name girl?'

It never occurred to me that I could lie, 'Willamina, sir'

'You work with the reels?'

'Yes sir.'

'Have you been at the mill long?'

'A year now sir, since last autumn.'

'That will be all, you may go.'

I hurried out in case he changed his mind. By the time I'd reached the last step I was running. Out to the fresh air. I ran and ran, down the hill, towards the trees as fast as I could. Until I couldn't run anymore and had to bend over, gasping to catch my breath.

At tea, the others talked about their afternoons. Having quickly given up on fish, Harry and his friends played a game of catch with some rags they'd begged from Mrs Hoyle and knotted together.

I was too scared to say what I'd done. I could see Ty was watching me, wondering if something was wrong, but telling my friends might put them in danger too. And maybe if I never spoke of it, the meeting with Mr Coleman might be wiped away as strangely as it had happened. Mr Coleman had been very drunk. Hopefully the memory would be murky enough that he'd not think to tell Wilks.

That night I couldn't get to sleep for hours, and when I did, I dreamed of Wilks coming for me. He and Greaves marching down the lines of benches to where we sat.

The next morning I watched nervously as we ate our porridge, barely taking my eyes from the door, but Wilks did not appear. We filed out of the hall, up the path towards the mill. Taking our places in time for the bell. Everything looked as it usually did. The spindles began whirling and we began working. I was more jittery than usual. Each click or creak behind me made me jump, but Wilks did not stop at my post as he walked the rows.

A week later Wilks did come. It was towards the end of the day. My crates had been changed twice and a third stood full: pristine, even reels coiled neatly almost to the top. As always, Wilks was already too close by the time I realised he was there, his voice in my ear, his breath curling down the side of my cheek.

'Complete that thread, then finish up. You're to come with me.'

I followed him down the length of the mill. My eyes on the whip hanging at the doorway. Steeling myself for what lay ahead. It wouldn't hurt so much this time. I knew what to expect. I was older and stronger now, and I knew it was worth it. Better me than little Harry. Far, far better.

But Wilks didn't go to the front door. Instead he turned left, up the stairs towards the office.

Mr Coleman looked livelier than he had the last time I saw him. The office looked messier. Once more there were stacks of books teetering on every surface. Papers spilled across the floor, collecting in piles around the table legs.

Mr Coleman glanced up at me then nodded at Wilks. 'That will be all Wilks.'

Wilks cleared his throat, 'Sir, shall I return presently for the girl?'

Mr Coleman shook his head no.

Wilks was clearly reluctant to leave me in the office. He cast a final disapproving frown in my direction before closing the door behind him.

Mr Coleman looked at me intently. I swallowed, staring down at Mama's shoes.

'Willamina is it?'

'Yes sir.'

'Can you read?'

'No sir.'

He sighed. 'To be expected, I suppose. Let us hope you're a quick learner. I've no time for simpletons.'

'Yes sir.'

From then on, Mondays I spent in the office. After breakfast I would go and knock on the office door and wait until Mr Coleman called me in. Inside it was always a mess. Like a storm had raged through, swirling the papers and books up into a rustling fury. As I had the first time, I always began with whatever was on the floor.

Once the books were back on their shelves, I wiped the surfaces clean and began sorting the papers I'd collected. This was when I had to pay close attention, because this involved the symbols. Mr Coleman gave me a list of symbols to look for on each piece of paper. When I found a set of them among all the other symbols on the page, I knew which pile to put the paper in.

It was like a game. One that I was dreadful at. In the beginning

I needed to run a finger along every line of symbols on every single page, sometimes more than once, to find the right set. Gradually I began to recognise some of them straightaway.

The symbols weren't called symbols. Their true name were letters. There were just 26 letters. Once I learned this, I had hope: even someone like me could remember so few as that. Groups of these letters were called a word. Words came in groups too; these were called sentences. With small dots to show when one finished. Each letter also had another version of itself, like a mother or father letter that showed the start of the next sentence. Once you remembered all the words you could break the code. This was what reading was.

I learned that words weren't only about rules and laws. Everything had a word. It was an astounding thing to realise. To look around you and know that everything you could see had its own set of letters. Even things that were not things had words. If you laughed that was a word. Or walked, or ran. You didn't even need to be able to see it. The wind had a word. Smells had words.

The whole world was made of words. Once I learned this, everything felt different. My head buzzed and sang from the power of it.

Words were not just for great men; even a farm girl could have them.

On a screwed-up piece of paper from Mr Coleman's bin, I wrote down the words I knew. My writing was ugly, much bigger than Mr Coleman's, even so I liked to see it. Each Monday I added as many more words as I could, and looked at them each night before the lamps were taken.

I hid away another sheet of paper when there was no space left on either side of the first. Soon I had five sheets to wrap with Mama's dress.

Some words like 'cotton' looked like what they named. A puffy word that reminded me of how it looked on a reel: cloudy soft outside with a thin wood middle. But most words, like 'delivery' or 'consignment' or 'batch' did not recall anything helpful, you just had to remember them.

I wanted desperately to share it all with my friends. These words felt like they were stretching out my thoughts: changing the shape inside my head. I tried to explain so Ty and Harry and Helen and Cal would see things differently too. To know the world as it really was. And how it could be for us too: knowledge was a code we could break and understand.

I laid my papers on the kitchen table at nights. Pointing out the little symbols and what they meant. Ty was able to sign his name so I thought he'd want to see other letters. I had found the word for 'cow' to show Harry. But my writing was too clumsy for them to understand. I couldn't explain it properly. Harry didn't see how my three letters looked anything like his Brownie.

No matter how much I tried to include them, Ty saw my working in the office as a bad thing. He saw how it set me apart from the other workers, here in a place where it was dangerous to stand out. At the mill we were to work, sleep and eat in a uniform sea of faces. At home on our farms we had never thought to wonder if we were different. But here fitting in could be a matter of survival.

Margery, the girl who worked to my right every day, had never warmed to me. Improving my speed at the cotton had made little difference to her assessment. She put it about that I had airs and thought myself above the rest, and this office business was firm proof. There would be giggles and sshs as I walked past some of the workers. Margery always in the thick of the circle. There were even whispers that I was now a spy for the mill.

But what worried Ty most was Wilks; the foreman clearly didn't like the arrangement either. Since I'd started in the office he had been checking my crates more often, and seemed to single me out wherever he could.

'I don't like it Mina', said Ty. 'The writing, the office. None of it. Wilks already had his eye on you.'

Helen agreed, 'No one else even goes to the office Mina. Ty's right, it can't be good.'

Ty shook his head, his eyes holding mine, 'It's not good. You don't belong in there.'

Ty sat across the table from me. I looked at his hands, clasped together in concern. I put one of mine over his. 'The office is the safest place in the mill.'

'Or the most dangerous.'

'I don't have a say in it, Ty. You know I don't.'

I *didn't* have a say in whether I worked in the office, but the dreadful truth was that I wanted to.

I counted down the days until I was back there. I saw how selfish this was. I knew Billy would be waiting for me. All that should matter was working the cotton and getting back to him as quickly as I could, but I was hungry for words. The more words I had, the hungrier I became. Hungrier than if they were food. I told myself it was to do my job better, to be less frustrating for Mr Coleman.

Deep down, I knew it was more, and worse. I wanted the words for myself.

I stopped bringing the pages to the others. I didn't talk about reading anymore. It made me sad to think it, more alone than I could bear, but maybe Ty also saw how the days I spent in the office put distance between us. While I was there with the books, my friends were sweating under the machines. Harry, Helen, Cal and Ty had become family. Ty and I both knew that what divided you from family was never a good thing.

EVERY

'What is it like?' I ask Dad.

'The morphine?'

'Yes.' Although I meant everything. The morphine, the pain, the knowledge of what was in his head, malignantly taking over, bringing death.

What was it like to sit here on this balcony and know that everything that he'd ever seen and heard and felt, would soon be gone?

'It's a clumsy drug. Feels foggy and disconnected. Like bad jetlag.'

'What about everything else?'

Dad looks at me, 'You mean the tumour?'

'Yes.'

'It's a fucking headache.'

There are currently twenty-three people at the house. A team of five are setting up medical equipment in Dad's bedroom downstairs. It is shiny, cutting-edge technology that they're running their thick grey and yellow cables to, but all that these machines can do is monitor. No one is talking about cures or recovery.

From tonight, Sylvia, a palliative care nurse, will be staying at the house. The term palliative is a polite way of saying we've shut the door on getting better. Like terminal no longer only means the inside of an airport. Sylvia's job is to manage the levels of pain Dad is experiencing. She will do this with morphine injections. Too little morphine and the pain becomes debilitating, too much and he'll be debilitated in other ways. Dad wants the smallest dose possible so he can still function, but it's a balance that's expected to tilt downwards as the tumour grows.

There are more questions than answers. We don't know how long the tumour has been there. Nor do we know exactly what it will do, or when it will do it.

What we know is that inside Dad's body, a battle is being fought and the good guys are not going to win. Once-healthy cells have gone bad. They have formed a shadowy mass, stretching dark tentacles into Dad's brain. Turning on their neighbour cells, becoming stronger and faster with each kill. The medical term for cancers like this is aggressive.

It's a hostile takeover. When the tumour gets to a certain size, Dad's brain will no longer work. The doctors don't fully understand brain function; they can't pinpoint which part holds what bit of him. We know that as the tumour gets bigger, Dad will get smaller, but they can't tell us what part of his personality or memory will go first. At some point, whatever's left of Dad will be overwritten by dark shadow. His memories, his loathing of mayonnaise and fondness for fresh figs. All of the skills and opinions he has built up over 64 years of life will cease to exist.

And that's the best outcome, other possibilities include a scenario where Dad loses control of his body first, so he is conscious but unable to talk, or move by himself.

My father does not want to be resuscitated. He has no interest in wearing nappies, and has been very specific about not wanting to be a vegetable on a bed.

They've been over the options. There weren't many. By the time Dad's symptoms – headaches, bouts of dizziness, an uncharacteristic craving for sugar – reached the point where they could no longer be dismissed, the tumour was lethal. Its tentacles coiled in too deep and tight.

Janelle and her team have consulted the foremost experts. Scans were sent to every relevant specialist they could find. Brain surgeons were flown in. The position of the tumour ruled out surgical procedures. Chemo was suggested, although only as a means of delay. Alternative experts advised unconventional treatments, more ways to slow down the tumour's path of destruction: wasp venom in Brazil, cider vinegar therapies in Switzerland. But these are only theories and projections. No one has any guarantees or cures, and Dad does not want to spend the time he has left hooked up to a cytotoxic drip in a chemotherapy ward. That is not the sort of time he wants to stretch out.

Right now, Dad and I are watching the sunset.

We're sitting on deckchairs on one of the balconies wrapping the ocean-side length of the house. The sunset is sticky gold and we're both wearing sunglasses. He's still half-buzzed on hospital sedatives. I'm hazy with jetlag. A soft breeze is blowing. We're sipping from tall glasses of carrot and ginger juice. He's drinking it because ginger is good for your immune system and there's an enzyme in carrots that cancer cells apparently hate. I just like the taste. Sipping my juice next to Dad, looking at the view together, none of this feels real.

Free from hospital wires, Dad's wearing his normal clothes. Apart from the bruising along the insides of his arms he is how I remember him. Out in the daylight his skin looks older to me, but so I imagine, does mine to him. It has been a while.

We have our deckchairs on recline, our feet pointed at the sky. It feels pretty relaxed. To look at us, you'd probably not think either of us has six days left to live.

Inside the house things are less tranquil. Sound is muffled by the balcony doors but on the other side of the glass there's a lot of movement, a sense of battening down the hatches against the coming storm. Every so often someone scurries past. A woman who I guess must be Dad's housekeeper is arranging extravagant bouquets of flowers on the dining table; the get-well cards have been stacked together in a pile. She's just finished working her way through the bedrooms downstairs, beginning with Dad's, changing the bedsheets, opening up the windows and airing out the wardrobes. From her brisk manner I'm guessing this refreshing was one of Janelle's suggestions.

Lenny, Dad's manager since before I was born, is over by the bookcases. He's on his phone, gesturing grandly at the books with a full glass of carrot juice. Lenny was waiting for us at the house. Hurrying out to the carpark as we drove in through the gate. His big, grizzled face a cobweb of concerned lines that creased into a grin when he saw me.

'Hey kiddo, long time. How ya doing?'

'Hey. You always going to call me kiddo, Lenny?'

'Damn straight kiddo. Come give Uncle Lenny a hug.'

By the sofas Dad's girlfriend Kara is discussing hair and make-up with her manager and her manager's assistant. Or maybe the second man is Kara's assistant. Either way, both men look nervous. There has been a critical shortcoming somewhere in the hair and make-up department. They are all drinking carrot juices, Kara sips hers angrily, insisting someone called Sebastian be flown in. I've no doubt this will happen, Kara radiates such self-assurance I have to remind myself she's only three years older than me. In proper light she is exceptional looking. Tall, gleamingly polished, her limbs have the otherworldly thinness of a model. She draws the eye with such pull, I keep finding myself staring at her.

Four men are checking security. Armed with high-spec binoculars and walkie-talkies they've taken turns climbing up ladders outside the property wall to see if there is any vantage point from which Dad can be seen. At one point this process involved two of them standing on separate ladders next to where we're sitting. There are high walls protecting the property and the way the house curves into the cliff keeps it hidden from the road, so we were already pretty secure. Only one of the neighbouring properties has even partial views of the house, but Janelle says there have been pigeons camped out front for two days now, so extra precautions must be taken.

There are also people working in the kitchen. I walked in to get something to drink and was greeted by piles of glistening vegetables and three startled faces. Carrots and ginger being fed into an industrial-sized juicer. It smells like they're now cooking dinner.

This house is big – my whole flat would fit into the kitchen – but it's not big enough to absorb this bustle. It feels more like a film set than a home.

On cue, lead director, Janelle, strides past. Pausing to adjust a spray of orchids before disappearing into the kitchen. She has two assistants trailing dutifully in her wake, a boy and a girl, both of them typing her instructions into their tablets and juggling glasses of carrot juice.

On the balcony, Dad and I sit side-by-side looking out. From our spot high up on the cliffs, gazing straight out, it's all sky and sea. Great and infinite blues, hazy with salt. Right now, everything feels surreal, detached with tiredness. From nowhere, comes the realisation I have a favourite view, and that this is it.

To the left is the farthest tip of Sydney's northern beaches. A narrow finger of land curving out to a heap of red boulders and Barrenjoey Lighthouse. Just 200-metres wide at its tapered arch, the peninsula separates the smooth deep waters of the Pittwater from the sand dunes and surf of Palm Beach. To the right, if you crane your neck, you can see the rock pools and spiky headland at the other end of the two-kilometre beach.

But look straight ahead and all you have is blue. The break of waves and the wild, untameable Tasman Sea.

This is the view I grew up with. This is the house I lived in until Mum died.

Blue was the colour of childhood. It's the colour of happiness.

Blue came before red, and grey.

A few years before I was born, Dad commissioned a bold, inventive team to build this house. He wanted his home to fit in with the landscape, not an especially common idea back then. Paint it the colours of the bush he told them: dirty greens and muddy blues. Much of the out-facing walls are glass, treated to reflect back the colours of the shrub and sky. It was a house of some architectural significance then, but to me it felt like a big bird's nest. We were three lucky birds living in our nest home out by the sea.

There are houses around it, more now than when I was small, some of them bigger and closer together. People overbuilding and sub-dividing their land as the real estate prices rocketed. Perched against the cliff-face, the house still feels nest-like. On three levels, it balances improbably on stilts. The back of it carved into living rock, the front facing out to sea. High enough on the cliffs to be secluded. Far enough from the beach that sunbathers are flecks of colour.

Inside it's a vaguely upside-down layout with the main living areas on the top floor, the level you walk into from the driveway. It's mostly open-plan: dining room area stretching into sofa area and opening out to the balcony, with a separate kitchen. Next level down are the bedrooms. Then Dad's studio, the cinema room and a laundry take up the last floor. The top two floors have wraparound balconies, but you can watch the blues of sea meeting sky from all three levels.

When Dad first brought the plot of land, it was mainly wild. Bush rambled down to the coral-coloured dunes. The few homes here then were weatherboard shacks and pastel-painted bungalows. White-haired retirees played golf on a casually mowed patch of grass next to the Pittwater. Thirty-three years has made a big difference. Billionaires and tennis stars live here now. A seaplane service takes regular flights back to the city for those whose schedules are too tight for the hour's drive.

On a map the Palm Beach peninsula looks bizarrely thin: a whisper curve of sand and bush-covered rock. It's hard to imagine how the roaring surf hasn't snapped it free or washed it away altogether. But time and tide have spared the peninsula, so it can't be as fragile as it looks.

The sun has almost set. Over the distant crash and shell-suck of waves I can now hear a vacuum cleaner whining inside. I'm wondering if Dad needs more painkillers. A gust of sea salt stipples a gauzy film over our sunglasses. Dad takes his off, putting his juice down on the table with a disapproving clink.

'You actually like the taste of this?'

'How you feeling?'

'Like I'd rather be drinking scotch.'

I turn to watch his profile, trying to read his expression, 'Dad I'm so sorry about all of this.'

He's staring out to sea, inscrutable, 'It is what it is, I guess. We'll have to get the film happening a lot faster than I planned though.'

'Janelle said it was pretty much done?'

'She means *Axlark*, which should have been finished weeks ago. It's the next one. Barely been started. We only got access to the diaries a few weeks ago.'

'The diaries?'

Dad points to the bookshelves next to Lenny. 'Our two-hundred-year-old production notes.'

I see a long line of brown leather spines. 'A historical? Didn't think you liked doing those.'

'I don't, the wardrobe always takes over. But this is something I need to do.'

I thought about all the stress, the months of preparation involved in getting a film off the ground. 'Dad, is a new project really what you want to be getting into right now?'

He's still watching the sunset, now a red oil slick on the water. When he speaks again, his voice is quieter. 'It's not just another film Evie. I promised Therese I'd make it.'

I'm surprised, not just by what he's saying. Dad never spoke of Mum.

'Is it something to do with Mum's great-uncle, that Parliament guy?'

I knew there had been a famous politician in the family, a few hundred years back. But I hadn't heard anything mentioned about him since I was little.

'Yes, that's right. Her great-great-great-granduncle Alden Rigby-Williams. Those diaries in there were his sister Claudine's, your great-great-great-grandmother.'

'Why did Mum want you to do this?'

'Alden was a reformer. He more or less invented child protection laws.'

'He saved children? I had no idea.'

Dad nods, then seeing my amazement says, 'We never really talked about your mother's family, did we?'

'We didn't even talk about Mum.'

Dad looks back to the horizon.

An image of blood flashes through my head. An arc of ruby red drops on concrete stairs. Then the questions, same as always.

Dad is the only person who can tell me what happened, what really happened that night. But he is moving to get up, closing down the subject, like he always does.

I jump to help him. He waves me away, preferring to lean on the glass instead, as he steps through the door to join the others inside.

'Dad? Can we talk about that night?'

He doesn't look back, 'There'll be time later Evie.'

MINA

The Office

Winter chilled and shook the trees. One morning we woke to a muffled landscape of snow. Then spring, summer, and autumn again, with its leaves flung up against the windows like outstretched hands. There wasn't cause to celebrate the seasons at the mill as we had on our farms. Whatever the weather outside, life inside was the same. Like reels of cotton, days at the mill fell in behind each other. Each one spooling indifferently into the next.

Each morning I followed the ringing bells with the other apprentices to our posts. On Mondays I'd slip away, head down, quickly as I could, up the stairs to the office. I'd find my friends again at the end of the day, quietly melting back into the throng.

I knew very well that the time I spent away from the mill floor would come from my quota. I did my best to close the gap, keeping my spindle lever fixed to full speed the rest of the week. Whirring through the cotton to pile up all the extra reels I could.

I'd stopped trying to convince Ty that my being in the office could be a good thing.

I hoped it had just become part of the mill's routine for everyone else.

One night came a lesson that showed me otherwise. I reached for Mama's dress, which I kept bundled together with the sheets of words I'd learned.

My bed was empty.

In panic I pulled loose the bedclothes. Frantic that our path home – the red dashes and crosses I'd pressed into the dress – and all the learning that was held on each sheet of paper might be lost too. Over and over I searched. Pulling up the mattress, searching between the wall and bed frames and under the surrounding bunks, until Helen stopped me.

Mrs Hoyle didn't know anything about it. No one had seen anything. There had been no sweeping in the dorms that day. All my belongings were simply gone.

The pages were a howling loss. The words had grown to twenty pages' worth of handwriting, the writing getting smaller and tidier as the pages progressed. But it was the dress I missed most. It wasn't just our way home, Mama's stitches had sewn memories of home into the cloth. Curled up tightly in my empty bunk I tried to tell myself it was only an old dress. That we would find another way to remember the journey home.

After that I stopped keeping a record of the words I knew. It turned out that I remembered them well enough without the paper, and it was not safe to keep them anywhere but in my head.

~

We worked the cotton, and years rattled by. Four of them had passed since we'd seen our homes. Harry had safely reached his ninth birthday and had been released from scavenging. Cal was seventeen, Ty almost eighteen. Helen and I were now in our sixteenth year.

In the office I'd lost count of the words I knew. This wasn't much cause for smugness: the more I learned, the more I understood what I lacked, but my filing had improved and Mr Coleman was less irritated with my handwriting. One afternoon I learned about maps.

There was a drawer of them in the office, rolled up in scrolls. I had known maps were a way of drawing out the world, now I understood how they worked. Once you could read the names of the places, you could follow the lines – some of them rivers, some roads and pathways – to wherever you wished to go. I found our village. No more than a squiggled line marked on one of the maps, but I knew now that even without my dress we could find our way home.

Running a mill involved a lot of paperwork. Everything that happened here was accounted for. Every crate of cotton coming in and going out had to be logged. Mostly we worked in silence. I tidied and sorted. Mr Coleman wrote in the ledgers, read the papers that had come in and threw them on the floor for me to pick up later.

I had a lot of questions, especially in the beginning, but Mr Coleman did not allow questions, so I had to wait for him to feel like talking or work things out for myself. The days Mr Coleman drank, taking sips from a gin bottle he kept in his drawer, were the days he was likely to explain things to me.

Those were the days he would also let me update some of the ledgers. But no matter how my handwriting improved, or however drunk he got, Mr Coleman never allowed me near the shelves directly behind his desk. These ledgers were forbidden, and punishment he warned me, would be fast and final. This must be where he kept his records of the workers. I hadn't found our cotton quotas anywhere else either, so I knew that's where these ledgers must be too.

Mr Coleman didn't own the mill. Like Wilks, he was an employee. The mill's owners were the Mercers, a family who lived two hours' ride away in London.

The Mercers had engaged Mr Coleman to run the mill and, 'not having an inkling of the business of cotton' the family made increasingly unreasonable requests of him. 'Living in their splendid house,' he said, 'they were entirely unconcerned by the exertion and sufferance involved in the making of their tidy monthly profits.'

He meant his own suffering. He rarely left his office or walked the factory floor and I never saw him touch a thread of cotton, but somehow Mr Coleman imagined every crate the mill sent to London was down to his own exertion.

The Mercers wanted more and more cotton processed and it was this burden that drove Mr Coleman to the gin. What started as a few nips here and there had stretched to the odd half a bottle. The waft of liquor creeping over the papers was becoming more regular. Some afternoons he got so far down the bottle, his nodding head would come to rest on whichever ledger was in front of him.

It was on a day like this that I decided to look inside the ledgers behind his desk.

I knew the risk. Mr Coleman didn't make empty warnings. If he woke up while I was reading anything on the forbidden shelves, the very least I'd have coming would be a whipping, and I could count on Wilks being especially severe. But night after night I had lain in my bunk thinking about these books. Somewhere within their pages must be our quotas: I had to know how much longer we'd have to work at the mill before we could go home.

Holding my breath, I edged behind Mr Coleman's chair.

I stood there for a moment, willing my heartbeat to calm, watching the back of Mr Coleman's head just inches away. Then slowly, gently as I could, I eased one of the thick black ledgers from the shelf.

From the first page onwards there were names. I ran my finger down the neat lines of Mr Coleman's handwriting. Hundreds of lives at the mill, each of us reduced to a line of detail and a worker number. The next ledger was the same.

I knew there were daily counts of how much cotton the mill produced. That Wilks and the other foremen kept track of how many carts each of us produced. What I couldn't see in either ledger was where these quotas were written.

Mr Coleman stirred.

I slid the ledger back into place and crept back to the stack of forms I'd been sorting.

From then on, every time Mr Coleman slept, I looked through more ledgers on the forbidden shelves. The sixth one I pulled was a record of the whippings Wilks gave out.

Later I found a slim brown ledger which held a record of the deaths at the mill. Miserably sad: each name next to how they had died and what age they were. Most of the names were written beside a single number: they had been young children under ten. If any proof was needed that scavengers were the ones most at risk at the mill. Here it was, black on the page.

Mr Coleman's handwriting ran to five pages of names, the ledger had a good twenty or so more empty pages, did he intend to fill them? How many more children would that add up to? How many horrific deaths? I wondered if anyone besides Mr Coleman had ever seen this book.

There was no sign yet of the ledgers I wanted to find. The ones tracking our quotas. The few workers who lived outside mill grounds and were free to leave were paid a monthly stipend. There were plenty of ledgers accounting these payments. Where were ledgers for apprentices?

Were the quotas the same for all of us? It made sense to me that our final target would be in keeping with the value of the farm we were each paying off, but was there a different rate for girls and boys? Did ages come into the calculation? And for scavengers or packers like Harry, Ty and Cal who didn't have reel-based quotas? How was their work measured?

I kept looking. I knew there was something I must be missing; not reading correctly.

I found my name and the age I'd been when we arrived here four years ago. Willamina Halewood, 12 years old, and tracked it across. I was worker 455, listed with our farm. Mr Coleman's writing stated that, at the time of citation, the land had 10 acres of workable fields, a cow, a plough horse and six hens. Papa and Billy were listed as 'two males remaining: an adult and a young minor'. There was no notation of what our farm was worth in either cotton or money. Alongside my details were similar ones for my friends, no values for any of their farms or work either.

I started again. Instead of snatching any of the ledgers in simple reach, I began going through the shelves tidily. From the top to the bottom, left to right, keeping track of which ones I'd seen. It was slow. Mr Coleman didn't sleep every Monday. When he did, it was not often for long enough to read much. It took me months, but finally I'd thoroughly searched the entire bookshelf.

There was no record that I could find of any apprentice's target quota or what they had amassed. With every other detail carefully accounted for, it seemed out of character for Mr Coleman to try to keep these figures in his head.

At the top of the shelves I'd found a thick roll of papers, tied together with a stained ribbon. Each sheet was wax stamped. Looking through, they described property details of farms similar to ours. Two rooms upstairs, one down. Acres of arable land, some with wheat fields. There were at least two dozen sheets. Ownership of all of them was attributed to the mill.

I saw that five of them had been signed over from a Mr RS Ruthers Esq. Landowner Ruthers. They were last dated four years ago, around the time we came. Could they be our farms? Had Landowner Ruthers sold our farms to the mill when he brought us here? Were we paying off our debts to the mill, not Ruthers?

That night I couldn't sleep. Possibilities rolling and lurching in my head. Could these ledgers be kept in Mr Coleman's private quarters; his cottage on the hill? But why? Surely our cotton quotas were no worse secret than the ledger of the mill's dead?

Other than by injury, no apprentice had left while we'd been here. New apprentices had come. One of the boys, a friend of Harry's, had been brought from a family who had already lost a daughter here. I knew I had pieces of something I couldn't quite assemble.

Just before the morning bell rang out, a thought came to me. A cold sureness creeping in over my bedclothes. There were no quotas. There would be no end to the debt. The mill had no intention of sending us home. Not until we were useless; broken and ruined in the back of the cart.

All those reels of cotton added up to nothing. They weren't a gleaming white path home. They led nowhere. They were simply stacks of crates to be sent to London. Everything had been a lie. Our competitions with each other to get faster and faster.

What did it matter how fast we were?

We weren't going anywhere.

EVERY

Later, after most of the Mitchell House production team have left for their own homes, the people who will be sleeping at the house assemble to eat dinner together at the long dining table.

Bedrooms have been assigned. I'm in the room that used to be mine, Janelle will be staying in the other ocean-facing room between Dad's and mine. There's some muffled discussion about whether Kara will be in with Dad. It's decided, in the end, that it may be better for her to have her own room. She and Dad's nurse, Sylvia, take the two guest rooms.

It's an early night and we're all in our rooms before midnight.

It's strange being back in my room. In keeping with the house's latest restyle of textured charcoals, the vibe is masculine minimalism. My teenage posters are gone. There are new dark wood built-in cupboards. The bed is bigger and now has a gunmetal-grey suede headboard. I run my hands along the pile, lifting a shadowy blur. I wonder who has slept in this room since it was mine.

There are five framed paintings on the walls now. Neat black frames where there used to be a mishmash of art posters and sketches held together by greasy pinches of Blu-tack. I was nineteen the last time I was in this room. Still sticking my own drawings and paintings to the walls. Tacking them up indiscriminately with prints by my favourite artists. I lean closer to see who's hanging now. It takes me a moment to recognise what I'm looking at.

More than a decade ago I painted these pictures on scraps of card, never imagining the possibility of them being beautifully trimmed and framed like professional, actual pieces of art. I stare at them amazed. Abstract shapes, in mostly dark palettes. It's fair to say this was Every Mitchell's moody period. Three of them are a bit rubbish, but there are two I still like. It's nice to see them. Whoever decided to keep these paintings, that was very nice of them.

Inside the built-ins, beside two extra pillows and a folded blanket, I find further evidence of teen me: an oversized AC/DC t-shirt and a pair of bleach-splattered jeans.

Lying in bed I listen to the beach below. The waves and sand lullaby of childhood. I wonder how many nights I'll be here in this room. Then jetlag closes in. Mattress and quilt come up over me and I sink, stone-boned through the layers.

Sunday, 4.09am

Four hours later I'm awake, alert and clear as though a bell has rung in my head. I lie there listening to the silent house. I'm hungry.

Upstairs, I switch the kettle on and check the fridge. It's immaculately stocked. Fresh representatives from all food groups neatly arranged on the shelves. Mostly healthy, more Janelle's doing than Dad's taste. I make myself a sandwich and take it over to the sofa with my mug of tea.

There's no fear of waking anyone. This house absorbs sound like deep space. Dad grew up in England, in old, wooden-floor houses where every step is a chorus of creaks and complaint. One of his first directives to the architects was that this home should be entirely soundproofed – from level to level, and room to room. Each of my footsteps dissolves soundless onto the, cool stone.

Outside is navy blue night-time. Stars unfurled to the horizon in an unmistakably southern sky. The dark is alive with spangled constellations. It's a night sky to put you in your place and remind you what a piece of insignificant dust you really are. I chew my sandwich.

Wind ripples through the Norfolk pines. Down on the beach the tide will have washed away yesterday's footprints leaving the sand smooth and clean. None of the houses have their lights on. No boats that I can see out on the water. Not so much as a blinking satellite overhead. All that's awake is the revolving beam of the lighthouse and me.

Mum loved this view too. What I'm looking at right now would have been one of the last things she saw. This is where she died, in this house. At the foot of the stairs. They weren't carpeted then. It was a different staircase. There used to be a raw spiral of concrete steps coiling through the house's three levels. One of those floating styles, coming out of the floor like a twirling ribbon. A set piece.

When I was little, I wasn't allowed to run down them. I always had to walk carefully, one at a time. There were thirty-two of them from top to bottom; two sets of sixteen. Everyone always said they were dangerous stairs to have with a baby in the house. Apparently there was always a plan to get someone in to replace them. But I got older, a toddler, then a child, and always so careful, so tediously cautious.

If I'd fallen even once.

Mum and Dad never needed to replace the stairs because I never once hurt myself on them. My pudgy little hand oh-so-sensibly gripping the rail each and every time I came up or down.

She must have caught her foot. We don't know exactly what happened. Somehow Mum lost her balance at the top of the stairs. Tripping and falling down to the bottom of the house where the cinema and Dad's studio are.

She lay there on the polished concrete. Her long hair splayed, a pool of velvety red blood inching out to frame her. It happened about this time, very early in the morning. But we didn't know straightway. Not for hours.

I don't remember everything from that day, but what has stayed with me is clear.

My alarm didn't go off until 7.25am. In the middle level of the house, my morning routine started as though everything was normal. I would have dressed for school and gone upstairs for breakfast – hand no doubt tightly gripping banister. That morning I had muesli: toasted oats with dark raisins and ribbons of dried coconut. I remember that distinctly because I saw it come up again later and have not felt like eating it since.

It's funny, what stays with you, what floats away. The bits you get to keep, the moments you hold in sharp focus. They're not the ones I'd choose. How did she smell? I could not tell you how that was. Ask me to draw a picture of those chewed-up twists of coconut and I could make it clear as a photograph.

It was quite normal not to see my parents on a school morning. I was 12. I could be trusted to get myself ready. To be waiting on time to be collected: uniform on, lunch made. It wasn't unusual not to see either of them until home-time at the school gates. No doubt I chewed my muesli unhurriedly.

I don't even know why I went downstairs. Maybe it was that I'd noticed Mum and Dad's bedroom door was ajar when I'd come out of mine. I must have expected to see them still up from the night before, watching films in the cinema room. That wasn't unusual either. Muffled with thick carpet and big sofas. Red wine smiles, Mum with her head on Dad's shoulder, curled around him like a cat.

The doctors told us she died quickly. The deep gash along the side of her body was window dressing. The real damage had all happened on the inside. Massive cerebral trauma. A blow to the left side of her head. The only outside sign of what actually killed Mum was a tiny curl of blood that ran from her ear to her neck, not quite long enough to reach the floor and join the rest of her blood.

Seventeen years later, the shame still feels hot. There's a sweeping burn of it at least once a day. To think of her lying there on the cold concrete while I dithered over breakfast upstairs. She wasn't dressed warmly, just a silky robe.

I never understood exactly what happened. How she fell so badly. Mum had studied ballet as a child, even drunk she was very sure on her feet. Or why she was alone. There were only three of us in the house that night, but where was Dad when she fell?

MINA

Harry

All I could think about the next week was getting back into the office. I was desperate to find something that proved the quotas existed. I told myself I just hadn't found the right ledgers yet. There could be a hidden shelf. Hollow compartments in the floorboards. Somewhere I'd not seen.

We had missed so much of our lives here at the mill. Billy would be seven now, a young man. Would he be tall and fair like Papa or dark-haired like Mama and me? Did he still save his favourite part of every meal to eat last? Would he still giggle if I drew circles on his palm? Or come running for hugs if there was lightening across the sky? I didn't even know if my brother would recognise me.

I couldn't let myself believe that we weren't working to pay off our farms, that all these years away from our homes didn't add up to something.

I realised one afternoon I could answer the question of quotas in some ways myself. I knew the price of cotton. It was a number I'd written down enough times in the office, and it had barely wavered in the years we'd been here. The mill wouldn't count the whole value of each crate we filled. There would be deductions for food, board; other costs I couldn't guess. But if I counted the value of half a crate, that would give me a rough sum I could compare to the value of our farms.

It took me a while, drawing marks in the dirt behind the apprentice's hall until I was satisfied with my sums. After the first year I had filled no crates on Mondays. None would be counted for the first month when I was too slow. Sundays were shorter, two-crate days.

I sat back looking at the numbers in the dirt. Three thousand, seven hundred and fifty crates of cotton. I had built a tower of crates. Helen's tower could be even higher. I wasn't sure how to work out Harry, Ty and Cal's quotas, as they had no crates to count, but there must be a way. We had come to the mill together, if any of us should stay back, it was me for the time I spent in the office.

Saturday afternoon the whistle screeched through my thoughts. It was the warning whistle. Someone had been hurt. The machines clattered to a stop around us. Greaves ran to get Mrs Hoyle and the wheelbarrow. It was quiet along the rows, everyone holding their breath.

Whatever our differences might be, when we heard that whistle everyone on the mill floor stood together as one. United in desperate hope that the injuries weren't terrible. That it wasn't someone too young, that they would be alright. That it had been quick.

As the barrow wheeled back, some of the workers looked away, flinching at the suffering, not wanting to see the extent of the wounds. I held my ground as the barrow neared my row, whoever might be lying in it, I never wanted them to see me turning away, shutting my eyes to their pain.

It was a child, a boy. Around the same age as Harry. The legs dangling from the wheelbarrow looked familiar. Harry had similar trousers. For a moment I hoped it wasn't one of Harry's friends.

Then I realised they could be Harry's trousers.

I screamed and ran to the barrow.

It was Harry. Crumpled and broken. His hair dark with blood, his clothes ripped open. There was blood smeared across his cheek and trickling from his mouth. His eyelids were fluttering.

'Move! Get back to your station,' barked Wilks. 'This doesn't concern you.'

I looked up at Mrs Hoyle. My face desperately pleading.

'Mr Wilks, this is serious,' she told him. 'I'll need her help.'

Wilks nodded us away, turning to yell at the other workers. 'Back to work, all of you, back to work now.'

Gently as possible we lifted Harry up onto the table in Mrs Hoyle's room. I was grateful he was unconscious; the pain of being awake would be too much. The wheelbarrow was pooled with his blood. Even as he lay there, more blood was running out over the table.

With a pair of scissors Mrs Hoyle cut the tatters of his shirt away so we could see where it was coming from. Everywhere. Harry's body looked like it had been through a wringer. Black bruises were coming up on any skin that wasn't bloody. When we moved him, his arms and legs swung loose, as though they had no tension. Worst were the wounds themselves. Ripped and twisted. It was as if the skin had come apart, leaving great valleys of gaping flesh. Blood pouring from so many places.

Mrs Hoyle stepped back, looking at him.

'Quick, Mrs Hoyle, sew up those cuts, before he wakes up.'

She shook her head. 'There's nothing we can do Mina, only ease his suffering.'

'You can sew him up. Give him stitches like you did on my back. Please try Mrs Hoyle, please try. We need to stop the blood coming out.'

'Mina, I could try to stitch together these wounds. But there's nothing I can do for the ones inside. There's nothing anyone can do. Ssh now, don't let him see you cry. He needs you to be brave. You can cry for him later, now we must be strong. It won't take long.'

'No, no, no. Mrs Hoyle. It's Harry. He can fight this. He can. He's breathing. Look, see how he's breathing and moving. We have to help him. Please Mrs Hoyle, please, stitch him back.'

'Mina it will only hurt him more. Too much blood has left his body. His insides are tangled. There's been too much suffering for his body.'

Harry was waking up, a thin moaning sound coming from him. His eyes fluttering open. 'Mina. It hurts. It hurts so much.'

Mrs Hoyle told me to get a small bottle down from the top shelf, the one with the red label. 'This will stop the pain', she told him, spooning the mixture into his mouth. He spluttered and choked but a good jolt went down. Almost immediately he stopped shaking.

I brushed the hair out of his eyes. He was pale. Far too pale, and he felt cold.

'Sorry Mina, I went too close.'

'It's okay Harry, don't talk, just rest now. You're so brave. So brave Harry.'

I covered his body as gently as I could with the blanket Mrs Hoyle passed me and kneeled down so my forehead was next to his. 'We love you so much Harry, you're such a good boy.'

I whispered in his ear about how we would go back to our farms soon. How he would be seeing his family and his cow again. That Brownie would be so pleased to see him. I told him that we would all leave the mill together very soon.

'Okay Mina.'

His eyes fluttered, his focus coming and fading. His breathing was now ragged. Uneven jags of breath that became a soft whistle I could barely hear. There was a sudden inhalation, and then nothing.

I pressed my face close to his, up against his neck. There was nothing, no sound. No movement. No breath.

Harry! His face looked so calm. So young. This could not be the end for Harry. How could this be his fate? Harry was too full of light to be dimmed here, in this cold, dusty room. There was too much life ahead for him. Far better it was me lying here than Harry. What had I to offer in comparison? He was the best of us all. I sobbed.

Later, when we washed him, we found that both legs and his right arm and shoulder were broken. No one had been working next to him. By the time the alarm was sounded Harry had been swallowed completely by the machine. It had taken long minutes to free him.

Wilks had put him back on a scavenger run. Nine years old was the cut-off age for working under the machines. Harry was ten, but

Wilks had stood him against the measuring wall this morning and decided Harry was still small enough to do the job for the day.

When we'd finished washing him, Mrs Hoyle sewed up his wounds to spare his mother from the worst of it. I washed the blood out of his hair, and brushed it neatly. Too neatly, it was the first time I'd seen it tidy. It didn't look right, so I ruffled it slightly. We wrapped him in the softest blanket I could find in Mrs Hoyle's cupboard.

Mrs Hoyle was going to tea but I didn't want to leave Harry alone. She said I could stay with him if I wanted. It would be alright to sleep on the chair beside him.

After she left, I knelt back down beside Harry, my head against his shoulder. He lay so still. With the blanket covering the wreckage of his body and his face cleaned, just a long, dark bruise along his cheek, he looked asleep. I couldn't believe the life inside this dear little body was gone from us.

And for Harry, all the things he would never see. His beloved Brownie. He would not pet her again. There would be no homecoming for him. He would never taste his mother's cooking. Instead, the last meal he'd ever eat was thin grey porridge. There would be no wife, no children of his own to raise. All that he could grow to be. The rich life he would have made. How could all of that be so suddenly gone?

This was not right. His life had mattered. Harry had been worth something far more precious than a tidy floor. The mill didn't see it this way. It would fire up again tomorrow as though none of this had happened. The machines would keep running, it didn't matter if that was through our bodies and bones. Wilks and Greaves and their men, even Mr Coleman, to them we were expendable. We were just a means of cotton.

I drifted in and out of sleep. Waking through the night to stillness and the silence of the room. The small hand in mine icy cold. In the morning when Greaves came to take him to the cart, I knew it was just his body.

Harry was already gone.

Nothing felt important for a long time after that. It was always Harry who had best dealt with life here, showing us how to make light of things where we'd seen only gloom. The four of us walked through our days heavy and hollow. The mill's routine folded around us, dragging us along with it, but the sadness was hard to shake, even if we'd wanted to. At breakfast and tea we ate quietly. Harry's place beside us howling with its emptiness.

Dozens of times I thought I saw him. Playing down by the river. His messy blond hair darting and disappearing into the mill's crowd ahead of me. His legs racing up the stairs to the boys' room. When I looked again, or ran after him, the hair was darker, tidier, or the boy was taller and it was just my mind playing tricks.

Three months after Harry died, I knew for certain that our quota ledgers did not exist. There was no need to keep records of our work because we were not paying off any debts. Whether we'd been able to read them or not, the pages we signed when we arrived had indentured us to Mercer Mill until the age of twenty-one. Indentured essentially meant the mill owned us. Until we reached twenty-one, we were as much the property of the mill as our farms.

The sheaf of papers I'd found rolled together were indeed land deeds. Mercer Mill had bought the farms our families lived and worked on from Landowner Ruthers. We were just collateral to the deal. During our years at the mill each of us would have produced enough cotton to cover many times over what the mill paid for our farms, but it was unlikely we'd be left with anything more than our freedom.

Helen and I had another four years here. Cal and Ty a year less. Harry would have had eleven more terrible years stretched out before him. How could we have even left him here alone?

Mr Coleman didn't see a problem in the arrangement when he'd confirmed it on one of his drinking afternoons.

'It's a good life here for you children,' he told me, slurring. 'A fine opportunity. We provide you all with food and lodging, almost certainly to a higher standard than most of you are used to. We give you a sound education in cotton. You could take the skills you've learned here to any mill in the country. Why, I doubt you'd find better training in any mill in Britain!'

I couldn't bring myself to tell the others. It felt kinder to let them think they were working towards something for a little while longer. We were sad enough already. Some nights Helen would climb into my bunk, like she had when we first got to the mill. We'd hug each other, and she would think I was crying for Harry. And mostly I was.

Harry had been gone eight months when I found out the mill would be building an extension. Mr Coleman told me another hundred workers, 'at minimum!' would be needed to fill it. Many of them would be young children. Children like Harry and my brother Billy. One of them *could* be Billy.

I sat with this news, fretting and pulling at it for days. My chest tight and ragged. The day the builders came, setting up the scaffolding along the back wall of the mill, I realised something that I'd known for a long time. Working in Mr Coleman's office, knowing what I knew. I couldn't just pretend things would be alright. The mill's owners, the Mercers, might be fine city dwellers but they were still a family. A family had children.

What family would let other children be killed in their name?

In the line for soup that night I whispered to Ty that I needed to speak with him. We agreed to meet at the willow. Down by the river and hidden from view in the long grass.

He was waiting for me when I got there. His back against the tree, watching the currents flow past. I sat beside him.

'You okay?' he looked worried.

'There's something I have to tell you. Things I've found in the office.'

'Office things?' He smiled, relieved that was all it was. 'Best keep it simple for me then Mina.'

In a rush, I told him everything. That there was no quota. That we had been lied to: there had never been a plan for us to pay off our debts. Ty looked back to the river. I watched his profile, outlined in blue with the dusk light. He didn't seem surprised.

'Ty?'

He flicked a piece of grass into the water, 'No one's ever gone home.'

'No. And none of us will. Not until we're twenty-one at least. The mill is just taking these years from us Ty. How can that be right? How many more children will die? How can any of this be right?'

Ty looked at me. 'What are you saying?'

'The owners must be told. They need to know how dangerous it is here. The mill can't keep taking little children and making them work as scavengers.'

'Told how? You ever see these owners come for a visit? Even if they did come, Wilks would finish anyone he caught trying to talk to them.'

'What if we went to them?'

'To the city! We wouldn't even know which direction to start out on.'

'Ty, you weren't there with Harry, you didn't see how hurt he was. You didn't see what that machine did to him.'

'I know…' Ty took a deep breath, his voice kinder when he continued. 'I'm so sorry you saw that Mina, but getting yourself killed won't bring him back.'

'What about the others who will be coming, when the mill's bigger? What about those children Ty? Someone has to do something. The Mercers need to know what's happening here.'

Ty turned to me, gripping my shoulders, our faces close. 'Mina these are wild thoughts, you know they are. Put the Mercers out of your mind. Harry's gone. All we can do is keep onwards, keep our heads down and do the work. We'll be home in a few years.'

A jolt of loneliness shot through me. I couldn't tell Ty about my plans. I'd been selfish to think I should. To him the journey that lay ahead would be unthinkable. He hadn't seen the maps, or how the city could be found. For him, London may as well have been a ride to the moon. Nor would it be fair to pull him into such danger.

There was no point talking about it anymore, Ty's words would only call to my fears, and I had enough of those already.

I reached to quiet him, my hand on his. Our faces were now close enough that I could feel his breath drawing in and out on my cheek. I looked down at my hand in his. Something felt different. There was a tightness firing and twirling in the air between us, in my chest, as I felt his hand grip mine. Maybe it had been different for a while. I saw that he felt it too.

For a long moment we looked at each other, trying to see each other's thoughts in the fading light, then Ty lifted my hand to his mouth.

I watched him run my fingertips slowly along the ridges of his teeth. The nip of his bite sent fiery sparks shimmering down my veins.

I gasped and he reached out, pulling me to him.

Over the years we'd hugged and knocked about. Ty's arms had been around me plenty of times, but this was charged and new. I felt the muscles moving under his shirt and pressed my body into him. He inhaled sharply, burying his face in my neck. The air around us sped and spun, then slowed down. Suddenly the world was only this. Skin, breath. The rush of water in the river running beside us. His lips on my skin. There was nothing else.

He ran a finger under the collar of my dress. Softly, so slowly tracing the line of bone beneath my neck, circling my shoulder. I watched his eyes, deep and dark, unreadable now. An aching breathlessness building inside me.

He paused, his voice low and soft. 'Is this what you want?'

I nodded, pulling him back to me, hearing the cloth of his shirt give way.

We tumbled backwards, down into the grass together; his mouth on mine a saltiness that tasted sweet. His body warm and strong, the full weight and length of it was a heaviness that felt both easy and unknown as it covered mine. It seemed a weight that could protect me.

Ty shifted and turned, lifting me so I now lay on top, pushing hard into him. I looked down into his eyes and we smiled at each other: slow, close smiles. We rolled together, spinning and swirling. The heat spreading out between us, wet and full of sweetness. His hands were rough but he held me as though I was precious. My body gleaming like the river.

Later, his finger traced a pattern on my skin. Lower than before, below my collarbone. Up and down and around. As though he might be making his mark, writing his name. For whatever it could mean, and for however long the touch of skin could hold, I did the same. Closing my eyes, I wrote Mina across his heart and wished this moment might keep us safe, binding us under the early stars against all that the world might unfurl.

We stayed there in the grass together until the bell for bedtime rang. My head on his chest, his hand in mine, the summer crickets calling out around us. I tasted him on my mouth afterwards, the heat of his skin still warm on mine as I fell asleep.

Two Mondays later I sat watching Mr Coleman's head flopped on his desk. I knew exactly where to find the name of the Mercers' house. Which map to copy out to guide me to London. I could see the slim brown ledger that held the mill deaths. I knew what had to be done.

Still, I sat there listening to Mr Coleman's snoring.

Taking the ledger would mean leaving tonight. A severe whipping would be the very least of what would be coming after that. And for what good I could not know. Of all of us, I was the one least qualified for the task. Lacking Ty's wisdom and strength, Cal's confidence, Helen's good sense.

It was Harry's bravery that I needed the most.

Eight hours later I lay in my bunk waiting.

The brown ledger was wrapped to my stomach with a strip of rag from Mrs Hoyle's scraps basket. The dress she'd given me was still too big, but walking under Wilks' whip today, the stolen ledger's edges hard up against my skin, I'd been very grateful for its loose folds.

I looked over at Helen, sleeping soundly in her bunk beside me. I hoped she'd forgive me for not confiding in her, not even saying goodbye. Sneaking off into the night was a betrayal of our friendship. It was a betrayal of all three of them: Helen, Cal and Ty – especially Ty. They wouldn't have let me go if I'd told them, but that didn't make this right.

As soon as he found out I was gone, Ty would know where. Hopefully he would understand why. I'd avoided his eyes across the table earlier. I knew there was a chance the four of us might never be together again. At breakfast tomorrow it would just be three. Like Harry, I was leaving them. Unlike Harry it was my choice to go.

I looked down the rows of bunks. I couldn't be sure all of the girls were asleep but every minute mattered now. If the cart took two hours to get to London, I would need a good five, maybe six hours' headstart on the horses. Hopefully Wilks wouldn't know I'd escaped until after breakfast. Once everyone was in the mill, he'd see my empty station. But by then I should have reached the Mercers.

My worst fear was that Wilks would send someone to our farm. Search it for me and take Billy in my stead. But if I didn't show the Mercers the ledger, that could happen to Billy anyway. The mill had no qualms in taking more than one child from a family.

I tightened the ledger under my dress and laced up Mama's shoes.

It was a good twelve-foot drop to the grass below, but with the door locked behind us each night, the window was the only way out. The window frame creaked as it swung open. As far as I could see, the other girls slept on.

I climbed up onto the narrow ledge. There would be no going back once I dropped from the windowsill. It was too high to climb back to from outside, and without door keys there was no other way in. I couldn't see how Wilks would forgive me for this. Nor Mr Coleman. They would view my going to the Mercers as treachery of the worst order and deal with it accordingly. I knew I had to face the possibility of never seeing Billy and Papa or the farm again.

I took a deep breath, taking a last look behind me. At Helen sleeping, at my own warm safe bed.

The landing winded me but nothing felt sharp or broken. I scrambled to my feet. The kitchen was dark. It didn't look like there were any lights on in the superintendent's quarters either, but that didn't mean no one was about.

To get to the woods I had to walk past Wilks' cottage. I'd hoped he would be asleep, but as I crept to the edge of the hall, I saw his lamps were burning. If he looked out of his window, there was no hope he'd miss me. It was a clear, cloudless night, the moon bright and still quite low. My dress shone like a white beacon on the lawn.

I tried to breathe down the rush of panic. If Wilks stood up, he'd look outwards before looking directly down. As fast as I could, I ran towards the glowing window, my dress flapping around me. Heart hammering, I fell to my hands and knees against the wall of his cottage.

Crawling under Wilks' window. I didn't dare raise my head to see if he was in the room, but I felt him there. Like a cold shadow seeping through the bricks. Every second I expected his voice behind my ear. His crop jabbing between my shoulder blades.

Finally, I was clear of his cottage. I ran across more open lawn to the path. Down the path, past the kitchen garden and, at last, over the fence and into the safety of the trees.

It was cooler in the woods. The temperature falling as soon as I stepped under the first branches and into the threshold of forest. The night-smell of trees and their secrets surrounding me.

From my bed to where I now stood had been the space of a few minutes.

Such little time to change the shape of so much to come.

EVERY

Sunday, 6.44am

When the sun comes up, blazing rose gold across the walls, I'm back in my bedroom. Flopped across the bed, waiting for everyone to wake up. I'm wearing the AC/DC t-shirt and bleach-splattered jeans I found last night, and listening to my old CDs.

I remember carefully rubbing away the knees of these jeans with a pumice stone when I was a teenager. Sprinkling bleach across the denim in what I considered an artful arrangement. The effect's not quite as impressive to me now, but they smell fresher than the clothes I wore on the plane.-

I found the CDs in the cupboard next to the jeans. Neat stacks of old music next to the three-piece stereo I was ridiculously proud of. Even the Sony logo looks retro now. But when I plug the stereo in, everything cranks into life. The LED display flashes, the triangular play button glows neon-blue and the little CD tray expectantly slides out.

I put on The Church's *Gold Afternoon Fix* and the sunny, shimmering guitars of *Metropolis* fill the room. Rich and bassy. It sounds wonderful. I slide open the balcony doors. Down on the water the blinking orange circle has cleared the horizon. Seagulls are wheeling and calling. The air smells new and clean. Mum and I used to dance around the kitchen to this song. Both of us singing along. *There'll never be another quite like you. I'm so involved with everything you do.*

—

By 9am, breakfast is in full swing upstairs. We're back to a full production. Around the table are Dad, Kara, Dad's assistant director, Joe, and both of Janelle's assistants, whose names are Nat and Nic or Nic and Nat. One's in satsuma orange, the other in chrome yellow and hot pink. They're on their laptops, tapping away brightly like two tropical lorikeets. There's a new guy called Chris the Editor who is sitting next to Joe and gazing at Dad like he thinks Dad is a golden god. Janelle's on the move, checking something in the kitchen. Carrying shopping bags downstairs. Kara's manager is slouched over one of the sofas, urgently whispering into his phone. These are movie people. You can tell by how flawlessly groomed the women are, and how much denim the men wear.

I take one of the empty seats at the end of the table. There's a selection of heaped bowls – fruit salad, yoghurt, muffins, muesli – although no one's eating. Riz, one of the cooks from yesterday, asks if I'd like anything hot: eggs? An omelette? Some grilled halloumi and rosemary tomatoes? We settle on a coffee.

Down the other end of the table Dad looks tired. Even so, listening to the conversations, it's clear the day he has planned won't be a restful one. He and Joe will be going over final edits with Chris. We're expecting Lenny with some people from the studio any minute. There have been changes, the usual last-minute tweaks. Kara isn't happy with some of her lines.

'Dad, is there anything I can help with?'

He doesn't hear. I wait a beat, then raise my voice to repeat the question. 'Maybe I could help with research on the new project? The location stuff? If any of the scenes are based in London…'

This time everyone hears. Eight heads turn to look at me. I picture what they see. My hair might be a bit wild: I didn't pack a hairbrush or any bands to tie it back. I didn't bring moisturiser with me either. My skin is scratchy and dry from the flight. I'm wearing the clothes of a sulky teenager from the 1990s. I realise I might not look as helpful as I'd like.

Dad smiles, amused by such an improbable idea, 'No sweetheart, you just relax.'

'Maybe you should be doing that too?'

Beside him Joe looks horrified. Everyone now appears to be holding their breath, waiting to see how my father will answer. Even the man on the sofa is watching intently.

Dad nods thanks to Riz who is refilling his espresso cup, '*Axlark*'s almost in the bag.'

There's a collective exhale through the room.

I persist, 'Can we spend some time together after that Dad? The two of us?'

'Yes... yes, definitely. Let's do that. Janelle, can you make sure there's some time?'

Janelle smiles, looking over at me. It's a dance we've played for years. We both know what this means. She'll come back to me later and explain how busy he is and how he'll make it up to me tomorrow. Which is fine, but how many tomorrows do we have?

'You look tired Every, did you get enough sleep?' she asks.

There are a few polite murmurs of agreement around the table, everyone taking a moment to review the shadows under my eyes. 'Yes, thanks Janelle. Just woke too early.'

'Jetlag? Sunshine's best cure for that, why don't you pop down for a swim.'

'Not sure I should be swim–'

Kara's drawl cuts through the debate on how I should spend my morning. 'Fooord can we go over that scene before the guys get here?'

Dad, Kara, Joe and Chris the Editor disappear downstairs to the studio. Riz starts clearing away the breakfast things and Janelle brings her laptop over to join her minions. Ten minutes later Lenny and the studio guys arrive and file downstairs in a swoosh of sneakers and denim.

I pour another cup of coffee. Today's newspapers are piled on the table beside me. I reach over to flick through them as I drink my coffee. On the front page of the second newspaper is my face.

You can see it clearly. It's taking up a quarter of the page.

In the showbiz section six pages in, the rest of my body is attached. I'm in the other tabloids too. *Ford Mitchell's daughter in frantic dash to his bedside.*

My stomach drops in a queasy rush.

The photos from the airport. It looks like I'm crying. Possibly angry crying. The pictures are laid out next to ones of Dad looking heroically urbane. There's a shot of us together on one of his sets when I was about eight. Another photo with Mum from a premier the three of us went to the year before she died.

I tell myself these are Sydney papers. Maybe international outlets won't have picked up the daughter angle. I'm hardly the story. I google the UK tabloids. I'm there. It's a smaller picture but still front page. I think about everyone at my office. My friends. The nice man at the cornershop. I'm clammy. The skin on my face feels hot and tight. Anyone who sees these photos now knows who my parents are.

I think about pigeons waiting for me with their flashlights outside my flat, my office. How long will it be before I can live in private again. If I keep my head down, keep out of any more of their pictures, will I be able to go back to a normal life?

I fold the newspapers back into their pile. It's unlikely anyone at the house would have thought to warn me. No one here would have thought twice about seeing themselves in a tabloid.

Janelle looks over as I get up. 'Evie, Nat's brought some things for you – clothes, something to swim in – I put them in your room. Anything else you need, just write a list. Nat can pick them up for you.'

The assistant in the orange dress smiles brightly. I thank her and mention to Janelle that I might go out myself later for some things.

'Hmm, might be easier to stay this side of the gate? Just for a bit Evie, with the paps outside?'

Apparently there are even more pigeons out front this morning. You can see them all on the security monitor, but I don't even want to look. Knowing they're there, waiting, watching, brings back a familiar claustrophobia. Waiting on Dad to find some spare time, hiding from the pigeons swarming outside. Even if the hotel room is really beautiful, if you can't leave, it's hard not to feel trapped.

I'm too jetlagged to think clearly, so I just do what I'm told, and go change into a bright yellow bikini.

At the bottom of the house, leading out from the laundry is a narrow passageway. Steep steps running downwards between property fences. It's private land until you get to the beach. Overgrown and reliably cobwebby, this path is one of my favourite parts of the house. No matter how many pigeons are out the front, it's always been secret.

Tiny lizards dart back into the undergrowth as I make my way down the path, their brown bodies fast and fluid as water. There's a heady, summery buzz of cicadas.

The sand is already scorching. It's weekend busy. Not like European beaches where sunbathers lay three fingers' width apart, but busy for here. Parasols and bright towels are scattered over and under bodies. Teenagers flirting and laughing. There's a sticky tropical scent of sunscreen and fizzy drinks. Up on the grassy picnic area someone is barbequing sausages and sweet onions.

At the water's edge toddlers in sun-safe rompers and hats are shrieking at the waves, wobbling buckets of sandy water back to their moats and castles. There's a platoon of kids learning how to be lifeguards: the little nippers, splashing about, having the time of their lives. I was part of the nipper squad here for a summer. I had to stop after pictures came out in *Hello!* and other parents complained about seeing their swimsuited eleven-year-olds in a magazine. But before then it was brilliant fun – I learned how to read the water, to watch for rips and see the tide turning.

There's a good surf up today. Waves are coming in evenly, dumping down a wide stretch of creamy whitewater. I wade in, diving under the first wave high enough to cover me. It's gaspingly cold. The Tasman Sea usually is. People stand on tippy toes to avoid those first splashes.

I push out through the waves. Jumping to glide over the ones still curling up, diving through the ones already broken. The pull and tug of surf is strong, real bones to swim against.

Out past the belt of swimmers, the sand bed drops away and the water quickly becomes deep. I don't feel the cold anymore. I feel light. Clean as an empty shell. Beyond the foamy milkshake of breakers, the water is smooth and glassy clear. I can see seaweed and rocks twenty feet below.

I float on my back, jellyfish light over the rolling swells of the beginning of each wave. Eyes stinging. Arms and legs starfish-wide. The water's salt holding me, my thoughts drift until I realise I'm thinking about blood. How red Mum's blood was.

When she was the age I am now, my mother had seven years to live.

From here I can just make out a reflective glint of window high above the beach. It's too far away to see anyone inside and even if it wasn't, our privacy is ensured by the trees and treated glass. It looks so peaceful, you'd never guess at all the happenings inside. This view has changed little over the years. The trees have grown and there are now more houses surrounding it, yet the house looks exactly as it did when Mum and I used to swim down here together.

My skin goose-pimples under the water's surface remembering all the blood. The close, earthy smell of it. How it was sticky but cold.

Washing it off later from the soles of my feet, and my face and hands.

I have to talk to Dad.

GREY

Blood has an almost identical composition of minerals and trace elements as seawater.

Those red currents swirling through your veins carry the same salts that ebb and flow in the ocean.

Ever wondered about that?

Here's another question.

If what you did mattered? If the weight of your decisions carried way beyond yourself? To the furthest shores you could imagine.

Would that weight make you more, or less?

And would you want to know?

MINA

Leaving the Mill

The woods were thick and overgrown. It was hard to see at first, but as my eyes began to adjust to the darkness my back straightened and my steps became surer. It was good to be moving, to have the canopy of leaves above me, to feel the muscles in my legs stretching as they were meant to. My breathing slowed and a mossy calm softened across my shoulders.

All of this, the faraway hoot of owls, the rustle of leaves and branches overhead, the snap of twigs underfoot, felt so familiar. It was easy to imagine these woods were taking me back to Billy and the farm. But from the map I'd drawn in Mr Coleman's office, I knew I was walking in the opposite direction.

Once I'd put a safe distance between myself and the mill, I headed towards the road. I'd planned on following it from the edge of the forest, so I could hide if I heard anyone coming. But after an hour of walking, the woods gave way to pastures. Trees and fields hadn't been drawn on the map, and now great sweeps of bare land, blue in the moonlight, stretched out on either side of me.

Leaving the protection of trees made me uneasy. I kept looking back over my shoulder, searching the shadows, but the road behind me was always empty. From the moon's position, I knew we were within the witching hours. Not many would venture out now. I used to watch the night shadows from our kitchen window, scared of what might prowl out there. That seemed a long time ago.

I looked up at the stars glinting in the skies above. I had come so far from home. The world was so big, so wide, and I was so alone in it. I'd not been on my own since we got to the mill, and here I was, more alone in all of this night than I had ever been. Each step taking me further away.

I thought how it would feel to have Ty's hand in mine.

With a full day already done, my body had been tired before I left bed. Out of practice, my legs now ached from the simple work of putting one foot in front of the other. My head hung heavy, my whole body longed to rest. My feet were throbbing.

I kept thinking about going back to the trees. Laying down and sleeping. It would be so easy to wake up tomorrow and make my life anew there. It would be cold, and lonely, but I would live. I knew how to find food; I could make a shelter. I could be safe and forget about the mill. Leave behind all of its heat and noise, its hurt. All I had to do was lie down and close my eyes.

A stone caught inside my shoe. I tried to kick it free but when it wouldn't budge, I sat to take the shoe off. Tiredness swept over me. Leaning forward I rested my head on my knees. I'd made good time, surely a few minutes rest would be okay?

I let myself tumble over. The grass felt soft and cool under my head. I looked up into the dark sparkling sky above me, the ground beneath cushioning my weariness, and let my eyes close.

Then I remembered what he looked like. His little body lying on the table. The blood in the wheelbarrow; matted and dark through his sunshiny hair. I heard his breathing, his last terrible moments of air. The chill from his skin when he was gone.

I pulled myself up, shaking my body awake. Blinking my eyes open.

Tightening the laces on both shoes, I set off again, swinging my arms to wake myself up.

A little later I came to a fork in the road, the path ahead dividing equally into two. I unfolded my map. The moon was smaller now: it wasn't easy to make out the map's lines. It seemed I should turn left.

But if I misread this, I wouldn't know until the following left turn which was another hour, maybe further, down the road. Doubling back would cost me hours of walking. Time I didn't have.

I stood wavering, struggling to decide. Wishing I wasn't alone in such an important decision.

Having to choose one, I started down the left road. The further I walked down it, the more sure I became that I'd chosen the wrong road. I almost turned back twice. I'd copied the map in a rush, on the office floor a few feet from a fitfully sleeping Mr Coleman. I could have easily made a mistake sketching out the little shapes and lines.

But, at last, I came to the second turn. Small and partly obscured in hedgerow but a road nonetheless. I was on the right path, and at this crossing was a milestone. I'd seen these markers before, but never been able to read what they pointed towards.

I ran my finger along the letters carved into the stone and knew it to be the word for London. The city was six miles away. Seeing the letters and understanding their message felt miraculous. Something like pride glowed in my chest. I was in the right place and I could read it to know.

I said the word aloud to myself, standing there on the empty road, alone in the middle of the night. *Lon-don, Lon-don.* This was a word I would teach Billy.

EVERY

Sunday, 1.30pm

Back at the house Janelle and the Ns are still on their laptops at the table. There's no sign of Dad or any of the studio people. They'll be downstairs. Huddled around the screens in the dark. Door closed.

I sit on the sofa, looking around. Wondering what I should do. Dad's not much of a hoarder. Books aside, the living areas are minimalist. Smooth, polished surfaces with just a few key pieces of personalisation. I realise I have no idea if the artwork and sculptures were acquired for Dad, or if he picked them out himself. Janelle would know. Is it weird that I don't recognise my own father's taste?

When she was here, Mum chose the décor. It was more of a family home then, less curated. There's a large black-and-white photograph of her now on the bookshelf. Mum used to say that worrying about how she looked was for work, not something she wanted to think about at home. She didn't like mirrors and never had any pictures of herself on display, so I'm pretty sure she'd never have allowed this photo, but it's lovely. It has a grainy faraway feel to it: the photographer either was Herb Ritts or someone trying to be Herb Ritts. Mum's looking out through the lens with such intimacy the picture feels alive, more of a window than a print. When I was younger, I used to wonder all the time if she could still see me, if she was looking over us somehow.

On the shelf below Mum are her ancestor's diaries ready for Dad's next project. I run my fingers down the line of soft-leather spines that stretch the length of the shelf. Janelle says Claudine wrote from childhood until her death at the grand old age of eighty-two, so this is what a human life looks like in books.

There's a small museum in north London that has kept these diaries safe. A few pages open under a glass box on permanent display, the rest in cool, dusty storage. Historic record of the family life of Claudine's brother, the great reformer Lord Alden Rigby-Williams.

Lord. Turns out great-uncle Alden was kind of a big deal. Also a lord. I might not have known anything about him but the internet certainly does. There's pages and pages of material. His public works: the reforms he made. The achievements of his life are a matter of undisputed record – Alden has several dedicated Wikipedia pages. But when I look for information about his personal and family life, I can't find very much at all.

Janelle says Dad's researchers had the same challenge, it's not just that he lived two centuries ago, Alden was notoriously private. That's why they had to wait for Claudine's diaries to bring flesh to the bones of Dad's project: all the personal, character-delving stuff needed to tell the whole story. Once access was approved, Janelle arranged for copies to be made of the complete set, hiring a bookmaker to bind each one of Claudine's diaries with an old-fashioned leather cover.

I pull one of the diaries out. It looks so authentic I feel like I should be wearing those white gloves people in films use to handle rare books. The copying has captured the night-sky blue of Claudine's ink. Drops of it splattering the page where she dipped her quill in the inkwell. You can even see the yellowing and cobwebby creases of the original, antiqued paper. It takes me a moment to understand the slanted loops and swirls of the elegant handwriting.

'We made our way to the tree. A sapling oak as Alden had described, growing in a small clearing by itself. The only comfort I could offer my brother was my hand on his shoulder. Alden knelt in front of the tree. With a penknife he carved her name – four dear, precious letters – deep into its bark.'

There's no explanation for why this was done or who the woman whose name was carved into the tree was, but the sadness in Claudine's words is unmistakable. It's strange to think this feeling, so real and tangible, has been preserved on the pages, locked to the handwriting for two hundred years. It's as real and alive as anything else right now.

I slide the diary back into its place.

'Janelle, do you think Dad would mind if I read the script for his new project? Be great to learn about Mum's family.'

'There's no script yet Evie, just notes and rough storyline, but I'm sure Ford won't mind you looking through them. And those diaries of course.'

By 2.30pm Dad still hasn't come up for lunch. I understand that this is not the time for long-term nutrition plans, but the doctors advised we keep Dad's meals regular. Riz and I make up a tray of juice and snacks. On the way down to the studio I meet Kara coming up. She stops in the middle of the stairs, blocking my way.

'He's busy right now Aavaree.'

I try to remember how other Canadians pronounce the word 'every'. I know I've never heard my name dragged out this harshly. There's something about her that makes me feel like a petulant teenager. The tray of lunch is getting heavy in my hands.

'The editing can wait five minutes, can't it Kara?'

'You know he wants to focus.'

'I *know* he hasn't eaten anything today.'

Kara shrugs her shoulders, 'Suit yourself.'

I catch myself rolling my eyes before stomping past her, down the stairs.

The studio door is ajar. I knock, then walk straight in, almost tripping over a thick yellow medical cable running across the room to Dad.

He's lying on the sofa. His eyes are closed and there's an oxygen mask over his face. The nurse is sliding a needle into a vein on the inside of his elbow.

Lenny is on his knees next to the sofa, holding Dad's other hand. Lenny turns to me: his face looks pale and very frightened.

MINA

London

I came to dwellings. Cottages, much like our own farms, began to dot the fields. As I walked on, the houses became bigger and much closer together. They sat in tight rows. Some were built so close together that a person could lean from the window of a house and take an apple from the sill of the next. Their fields dwindled to walled plots too small to grow more than a brace of beans. Perhaps dispirited by this lack of land, few residents seemed to have tried growing even that. The gardens of some houses were raising only flowers, from what I could see, entirely inedible ones.

Now there were houses with no land at all. I couldn't understand why anyone would want a big house if the bargain was no garden. Were the people here blighted with bad soil? That could be the reason for so few trees. I'd walked ten minutes without seeing a single one. The trees I did see weren't flourishing: their lower branches ripped away, for firewood or by accident I couldn't tell.

A wide ledge ran along the road's edge. I stepped up and walked along the ledge, hoping that was its purpose and that I wasn't doing anything to anger the people who lived in this strange place.

The sound of my footsteps echoing down the empty road was eerie.

I came to a road lined with lamps. Each one fixed to the top of its own tall post, casting down hazy loops of light. Outside! Who were they burning for? There was not a body in sight. It was troubling, as if all the people had been spirited away. I told myself someone had just forgotten to snuff them, and hoped desperately that this was true. I stepped from circle to circle imagining the scolding that person would get from Papa. He would find it too wasteful to endure, all these lamps firing through the night, not illuminating a single kitchen table between them.

Light would be coming from the day soon too. I pulled out my map again, already knowing it wouldn't be help to me now. The original I'd copied it from had outlined the road leading to London but hadn't given much detail about what to look for once I got here. Just a drawing of three houses at the foot of the map, beside a wide looping river and bold lettering proclaiming them to be London.

The Mercers lived in a house called 47 Berkeley Square. There had been no other description, or account for how I could tell theirs apart from the other houses, but if I found the London river, then walked along it to the three houses, one of them must be 47 Berkeley Square.

I kept heading downwards, my ears tilted for sounds of wet.

Other roads began branching off the one I was following. I saw that some of those roads were crossed with further more roads. Soon, every road I looked down sprouted more roads. Dozens of roads and hundreds, perhaps thousands of houses. All of them so similar, how could anyone living here find their way home? Gloomy smells of coal fire and cabbage sifted through the air.

For the first time I understood the size of what lay before me. London was monstrous. Like a huge hungry mouth, all of these rows of houses its overcrowded teeth.

Water seeks lowest land so I knew I had to do the same. I kept walking straight and downwards, only crossing and turning from a road when it veered too far left or right. The further inwards I travelled, the worse London smelt. A reek of people, of waste, food, shit and animals swelled around me. I looked behind: where I'd come from was interchangeable with what lay ahead. With few trees to mark the way, the city was a twisting labyrinth. Expanding and closing in around me as I walked ever deeper, down into the mouth of it.

To keep the fear at bay, I imagined a thread from my dress tied to the first house I'd come across, back where there were still field and trees. I pictured the blue-and-white thread spooling out from my skirts, back along the roads I'd travelled. Hanging there, waiting for me to follow it safely out.

Dawn had broken and the city was coughing to life. From within the houses now came sounds: raised voices, pots banging; I heard a baby crying. Kitchen fires were being lit and breakfasts being made. Smells of lard and porridge wafted out.

I was afraid to meet the people behind these walls. I was a trespasser with no right to be walking their lamp-lit roads, and with lives so different from ours, how could we be similar? Would these people know me as an intruder and chase me away?

The first city dwellers I saw were men. Six of them marching down the road towards me.

At a distance they made dreadful outlines. Strange bones protruding from their shoulders. As they came closer, it was a great relief to see that each man carried a ladder hoisted over his shoulder.

Pressed against a wall, I watched the men pass. They trooped by without a glance. Their number dividing as they went, a man turning down each road they crossed. I saw one of the men lean his ladder against two small bars at the top of a lamp's post. He'd scampered up it, turned out the flame and was down again, repeating the process on the next lamp by the time I realised what I was seeing. As the sun rose, these men had come with their ladders to turn down the lights.

I watched him a few moments more. He was clearly flesh and blood, the same as any other man. Swift and sprightly, up and down he climbed along the road. His ladder an extension of himself the same way the scythes and hoes were part of the men back home. Being fearful would not help me reach the Mercers. I took a deep breath, stepped from the shadows and followed him to the next lamp to ask where I would find them.

The man answered without taking his eyes from his task. He didn't know the Mercer family or which house I was looking for, but if I was wanting the river he said to keep going straight. It was ahead, just after Cintpaws. I asked what Cintpaws was, but he laughed and said I couldn't miss it.

I passed other people. More lampmen with their ladders, a woman and a little boy. Then many more people, all of them in a hurry, as though they shared a meeting they were all late for. That I was a stranger seemed not to matter, for no one paid me any notice unless I spoke to them. No one knew the Mercer family. Nor could they tell me where 47 Berkeley Square was, but the way to Cintpaws and the river was always ahead.

I came to a rise in the land and looked over the hill to a sea of chimneys, rolling out in all directions. Countless grey funnels of smoke climbing up through the sunrise. Where I stood a signpost told me I was in Islington. Was this not London? Was this another city? Had I misfollowed the map and lost my way so disastrously? The next person along the road calmed my panic.

Islington was a village *within* London.

The scale of this place was unimaginable. Village after village with no space between.

I began to realise that 47 Berkeley Square could be more than just the name of the Mercers' house. It might also describe its location. Many of the roads I walked down had names. Either on a signpost at the beginning of a road, or tiled high on its first house. Some houses had numbers: on the doors or at their gates. Within the maze, could this be a way of telling where you were and how to find it again? How clever if Berkeley Square was a road and 47 was its number on it. Twice I came across a name that was close to Berkeley, but not quite right. I checked carefully, sounding out the letters to be sure, before walking on. There was still no sound of water.

In the distance up ahead, I saw a huge building. A great dome that curved up towards the clouds, rising clear above the skyline. Pure white as though carved from fresh-laid snow, the building dwarfed its neighbours, making everything else seem no more than sheds for livestock in comparison.

Magnificent at a distance, standing beside it and gazing up, the beauty of the building took my body's breath. Cintpaws. Even spelt as it should be, St Paul's was a name that in no way spoke of its vision. I had not the words to name its grandeur.

I can now describe the statues and wide stone steps. Today I know what to call the marble pillars and turrets, the sky-piercing steeple, the panels of carved roses, but I'm no poet and these words still can't frame the wonder that battered and lifted my heart that morning to stand beside such a building. The sun itself seemed to shine brighter on its glorious symmetry. That such beauty could be hewn from human hands amazed me. People must have assembled these stones the same as any other building, but what fineness they were in this form. I stood there staring up at it as people bustled around me.

As promised, the river flowed nearby. But not the waterway I'd expected. Tea-coloured and vast, it must have stretched a thousand feet from shore to shore. People were rowing themselves across its murky depths in all sorts of craft. There was also a great bridge. Long enough to reach the distant riverbank, strong enough to support houses. And these houses, built over the swirling currents, were not flimsy straw shacks but heavy, brick-worked structures five storeys high.

Everywhere I looked someone was moving: working, rowing, unpacking cargo, yelling to someone else. Sprawling and chaotic, it was fascinating to see. Moored to the riverbanks were clippers with billowing sheets of fabric secured to their masts. Crates of food, sacks of coal and grain, bundles of wood were being unloaded. A city this size would need a lot of feeding, and this was clearly the entry point of its appetite. A muggy stink of waste and rot wafted up.

Just as the river was far from the cress-laced waterway I'd imagined, neither were there only three houses. Dozens of buildings bunched along both sides of the river's shoreline.

I realised I might not even be on the right side of it.

Panicked, I called to a man driving a cart of vegetables.

Like the other people I'd asked, he didn't know the Mercer family or the road they lived on, but he was sure it wouldn't be here, not on the river. If it were a fine family I was after, he said, my best bet would be up west, away from the whiffs and pongs.

I was welcome to follow him to the markets. Someone there would point me in the right direction. He jerked a thumb at his overladen baskets and sacks: there was no room for me to ride in the cart but with his horse pulling slow as it was, I'd have no trouble keeping up.

I looked back at the river. Having taken so long to find it, I didn't want to lose sight of it, but what the man said made sense. The water smelt as brown as it looked, and the houses lining its edges seemed more like work buildings and warehouses than homes for fine families.

The market was as busy as the river, but rich with a far lovelier smell of cut greens and fruit peelings that made my stomach rumble with hunger. Across the cobblestoned square the workers laboured as quickly as we did on the mill floor. Instead of cotton that could feed no one, here they worked with fruit and vegetables. Potatoes, beans, oranges, shiny apples were being unloaded into neat piles. Round green cabbages were flying, tossed through the air. Rather than offering a range, each stall seemed to have agreed to specialise in a particular fruit or vegetable. One stall was selling nothing but herbs and lettuce. Another only bunches of flowers.

Buying flowers seemed an odd thing to do when you could have them for free, then I remembered there were no fields or forests here for people to pick them from. And these were beautiful flowers. Flowers the like of which I'd never seen. Pails of red, pink and purple; shapes I'd not known existed. I stopped to breathe in the cloud of powdery sweetness. A girl looked up from bundling bunches of lavender together.

'Morning miss, looking for some lovely fresh blooms? Bouquets for your mistress?'

'I'm sorry, I've no money. I'm looking for Berkeley Square, do you know it?'

'Berkeley? Think that's up west… Here, Maud,' she called to a girl stacking crates a few yards away. 'This one's for Berkeley Square, isn't that just up from our Wednesday delivery?'

'Aye, that's the one. Just up from St James. What's she wanting there? She off to work?'

Both girls looked over expectantly.

'I'm trying to find the Mercer family.'

'Fine people are they, then?'

'Must be fine people, Beth,' Maud answered for me. 'No other kind up west.'

The girls nodded knowingly at each other before turning back to me, 'Just keep going up that way Miss. You see the big park, you've gone too far. Straight as the crow flies, should take you no more than half an hour.'

'Thank you very much.'

'And Miss…'

'Yes?'

'Don't forget, if your new mistress likes flowers, she won't find better than our peonies.'

It seemed simplest to nod and tell her I wouldn't.

As I walked off, I heard Maud's voice. 'So she *is* going for work then?'

Berkeley Square was an oval not a road. An oval of large and extremely elegant houses. Each one grander than the last. Some six storeys tall, almost the height of the mill but of far richer design, with swirls and finishes as fine as lace.

At the heart of the oval were trees. Fifteen, maybe twenty trees, the most I'd seen since entering the city. An iron fence enclosed them, as though the trees might otherwise wander off like a flock of untended sheep. Or was it that they were so rare, the railings were needed for their protection? But no, there was a gate and it was open. No garden crops grew but the oval was well-tended, its grass clipped winter short and the trees straight and strong. Benches to sit on dotted a path that ran down its centre. That the Mercer family should wish to be near leaves and branches reassured me. Fine though the houses were, these trees felt someway like common ground.

Berkeley Square. I was giddy with relief to be here. To have found it.

Where I stood was number fifty-eight; just doors from the Mercers.

I raced around the curve of houses, each a lavish palace, counting down the numbers. Elaborate wrought-iron archways led to doorways large enough to enter on horseback. Fifty, forty-nine, forty-eight... There was no mistaking number forty-seven: a large brass plaque fixed to one of its four white pillars announced it.

No. 47 Berkeley Sq.

Unwrapping the ledger ready to present it, I stepped up onto the marble steps and pulled the brass knocker down – too softly, it had hardly made a noise. I pulled it again with a steadier hand, then took a step back and looked up at the windows above. My heart hammering as I waited.

There was no sound within. Could they be out? It would be well past seven o'clock now but the Mercers could hardly have livestock or crops to tend. I listened at the door. Only stillness.

Dread bubbled up, had I definitely taken down the right name for the Mercer's house?

I knocked again, more firmly still. The cracks reverberating out to the trees. This time I heard footsteps – sharp clicks coming towards me across a polished floor – and jumped back just in time as the door swung open.

A distinguished gentleman, suited in crisp white and black, stood in the doorway.

'Yes, can I help you?' he frowned.

'Morning sir, are you Mr Mercer sir?'

'Of course not. Mr Mercer does not answer his own door.'

'I'm sorry sir. Would I be able to speak with Mr Mercer?'

When the man just glared at me, I added, 'Or, perhaps another member of the family?'

'On what possible business?'

'I work at Mercer Mill,' I held the ledger out as proof. 'I've brought something for them to see.'

'Who sent you?'

'No one sir, it's about their mill.'

'Out of the question.'

Before I could say anything more, the door swung shut in my face with a resolute clunk.

I stepped back, stunned. Not finding the house, being caught by Wilks, not being capable of the task… I'd had plenty of fears, all of them growing as I walked through the night, but it had never crossed my mind that I wouldn't be able to see the Mercers once I got here. My eyes suddenly blurred with tears. What should I do now? What *could* I do? I was so tired.

I looked down at the ledger in my hands.

The footsteps came to the door much quicker this time.

'Sorry sir, really I am. I wouldn't disturb if it wasn't of the greatest need.'

The butler sighed, weary as the night is long. 'The family do not entertain unexpected visitors. And certainly not the likes of street waifs. Be gone girl, or I'll have the constable called.'

I stood looking at the closed door. After a few minutes I slowly walked down the steps, across the road to the garden oval and sat on one of the benches. Looking up at the trees, I was overcome with tiredness. My feet throbbed and my stomach growled with emptiness. Ty had been right. Running from the mill in the dead of night. Walking to London; thinking I could knock on such doors. How could I have been so stupid? I'd put Billy in harm's way. Hurt my friends, Ty. For what?

Opening the ledger, I traced my fingers over the names. I pictured their faces. Their little bodies wrapped up in the back of the cart. The feeling of Harry's small cold hand in mine.

The curtains moved upstairs in the Mercer's middle window. The people who could end this misery must be home. They were just yards away, beyond a thin sheet of glass and a fall of velvet.

What I held in my hands was too important for me to turn back now. I was not equal to this undertaking, there was no doubt of that, but there was no one else here.

I fixed my dress, tidied my hair as best I could, and walked back to the door.

Raising the bronze knocker down firmly on its plate, I hid my shaking hands in the folds of my skirt.

The third time he opened his door, the butler gaped at me in open disbelief. I rushed to speak before he could slam the door again.

'Please sir, my apologies for being here unexpectedly. May I make an appointment to see Mr Mercer?'

'Are you quite mad?'

'Just a moment of his time? It is of grave importance. Or any member of the family?'

'Absolutely not.'

'I'll wait until a time that's convenient for them.'

'Not on these steps you won't.'

A few hours later a coach and horses pulled up in front of No.47. I saw two ladies and a gentleman come out of the house and climb inside. I ran from where I was watching across the road, calling and waving like a madwoman, but the coach was already drawing away as I reached it. I caught a glimpse of one of the passengers, her face pointed determinedly ahead, but I couldn't tell if they heard me.

Not wanting to risk missing the Mercers twice, I stood waiting for their return at the railings by their steps. Alternating my weight from one foot to the other to ease the throbbing in my tired feet.

Looking down at Mama's shoes I wondered what she would make of this place, the people who lived here. Those I'd come across as I walked through the city, at the market square and down by the river had paid me little mind, treating me as though I could be one of them. But here the residents saw my difference more clearly. I did not belong, and the ladies and gentlemen sweeping by in their beautiful clothes looked at me with cool, undisguised disapproval.

Living inside such grand homes, dealing with such finery as a matter of daily course, how could they not? To a man, they were suited and gleaming from head to toe. The ladies layered in silky fabrics with gloves and parasols. I stood as tidily as I could, and tried not to stare at their elegance.

Two women were walking a small dog on a leather strap. It trotted along between them, its fur cut in a peculiar way. I was so taken by the dog and its strange haircut that I stepped backwards, directly into the path of a gentleman.

'Oh sir, I'm so sorry sir.'

Given the refinement of his suit, I expected him to rush on without glancing back but his eyes were fixed in horror to my dress. Was it so hideous?

Tipping his hat finally, he cleared his throat, 'Not at all Miss, the fault was entirely mine.'

We nodded good day to each other and he continued on.

Sometime after sunset, the horse and carriage pulled back up at the steps. The driver climbed down and opened the carriage door. I couldn't see into the interior but readied myself to speak with whoever emerged. It was the two women who had left earlier.

I rushed forward but the coachman barred my way, his arm out across my chest, holding me back. The ladies hurried past, up the steps and into the open doorway without hesitating or seeming to hear my pleas. The butler glared as he pulled the door shut after them. This was more or less repeated an hour later when the carriage returned with the gentleman. But this time the driver shoved me hard enough that I fell backwards onto the footpath.

I picked myself up and walked back to the trees. Sitting on one of the wooden benches, I watched the cracks of light coming through the curtains at No.47.

A few hours earlier the lamps along the road had been lit. Beginning at the top of the oval, two men had taken a side each, timing their ladder ups-and-downs almost perfectly, meeting at the bottom of the oval within moments of each other. Through the trees, the lights flickered prettily, encircling Berkeley Square like a twinkling necklace.

It was quiet in the square now. The lampmen long since gone, and there was no one else walking the paths. It was cold on the bench, cold and hungry. I rested my head on the back of the bench. How could I speak to the Mercers? The ledger was too important to leave on their doorstop. The chance of the butler giving it to them seemed slight. Even if he did, the ledger would need explanation. I pulled my dress tighter around me against the night's chill. There had to be a way of getting a message to them.

A better way that I was not thinking of.

When morning came, I waited for the lampmen and their ladders. The man I spoke to plainly thought me odd, but nonetheless he let me climb his ladder. Despite his hurry, he kindly waited until each of the sticks I'd collected under the trees had caught fire and blackened thoroughly.

I'd thought to use some pages from the ledger itself. There were plenty that were empty, but all the pages were bound together and I dared not rip one from the back of the book and risk losing any from the front. My dress was the only thing for it.

In the night I'd ripped a panel from the side of the skirt. The frayed gap made me look even less presentable but the thick cloth would do the job well.

Quickly, while the sticks were still warm, I wrote on the white underside of the fabric. Running over the words until they were charcoal-black and clear. A simple message in large enough letters that the Mercers could see from behind their windows.

Children are dying at the mill.

I was able to stand outside the Mercers' house for most of the day. The sign held high above my head so the family could best read it from their upstairs windows. My arms shook after a few hours but not so badly I couldn't keep the cloth taut enough to show the words.

The ladies and gentlemen walking by openly stared now. I had tried to letter the words as neatly as I could, but rather than arouse concern or curiosity, the sign made them angry. They tutted and scowled as they passed, 'Well I never.' 'What gall!'

Late afternoon two men in blue uniforms came. They told me they had been called for by the residents of No.47. A public disturbance, I was to leave immediately and not come back. Otherwise they said, it would be Bedlam for me. I didn't know what this was, and tried to explain that I meant no disturbance or disrespect. That I worked at the mill for the family and only wanted to speak to them. An idea that made the men laugh: 'Wants to take tea with the Mercers, she does.'

'C'mon, we'd better take her down.'

'Please, if I could show Mr Mercer this ledger? It's so important.'

They laughed again, each of them taking hold of me, paying no notice of my pleading or promises to leave of my own accord. I tried to twist free but the men would not let go, laughing all the more at my struggle and how I gripped the ledger, as if this were further proof that they were right to take me. I looked up at the windows of No.47 as they dragged me out of the square. The curtains twitched.

The road the men were taking me down was busier. Horses and carriages, people everywhere, some in fine clothes, most not. We passed a tiny girl selling posies of violets from a wicker basket. She couldn't have been older than four or five, but clearly all alone. Her eyes enormous and emotionless in her small face as she watched the men drag me pass.

Suddenly, the thread I'd imagined running from my dress to guide me safely back through the maze of streets snapped and blew away. With so many people here, did some get lost? Swallowed by the city. Vanished unnoticed into its cracks.

Wherever we were going, I knew very well that when men came to take you, grasping and pulling, it was never to a good place. I had known there would be a high price to pay for jumping out of the mill's dormitory window, but being locked-up, alone and so lost from home, was worst of all.

A gentleman stepped in front of us, standing squarely in our way.

At first I hoped it was one of the Mercers, having seen my sign, at last wanting explanation, but as he spoke, I realised it was the gentleman I had bumped into the previous day when I was distracted by the little dog.

'Thank you constables, I'd be much obliged if you would release the young lady.'

'She's touched sir; we're taking her down to Bedlam.'

The gentleman narrowed his eyes. 'That won't be necessary, she's in my employ.'

The constables looked doubtful. 'She's been telling stories about working for No.47 sir, we don't know which is which.'

'You may escort her back to my residence.'

It was obvious the constables were reluctant to do so, but neither did they want trouble with such a well-dressed gentleman. 'As you wish sir. She may be your servant, but if she bothers them at No.47 again, we've no choice but to take her down.'

'That won't be necessary.'

'For her own good sir.'

The gentleman's residence was back in Berkeley Square. A corner house of six floors that was just across the park from the Mercers' and even larger and more intricately decorated.

As with No.47, No.23 Berkeley Square announced itself with a polished bronze plaque. Marble steps led us under a wrought-iron archway to the imposing doorway. But this door was being held open.

Inside we stood in a grand room. Glittering shards of glass hung from the ceiling and a chequerboard of black-and-white tiles shone across the floor to a wide staircase that curled up and around to the floor above. A small table held a vase puffed with enough blooms to stock Maude and Beth's entire stall. To each side were rooms, all velvet drapes and fine upholstered furniture.

The house also clearly impressed the two constables. They quickly unhanded me, assuring the gentleman they would be honoured to assist with anything further. Anything at all. Their eyes gleaming from the treasures they saw. They were bowing so low, they almost scraped the tiles as the front door closed behind them.

The gentleman and I stood looking at each other.

I thought about how I must look against such surroundings, my ripped dress and untidy hair, my charcoal-smudged hands.

'Sir, I am not your servant.'

He laughed. A great belly laugh that echoed in the hallway.

'I'm well aware of *that*. Tell me, where on earth did you get that dress?'

GREY

Yes, I fiddled. Tweaked things. I couldn't help myself. I knew how high the stakes were.

Zaffre-blue lilies entwined on cream calico. It sounds prettier than it looked. The cut of the thing didn't help. Loose and shapeless – an ugly sack over too-thin limbs.

Getting involved is a big no-no. I have a job, and it is to watch. To keep an eye on things and tally up the wins and losses. This is not the same as shifting the path ahead.

But a balance must be kept. Light and dark, spinning stardust on a plate.

If dark outweighs the other, all of us will fall.

EVERY

Monday, 4.15am

Jetlag isn't usually a problem. But here I am. Awake again. Suddenly as alert as the surface of the sea. I listen for what has woken me, but only the usual sounds of night come through my bedroom's open balcony. Wind rustling through the pines, distant echo of bats, a koel's mournful call. The steady heartbeat of the waves.

Upstairs I plunge some coffee – the same watery black as the sky – and take it over to the sofas. Dad doesn't remember what happened yesterday. Lenny says the two of them were talking, everything seemed normal. Then Dad reached across the editing desk and just buckled over.

Janelle rang the hospital and the two of us listened to the doctor's response together on loudspeaker. Blackouts like this are not unusual, but what it means they can't say. Nor can they advise on what might come next. Dad may or may not collapse again. He may, or may not, be able to get back up next time.

At this stage everything is normal.

It is a waiting game with unknown rules and one-sided scorekeeping.

I pad about the house. Empty-eyed and jarred out of time. Waiting for the sun to come up and bring me back to the day's loop. One of these mornings, one morning soon, will be Dad's last.

As I think about it, the finality of it, I realise my father's last dawn could be the one about to unfold in front of me now. It's a sharp, hollowing thought, a hurt that scrapes my insides. Storm-cloud-coloured bruises on a white sheet. Small bloodied footprints over cool concrete. Ruby red on polished grey.

Later, when the sky is a perfect cornflower blue and the sun high and small, it's business as usual. There's no mention of yesterday's collapse. Roxy Music's *Avalon* album is playing throughout the house and things couldn't feel breezier. Everyone's cracking on like all of this will last forever.

Over plates of grilled breakfast Dad and Joe are discussing the work ahead. They're planning to be down in the studio all day. Kara still wants something tweaked to the final cut. Her manager is suggesting they add it and see how it fits. Joe doesn't look convinced. Lenny is on his way over. Chris the Editor is parking his car now.

I watch Dad carefully as he talks with the others, trying to assess how he might be feeling. He looks tired but his speech is clear and fluent. He could be moving a little slower. Although that could also just be the morphine. It's macabre, this watching, waiting for signs of decline. I need to stop.

Chris arrives and all five of them head downstairs to the studio. The day rolls forward. Janelle and her assistants have now formally set up office at the dining table. Stacks of files and five laptops between them. Janelle is typing briskly. Nat and Nic are on their phones. Janelle's legendary rolodex is out. There's talk of flowers and a guest list. I ask if there's anything I can help them with but whatever the party is that they're planning, Janelle tells me it's all in hand.

I look out across the bay. I should keep busy too, try to distract myself. I'm just about to slide out a couple of Claudine's diaries when my phone starts vibrating in my pocket.

As I answer the call, I realise that the event Janelle and her assistants are planning is not a party, it is my father's funeral.

'Hello?'

'Hey Evie.'

As with Janelle's call four days ago, there's no need for this caller to say who they are. We haven't spoken for years but I recognise his voice before he's finished saying my name.

'Hi Jake.'

'Hey. Saw you in the papers. You're back?'

He says it would be nice to see each other. He can come pick me up: when would be good?

I look around me. Jo, Dad's housekeeper dusting the bookcase. Riz in the kitchen preparing a lunch that will be eaten in front of the screens.

'Evie?'

I ask Jake to hold the line for a second. It feels wrong to even consider leaving the house, but Dad won't be out of the studio before this evening. Me drinking cups of tea and staring anxiously at the view won't stop anything bad from happening. I know I'm not ready to listen to the catering details for what Janelle and her assistants are organising.

I unmute the phone, 'Jake, how about now?'

He laughs, 'Sure. What's the address?'

He can be here in 40 minutes. I tell him about the pigeons outside.

'Pigeons? You mean paparazzi? No worries, I'll bring the pick-up.'

An hour later, I'm crouched on the floor of a truck, watching Jake reverse and swing out of the drive. The truck is painted *Gingko Gardens Design & Landscaping*. There are bundles of bamboo poles tied down in the back. It's the ideal cover. I sit up once he tells me we're clear.

'They always there? What do you call them again, vultures? Crows?'

'Pigeons. Think so, at the moment. You can't see them from inside unless you check the monitors.'

'Must be a hassle though. Dealing with that every time you leave the house?'

I nod at the logo, 'Gingko Gardens? I like it.'

He pauses, changing gears, checking his rear vision mirror

before answering, 'Yeah, thought it sounded more respectable than Jake Riley Gardens.'

'Remember the tree outside our flat, the one with those pretty fan-shaped leaves that used to blow into our windows? That was a ginkgo, wasn't it?'

Jake keeps his eyes on the road, 'Mmm hm. An Autumn Gold.'

I watch him navigate the bends and winding road, back down the peninsula towards the city. We wind down the windows and our hair whips around our faces. Patches of sun flash across my arm.

'Where do you want to go Evie?

'Wherever, doesn't matter, just not too far from the house.'

'You had lunch?'

'Not yet.'

'Still like Thai?'

Jake and I met eight years ago at a comedy night in South London. It was a friend's birthday; she and Jake worked together. There were lots of people but I noticed him right away.

A month later we found ourselves sitting next to each other at a dinner party. By the second glass of wine neither of us was talking with anyone else at the table. He was over from Sydney for six months and making the most of it. He was seeing a few women. They all knew about each other. They were sophisticated women. One of them was a Spanish artist fourteen years his senior. Everyone was having fun.

As friends Jake and I spent time together: a walk on the heath, we saw a band at Brixton Academy. There was a play in Islington. An exhibition at the Tate. In a pub one night he leaned forward, his voice close and deep over the noise of the crowd, and told me that he liked me, *really* liked me. I told him I liked him, *really* liked him. We smiled happy little nervous smiles at each other. I was not a sophisticated woman, if anything was to be with us, it would be exclusive. He said he understood. He wanted that too.

Outside the pub it was snowing that night, we kissed goodbye on the cheek as friends would, as we usually did. Keep warm, pull your collar up he said, adjusting my jacket. Then he kissed me, not as friends do. His arms pulling me into the warmth inside his coat, his mouth on mine. The snow swirling around us.

We moved in together a month later. An attic flat just off Great Portland Street with a view of London's crisscross of rooftops. The rent more than we could afford. The living room and bedroom combined. All the ceilings sloping so he hit his head at least once a week. We didn't have a TV. We read books, drank red wine and stayed up all night talking. We ate a lot of tinned tuna and green apples.

He showed me a different London. A place of literature and history. We walked down streets that had once carried du Maurier, Huxley, Woolf and Orwell and it all felt giddily alive. We had no money but everything felt richer. We caught the train to Paris and spent an hour staring at *L'Origine du monde*. We swerved the *Mona Lisa* crowds to stand in awe at the feet of Canova's marble Psyche and Cupid.

We knew we were being pretentious and young. For centuries people had loved like us, we knew we were nothing new. Still it felt like we were walking on our own moon. And for four years that's how it was. Until London finally became too grey for Jake.

He'd never meant to stay. He was tired of the crowds, the queues, the endless waiting. The slow, unassuming rain. You don't notice it, and suddenly you're wet through. That's London he said. It's a city that drowns you in mist while you're standing in line.

We were walking through Hyde Park. Shuffling through the piles of autumn leaves, under low, slate-coloured skies. I remember it very clearly, the details crisp and sharp. He stopped and turned to me, as it began to rain. He told me he couldn't do another winter. Not another five months of gloom and living indoors. He needed sunshine and wide-open skies.

'Let's go home Evie', he said. 'It's time.'

As the rain came down harder, we sheltered under the canopy of a huge oak tree that stood in a clearing by itself. Jake's arm around me, my head against his shoulder, the air filled with the sweet mossy scent of rain.

A girl's name had been carved deep into the trunk of the tree we were leaning against. I remember tracing my finger along the smooth groove of the four letters, avoiding his eyes as my veins ran cold. Knowing that I wasn't ready to go back to Sydney. Not even for Jake.

Jake parks the truck at Milsons Point, near the harbour's edge at the foot of the bridge. The restaurant's bi-folding windows are open; incense wafts out on the breeze mixed with stir-fried galangal and lemongrass. There's only one other table occupied, which seems quiet, then I realise it's almost 3pm.

We take one of the dark wooden tables in the corner. We look at each other. He looks good. Brown and strong from working outside. There's a kind of contented ruggedness about him now.

After so long; so much distance and thought, it's hard to believe he's this close. Sitting just inches in front of me. His arm stretched out, almost touching my glass. The southern cross of freckles just above his wrist as I remembered it. I resist the urge to run my finger along it, taking a sip from my wine glass instead.

'It's good to see you Evie.'

'Thanks for coming to pick me up Jake. This place looks good.'

He fidgets with his glass. 'I'm sorry about your dad. He's going to be okay?'

I'm not sure how to answer. I just shake my head.

Jake looks surprised, 'It's true? What's in the papers? He really is…?'

'Dying?' I try not to sound melodramatic. 'Think so.'

'God, I'm so sorry Evie.'

I take another long sip of my wine. Passionfruit, gooseberry tart. I can feel it percolating, a fuzzy detachment bubbling up from the floor to my head.

I reach to refill our glasses; Jake's hardly touched his.

'I'm the driver,' he smiles, his hand over the rim.

After lunch we walk down to the water's edge and sit on the clipped lawn across from the Opera House. I've been checking my phone every few minutes, fiddling with the volume, paranoid about losing reception. Janelle said she'd let me know if Dad came up from the studio early. There's been no word and I'm on full bars of reception, so there's no rush getting back. I send her a text just to be certain.

We watch the sailboats and ferries bustle past. A million diamonds sparkle, shimmering off the water's surface. Across the harbour, there's a vast white ocean liner rising up from the water, dwarfing the port building it's moored beside.

After Jake left London, we kept in contact for a while. I wanted him to be happy, of course I wanted him to get on with things. But it hurt. Like watching the life you should be having, with better weather. It was hard for him too. In the end, it just felt easier on us both not to answer when he rang.

The sun's hot. I lean back and close my eyes, feeling the stubble of cut grass through the cotton of my shirt. I drank Jake's wine as well in the end, finishing off the bottle, and the alcohol is creeping like sugar through my veins, rounding out the sharp edges, making everything seem both more, and less surreal. I can feel myself slipping, almost overcome with tiredness.

I drift with it. Listening to the parrots mocking each other in the palm trees behind us. The faint slosh and slap of the water against the seawall. The sun drawing patterns on my eyelids. I wonder if morphine has this effect too: bubble-wrapping you from your feelings. I think about Dad locked away in the dark, with all of this life and warmth out here.

Jake's voice pulls me back. 'You okay Evie?'

I shake myself awake and prop up on my elbows, 'Sorry, just a bit jetlagged.'

'Yeah, you never could sleep when you were worried.'

'Guess not.'

'You still happy in London?' He's watching me closely.

'Do you miss it Jake?'

He smiles, turning back to the water, letting me avoid his question, 'Some things I miss, definitely. But this is where I should be. What about you Evie, wouldn't you rather have all this?'

He's gesturing at the sea, the blue sky, but I'm not sure that's all he means.

I get to my feet, brushing off the grass, 'Let's walk. I need to walk off that wine.'

We follow the esplanade under the bridge, past the old Olympic wonder pool and Luna Park, the fairground rides looping up high above the fence in a sickly gust of candyfloss and pink disinfectant.

The boardwalk narrows to a thin path around the cove of Lavender Bay. A flotilla of yachts is moored here, their hulls slanting like ducks in perfect synchronisation with the tide. I check my phone, sending Janelle another text as we watch three men in a dinghy row out to one of the yachts.

'I want to show you something.'

I raise my eyebrows in mock alarm and Jake laughs, 'Ssh, you'll like this.'

At the curve of the bay there's a steep flight of steps leading up under an arch. It's a little overgrown with vines; branches from the trees above hang low. The archway and the railings are remnants of the Art Deco architecture era built around the harbourfront in the twenties.

About halfway up, there's a gap leading to the lawn of someone's private property.

Jake steps through it.

'What are you doing!?'

He grins at my primness, 'C'mon Miss Goodie-two-shoes.'

Across the lawn is a little trail of stepping stones, we follow it down and into a grove of fruit trees: lemons, grapefruit, figs. There are tiny seats carved out of chopped logs and meandering paths of chipped bark. Sculptures sit on concrete plinths. Oversized ferns line the paths. A spray of daisies grow out of a wheelbarrow. It's all higgledy-piggledy but lovingly disordered. It feels like a garden designed by children.

'This can't be public.'

'It is. Sort of. It's the Secret Garden, but anyone can come here.'

'What do you mean?'

'It used to be a junkyard, overgrown, full of rubbish people used to dump. Fridges and mattresses, stuff like that. There was a railway line here originally but it stopped running about ninety years ago. Then the plot was derelict for years.'

He points to a house higher up, overlooking the garden. 'Wendy, the woman who lives there, started clearing and planting it out. Her life wasn't great at the time; she says she wanted to create something beautiful. Gradually people started helping her. Dragging out the junk and bringing the odd plant.' Jake nods to a lavish cluster of bird of paradise. 'Those were ordered for a place in Balmain, at the last minute the couple decided they were too orange for their garden, so I planted them here.'

'The council haven't noticed all of this?'

'Course they have. Right on the harbourfront, with these views? This land would be worth millions. It's probably been earmarked for development for years. But the council know they'd have a fight on their hands trying to bulldoze it now. There've been petitions. The Secret Garden has become part of the local community. People have got married here.'

We sit on a small bench under a frangipani tree. Looking out over the water from a secret garden, somehow secluded on the shore of one of the world's most famous harbours. Through the creamy sweet of the frangipani petals, I can smell Jake. It's a smell that makes me want to close my eyes.

'How's your work going Evie? You still volunteering at that children's centre?'

'Most weeks.'

He smiles, 'It still making you cry?'

'Yep. Most weeks. Every week there's an awful story. Another poor kid. Here we are, it's the twenty-first century and there's still no country in the world where children are safe. How can that be?'

'But people like you, fighting the good fight?'

'Jake I'm not doing anything. There's so much more I'd like to be doing. We need better laws, better, updated laws to keep children safe and a lot more money spent.'

'What about your art, how's that going?'

I shake my head. 'Haven't painted for years.'

'That's a shame, you were pretty good.'

Jake drops me off a couple of hours later. He cuts the engine and leans back in his seat. I ask him if he wants to come in for a coffee, but he doesn't want to intrude. He hasn't met Dad and thinks it would be disrespectful with what's going on. There's no point trying to explain how many people are traipsing through the house all day.

We sit in silence for a moment, fiddling with our seatbelts, both of us keeping our eyes fixed ahead to the garage door.

'How are you and your Dad?'

I look over, not sure exactly what Jake means. 'Okay. He's on drugs, but there must still be a lot of pain...'

'No, I mean, are you talking? *Have* you talked? You know, about everything?'

'It's hard. There's been a lot going on. He's been pretty busy with work.'

'*Work?* You need to talk to him Evie. He's the only one who can tell you about that night. Whatever happened, you should know. Evie, this is your dad. Your mother. It's your life. For fuck's sake, what's more important?'

MINA

Lord Alden Rigby-Williams

It was a miracle of chance that happened that afternoon. In a city
of more than a million souls, only a handful would have been in a
position to help me. Fewer still who might have any inclination to
do so. Somehow, I had stepped into the path of Lord Alden Rigby-
Williams.

A Member of Parliament, Lord Alden was a high-born
gentleman who had found a liking for balancing the occasional
scale. Some years before he had campaigned on behalf of the
inmates at Bedlam. He'd seen inside its walls, and sworn to do what
he could to keep anyone free of such misery. The wretched inmates
were chained like dogs, kept in their own filth, cold and starved. If
they weren't mad going in, it didn't take long before they were so.
An outsized portion of the inmates were women. Carted down to
Bedlam's dank bowels for far less offence than petitioning a well-
to-do family with a sign written from burnt twigs. From his parlour
window across the square, Lord Alden had seen the constables
arrest me and knew where they would be taking me.

But the odds of what had first caught his attention were more
extraordinary. My ripped and very much unloved dress had
somewhere, somehow been cut from the same cloth that upholstered
a footstool once belonging to Lord Alden's grandmother. How this
was true couldn't be imagined, but I know it was, for he showed me
the stool himself. He'd sat on it as a boy, reading to his grandmother

after her eyesight failed. They were fond memories and he was given the footstool as a keepsake when she passed. It still sat in a room upstairs, the twisting blue lilies unmistakeable.

All of this I learned later. Standing in his luxurious hallway that afternoon, watching him laugh, I had no inkling of the gift that had been handed to me. Lord Alden was a stranger in fine clothes. I was on the wrong side of a large door in a foreign place. Tired and hungry, I was a long way from anything I knew. No one I knew had any knowledge of where I was.

'Thank you. I'm most grateful to you sir. If I may excuse myself now?'

He stopped laughing, the amusement lingering as he nodded to the sign I'd made. 'Who paid you to stand with that?'

'No one sir. ...Sir, if I may let you get on?'

His eyebrows rose with interest, 'You wrote the sign yourself?'

'Yes sir.'

'What connection do the Mercers have to this?'

'It's their mill. They own it and it's very dangerous. If I may leave now sir?'

'Leave? Of course you can *leave*. Keep well clear of that house though. I assure you Bedlam is not somewhere to be trifled with. Those constables will have you down there without a second thought.'

'I must speak with the Mercers sir, it's a matter of life or death.'

He looked at me thoughtfully, 'Perhaps you have time for some tea first? You might be kind enough to tell me about these children who are dying?'

I looked at the door.

He smiled kindly, indicating a table not far within the next room. 'We can sit just there.'

The table was polished to such a gleam I could see my own face peering up at me. The seats were cushioned softer than a pillow. My feet sunk into deep rugs. The curtains, the upholstery, the floor: everything was so soft.

A woman in a pinafore so white and crisp I blinked to see it, brought a silver tray with tea and biscuits. Light as clouds in my mouth, the biscuit had been ground so finely, it hardly needed chewing. Hungry as I was, it took all the manners Mama taught me not to wolf the plate of them.

I kept the front door in my view while we talked, but it became increasingly difficult to entertain dark thoughts about this man. I had walked through one night and spent the next curled on a park bench, but he seemed not to notice how out of place I was on this soft chair in his beautiful house.

And he kept asking me questions. Straightforward and plain, like I was a person who had words worth hearing. I was shy to speak at first, to talk freely with such a fine gentleman, but Lord Alden's questions were hard to skirt. The more I told him, the more he wanted to know. Slowly I found myself telling him everything.

I told him about Harry. How dear Harry was, and how painfully he had died. How his death should never have happened. Why the Mercers must be told so no more children would be forced under the machines. Lord Alden read the ledger pages carefully. His manner was precise, but not unkind, clarifying my answers until he was satisfied of their detail. Why were we working at the mill? Where had we come from? I told him about Billy and my father. My life before we had been taken.

The room's lamps were lit around us, still he asked me questions. The pinafored woman stood at the door, 'Pardon the interruption my lord. Will you be wanting dinner at the usual time?'

Lord Alden checked his pocket watch with surprise. He leaned back in his chair, looking at me, at my sign, now folded beside my feet on the rug.

'Thank you Mrs Peel, yes. Please set for two, perhaps we could have it in here tonight.'

He turned back to me. 'You will join us for dinner Miss Halewood?' It wasn't a question.

Dinner was wonderful. Food enough for a family of six was brought for the two of us, and not a single bowl on the table. Beginning with a basket of tiny breads, soft and warm on the inside, Mrs Peel served the meal in front of us onto lovely flat plates. I thought of my friends back at the mill, with their bowls of miserable broth. This food was too good not to share.

Watching me eat some beans, after I'd speared too many and dropped half of them back on the plate, Lord Alden laughed. 'When was the last time you ate?'

Aside from the biscuit, it had been tea time at the mill two days ago, so I just told him the truth. 'I've never eaten the like of this sir.'

He looked down at his plate, then back to me.

And that was that. He said he would help. Nothing would be the same again.

It makes no difference whether or not we can see it coming. Change splits the ground beneath our feet all the same. Why would Lord Alden help me? I asked him later, how he could take on such a thing so very lightly?

He just shrugged and smiled as if it hadn't even been a choice.

After dinner Lord Alden sent his calling card over to the Mercers, requesting an audience at their earliest convenience. His man returned with a similarly embossed card bearing message that Mr and Mrs Mercer – and both of their daughters – would be greatly honoured to receive Lord Rigby-Williams and his guest tomorrow. The Mercers hoped eleven o'clock would be an agreeable time?

Lord Alden suggested meantime that Mrs Peel might see to one of the guest rooms – assuming I hadn't arranged alternative accommodation for the evening? He hesitated, considering something delicate. 'Might it be sensible if Mrs Peel also rustled up another dress for the visit tomorrow? Much as I appreciate the heritage of this one...'

Mrs Peel ran me a bath. I imagined she was as surprised by having to do so as I was to be stepping into it. But she seemed a generous woman, even when we were alone, and appeared to be taking this course of events in her stride. The bath was steaming water in a pan large enough for my whole self to sit comfortably inside. Mrs Peel brought me warm robes, took my dress away to be washed, and asked what preferences I had for a new one. A girl would come shortly to measure me.

That night I slept in a bed the size of our bedroom back home. The scent of lavender soap still on my skin and the grandest feast I'd ever seen in my belly. Pillows soft as swan's down against my cheek, and the overwhelming generosity I'd been shown swirling through my head.

The luxury was wasted on me. My body was clearly not made for such riches. I slept fitfully, mostly dreams of Billy and Harry, but Ty too. I knew they were just dreams but it was hard to discount the disappointment in their eyes: how could I be enjoying myself with what was at stake? Several times I startled awake, a churning dread in my stomach.

The next morning a dress was hanging inside the door. The shade of a summer sky, with creamy coloured underskirts, it was so lovely I was nervous to touch it, let alone try it on. But there was no other clothing for me to wear and I could hardly hide in this room all day.

It seemed incredible that a dress for a fine lady could fit me at all, but it did. Coming close to the ribs then falling smooth to the floor, amazingly, the dress fit me very well.

I opened the door and peered down the corridor. There was no one there, but from the noises coming from downstairs, the house was already busy. I could hear people bustling to-and-fro, the front door opening and closing. I tiptoed down the carpeted stairs, expecting cries of 'stop thief!' at every step.

A girl arranging a fresh arrangement of flowers directed me to a room where Lord Alden was taking breakfast and reading papers. He looked up as I came in. 'Oh good, Mrs Peel said she was able to arrange a dress. Less memorable certainly, but suitable enough?'

'Yes sir, thank you. Thank you so much. It's a great kindness I don't know how I'll be able to repay.'

'Fiddlesticks. Some eggs?'

I sat and a plate was brought for me, tea was poured. A serving of buttery eggs, big enough for several breakfasts, was piled on my plate.

'Did you sleep well?'

'Thank you sir, your house has every comfort.'

'Good, good. Now, I've been thinking we should leave the ledger behind this morning.'

'Oh?'

'Yes, better to start discreetly. No need to spook the horses just yet.'

I wasn't sure what he meant, but perhaps it was a reference to the fact horses were brought from the stables to take us to the Mercers' residence. Their house was barely a minute's stroll across the square, but Lord Alden said we should make every effort to appear civilised.

And so we circled the trees and came to a dignified stop on the opposite side of the square. The coachman held open the carriage door as the entrance to No.47 swung open. Lord Alden offered his arm to help me down, and I stepped under the Mercers' archway and past the horrified butler.

The Mercers' house was almost as grand as Lord Alden's; it also had a curved staircase and hanging glass pieces. We sat on well-padded chairs facing each other. Lord Alden and myself on one side, Mr and Mrs Mercer and their two daughters on the other. The daughters were perhaps a year or two older than me. Both seemed very interested in Lord Alden, watching him like two hungry geese eyeing up scraps of food.

Tea and biscuits were served and polite conversation was made. There was talk of the great honour Lord Alden bestowed with his visit. And the honour felt in return at being so graciously received by the Mercers. If the Mercers knew me as the girl who had stood outside their home the day before, they gave no indication. Mr Mercer finally brought observations on the weather to a close. 'Is there, perhaps, a way in which we might be of service to you this morning my lord?'

'Indeed, thank you sir, I wished to acquaint you with Miss Halewood. The young lady has travelled to London with news from Mercer Mill. She is in work there, you see, and has first-hand accounts I'm sure you'll be grateful to know.'

The three women exchanged quick disappointed glances. Mr Mercer himself looked mildly annoyed, 'News from the mill you say? How unexpected.'

Lord Alden continued, 'Yes, if you'll permit me to speak plainly, it's possible the men managing the mill are overlooking certain hazards. Sadly there have been casualties. Miss Halewood has come with the express desire to apprise you of this situation, for the casualties have frequently been young minors.'

'I see.'

'Indeed sir,' Lord Alden asked. 'I wondered if there might be a way to address these hazards? For myself, I should be delighted to lend whatever assistance I can.'

Mr Mercer now looked positively furious, his cheeks reddening as he spoke. 'I thank you for your interest my lord, but I'm in regular correspondence with the mill. If there were any unnecessary casualties, I would know of it.'

'But Mr Mercer sir it's true,' I blurted out. 'There's been many children killed at the mill. It's too dangerous sir. If you could see where the little ones have to work.'

Mr Mercer scowled at me before addressing Lord Alden. 'Really my lord, it's kind of you to trouble yourself with these humble affairs, but my man at the mill is quite competent.'

He paused, looking at his increasingly fretful daughters, before continuing in a conciliatory tone. 'Perhaps we could invite you back on a more agreeable matter my lord? We're holding a small recital next week, nothing outlandish: family, a few good friends. My daughters are both excellent singers. We would be greatly honoured by your presence.'

Lord Alden and I were back in the carriage within minutes.

We sat side-by-side, heavy in our seats. 'What else can we do?' I asked.

'We can call back on the Mercers, call upon their sense of decency. I spoke too plainly.'

'Shall we do that this afternoon?'

'It would be better to wait a few days.'

This panicked me. Already I'd been gone too long from the mill. The risk I was putting Billy in would be growing every day I stayed away. 'My lord, I must be back before then.'

Lord Alden looked sympathetic. 'We cannot force their hands Miss Halewood. It is their business how they run their mill. There is no law that says otherwise.'

As we got out of the carriage, I looked back across the square to the Mercers' front door. I realised there would be little chance of changing their views. We could go back and plead with them again, but when I had looked into their eyes, I had seen how disinterested they were in warnings from the mill, or the safety of the children working there. Mr Coleman had been right: The Mercers were not concerned about what it took to provide their cotton.

I should leave for the mill as soon as I could.

I was about to thank Lord Alden for his kindness when something that he'd said struck.

'But if the mill was doing something unlawful, it would have to stop?'

'Of course. That's what laws are for.'

'What are the laws that protect children?'

'From what, mills?'

'Yes, and the machines.'

'None. None I know of.'

'Are there laws to protect children from the adults they work for?'

'Laws govern adults. It is for adults to ensure the children in their care are protected.'

'What if they don't? What if the adults *aren't* protecting the children?'

Lord Alden raised his eyebrows, intrigued. 'I have copies of the laws in the library. Let's see what there is exactly.'

Lord Alden's library was incredible. There were thousands of books, from ceiling to floor, stacked immaculately along every wall. Two long adjoining rooms of nothing but books. Where Mr Coleman's office had several hundred, here was a forest of books. Each one beautifully leather-bound. Their spines shining with gold. I stared mouth open. In awe of all the knowledge that must be contained within these shelves. All the new words that could be learned. Was there no limit to the knowledge that could be held within a single human head?

We sat at a table in the middle of the first room, leafing through the books of laws which Lord Alden thought could be most relevant. There were a lot of laws. Some were strange, but most were of such simple sense it was hard to understand why they needed to be committed to a book at all.

There were numerous laws detailing how a male could rightfully relieve himself in a public thoroughfare. Laws regarding the keeping of adult pigs indoors. I also read about which days the King had sanctioned the trading of potatoes.

As the day wore on, the pile of books we'd looked through grew higher and higher. We'd not come across a single law that would be helpful to the children at Mercer Mill.

Just after five o'clock, Mrs Peel knocked at the library door.

'Ah Mrs Peel, a mind-reader as always. More tea would be outstanding.'

'I'm sorry my lord, there are two constables here.'

In the hall behind her were the two men who had tried to take me to Bedlam.

'Apologies for disturbing Your Lordship, we've come about the girl. She's to go back to the mill. She's got away from her duties, you see.'

Lord Alden stood up, 'Are you intending on taking her to the mill now?'

'No, no, just to the station my lord. The mill's sending a man for her in the morning.'

'Miss Halewood will remain with us this evening. The mill's man can collect her from here just as well tomorrow.'

'Sincerest apologies Your Lordship, that won't be possible. The Mercers were quite clear on that point. She's caused the family some bother already. Best for all concerned if she comes along with us now.'

I stepped forward. A few hours earlier I'd read laws relating to the harbouring of criminals; punishments were cruel. Whether they were ever meted out to lords wasn't clear, but I didn't want to risk involving Lord Alden in any such pain and humiliation.

'They're right my lord, I did leave my duties. Please let me go.'

He looked at me incredulous, then snapped at the constables, 'This is ridiculous. What difference can it make where Miss Halewood spends the evening?'

'Out of our hands. Entirely out of our hands. Couldn't be sorrier my lord.'

The constables locked me in a small room, three grimy walls; bars along the fourth side. There was a pail and sleeping pallet but they smelt very bad, so I kept to the other side of the room and sat in the corner. It was dark and cold.

Huddled against the stone wall, I thought about all that had happened since I left the mill. My running away, walking through the night and waiting outside the Mercers' house. It all felt so useless. Not a step I'd travelled had worked to slow the mill. Even as I sat here, its machines would be roaring, children suffering beneath them. I had left the ledger on the table of Lord Alden's library. Would it be tidied away, slid into one of the shelves? Harry's name – and the names of the children who had died before him – buried with the laws that had failed to protect them?

The darkness of the cell, damp and foul-smelling, closed in around me. Who was I to have thought I could change anything? What difference could a farm girl possibly have made? I pulled my skirts tighter around me. I was still in the dress I had worn to please the Mercers. There had not been chance to give it back to Mrs Peel, or thank her, and I felt very sorry for that.

I played with the skirt, folding and unfolding the thin, silky fabric between my fingers. It was far too pretty for this filthy floor. And much too delicate for Wilks' whip. This dress would be ripped apart far quicker than the one that Mama made for me had been. I didn't want to think about the skin underneath it.

It would be Wilks coming for me in the morning. I couldn't imagine him sending anyone else to deal with such treachery. I dreaded seeing his face, and what would follow. The cart ride back to the mill, the leather cuffs hanging from the fence. Would he punish me so severely that I wouldn't be able to work again? Whether or not I survived the pain and blood, I knew my time in the office would be over. I would not be allowed to touch another book again.

I hadn't thanked Lord Alden either, not properly, and felt very bad about that too. As the constables had bundled me out and down the stairs of his house, Lord Alden looked angry. I must have seemed very ungrateful. Instead of telling him I would never forget how generous he had been, I'd fumbled uselessly with my goodbyes.

For some hours the station was busy, I could hear people coming and going. A man was crying in the cell next door. Then it quietened down. I shivered, rubbing my arms for warmth. It was colder in the stone-walled cell than it had been out on the park bench two nights before.

Too cold to sleep, the night dragged on, dark and heavy.

To keep my mind from the cold, and what was coming with the morning, I tried to remember the roads I'd walked down. I pictured them from above, as though seeing them from the wings of a great raven.

I closed my eyes and imagined nestling into downy warmth. I felt the strings of vast muscles tighten and release under me as the bird lifted up over the rooftops. Back to Berkeley Square and Lord Alden, then along to the flower girls at Covent Garden. I felt the wind on my face and heard the steady heartbeat of coal-black wings stretching out on either side of me. I ran my fingers down the water-silk ridge of feathers and saw the blue-green sheen across the bird's back as we caught the light, circling the glorious dome of St Paul's.

Higher we flew, ribboning up through Islington, above the rows of houses, until finally gliding out into the open fields and fresh air. The woods, rustling and safe with green. Then the mill. Ty,

Helen, Cal and Harry. Harry alive and laughing. His hair a halo of sunshine. Airborne together, the five of us soaring free. Swooping and diving back along the dirt paths homewards. No need for maps or bloodied dashes. Held aloft through warm currents of air. Home to Papa and Billy.

Smiling in the dark as I imagined this, the sweetness of Billy's hug. I knew it was unlikely that I would ever see my brother again.

Morning finally came. The station bustled again, but there was no Wilks.

I paced, and then sat quietly, waiting and shivering. The man in the next cell was dragged out, crying now for justice, for mercy. That he was innocent.

Around midday one of the constables came swinging his big loop of keys to unlock the bars. 'Up you get Miss, time to go.'

I stood and followed the constable down the corridor. Heart pounding in my ears.

As we walked, the stained bricks of the station walls came into sharp detail. I noticed the layer of dust collecting along the skirting board. The crack that ran across one of the paving stones, a tiny chip of wood that had been caught there and worn smooth. Grimy handprints along the wall: prisoners before me desperately trying to brace themselves against the door frame.

Taking a deep breath, I looked up, steeling myself to face my fate. But it wasn't Wilks waiting for me.

The man standing there – his manner and fine suit in fantastical contrast with the station – was Lord Alden Rigby-Williams.

I'd not imagined how we would meet again. To be seeing him here instead of Wilks was so overwhelming I could not speak. I stood there blinking in astonishment.

On the way back to his house Lord Alden explained what had happened. After I left, he had called on the Mercers again. 'What choice was there? After Mercer had sent men around for you. Had you dragged away like that in the night!'

Conversation had been charged, but the two men had, at length, settled on an arrangement where Lord Alden would purchase the farm my family lived on. The papers were sent for, and had been brought down from the mill this morning.

Lord Alden had ridden directly to the station as soon as the signatures were waxed.

It took me a minute to understand what he was saying. I would not be going back to Mercer Mill. Not ever. Billy would never have to go near it. My family was free from Wilks.

'My brother will always be safe?'

Lord Alden smiled, 'From the mill, yes. The sale is final. You and your family should not have to deal with the Mercers again.'

Such a thing seemed as fanciful as flying home on the back of a giant bird. 'How can I ever thank you for this? It's a debt far greater than I can ever repay.'

Lord Alden looked at me for a long time before answering, 'Miss Willamina, this is a small thing that I could do, and I was very pleased to do it. Making your acquaintance has been a pleasure I have enjoyed very much.'

I learned much later that Mercer had demanded many times over what the mill had paid for our farm, arguing that included in the sale were the indentured years I would have spent at the mill.

I'd assumed I would be working those years in Lord Alden's household. Hardly fair enough recompense for Lord Alden's generosity, but I promised to work as diligently as I could. A notion that amused Lord Alden. No, he'd have his coachman Farris drive me home tomorrow in the carriage. I could take the deeds to our farm with me; they'd be of little use here.

The following morning Lord Alden bid me farewell on the steps outside. It was a cold day, the sky a low, wet bruise of grey. He helped me up to my seat, signalled to Farris and tapped on the door.

As the carriage pulled into the street it began to rain. A stony, full fall of water, dripping from the railings and pouring down from the roof, but Lord Alden was still standing on the steps, one arm raised to send us off, as we rounded out of the square.

I watched London tumble and climb past the window. From the comfort of the carriage's padded seat it was easier to appreciate the city's prettier qualities: the grace and detail of its architecture. Nonetheless it was still a great freedom when the houses finally thinned to fields, and to be out on the land once more. As completely as it had come, the sky lifted and the rain cleared, for which poor Farris must have been glad, driving in the rain couldn't be comfortable.

The weight of my luck was overpowering. The sheer impossibility of Lord Alden's kindness. For all the countless times I had imagined it, and all the ways that I had travelled it in my mind, riding home in a lord's carriage was not a possibility I could have ever dreamed. Yet here I was, a free woman, indeed freer than I had ever been. A blanket across my knees, on the seat beside me a roll of parchment declaring me landlord of my family's farm. Billy and Papa only hours away.

Farris stopped at a wayside inn around lunch time, we stretched our legs while the horses rested and fed. It was around five o'clock when the trees began to form familiar shapes. The lay of the hills and the curve of the fields wrapping around us in dear, so very dear, welcome.

Each tree recognisable as part of my family.

By the time we pulled up outside our cottage, my heart was swelling fit to burst.

Stepping into the cottage conquered me completely.

Of all the senses, it is smell we are most powerless against. The memories it returns; the doors inside a body it can unlock. It is a marvel, the weight of what we carry around within ourselves unknowingly. The deep, wordless feelings I'd wrapped away years ago, suddenly released by the scent of drying thyme. The layers of life lived here, the patina of winter fires, Billy's first steps, Mama's voice calling us in, Papa laughing at my childish stories. The fine sweetness of Billy's hair when he was a baby. Such precious life, and all of it has a perfume.

Five years had been a long time for me, but it had changed Billy and Papa too. Billy was so tall. He had shot up like a young tree. I couldn't stop hugging him, reassuring my arms I was really here with him. His hair was darker but he was still very much the brother I remembered. Shining eyes and a bundle of energy and questions.

Where I had been, and what I had been doing weren't easy to answer. I didn't want to tell them how bad it was at the mill. The whippings, how we lived there. Wilks. What would be the point? It could not ease any of the suffering that had happened. My family knowing would only bring more hurt. I could see Papa had been angry and sad for a long time. He looked older than his years, his face now deeply lined. Papa would have felt responsible, but none of it was his fault. And once we were gone, there would have been no getting us back from the mill.

After we were taken: Ty, Cal, Helen, myself, and Harry, there had been frantic searching, most of the village out with their lamps all night. It was only later when Landowner Ruthers returned, after his barn had been burnt to charred stays – a crime punishable by hanging – that our disappearance was explained.

We were safe and well, Ruthers told them. In lieu of the hefty land debts our families had accrued, we would be acquiring a trade in a mill not far from London. Should we choose to, once we had completed our indentureships, we would be free to leave our employment and return to our farms. Until that time, we were not to be disturbed.

Standing in the village square, with everyone gathered, Ruthers had used the opportunity to call for volunteers. There would always be plenty of good work at the mill, he told them.

In the months after that, there had been a lot of coming together. People from nearby farms visiting more often, families comforting each other. Helen's mother, Rebecca, was living with Papa now. It was a shock, but then I realised I could only be happy for them.

Mama wouldn't have wanted Billy to be without a mother. Like my father, Rebecca was a widower and with her daughter gone, she was alone. Watching the three of them together, there was clearly a fondness that would be childish to begrudge.

It was far easier to hear all that had happened here than to talk about where I had travelled to. We had shared words for here. Even without saying much about the mill and our lives there, or how we lost Harry, I struggled to describe anything properly. The city, St Paul's, Lord Alden, the property deed that was now strapped to the rafters overhead, even my fancy new dress was hard to explain. How could my family understand an entirely new world, having never seen anything like it? I reminded myself that there was no rush. We would have plenty of time together to speak of everything.

The next morning I woke early, earlier even than Papa, and tiptoed past everyone sleeping and out into the morning. The sun was just clearing the line of land. The grass dewed and sparkling. I wrapped my old coat around me. I'd found it hanging still with the other coats, as though I'd been expected home any minute, and felt a rush of affection for Rebecca. It was a good thing for her to be here.

The coat used to be too big, now it was tight. I rubbed the little robin Mama had embroidered on the lapel, its stitching more precious than any city silk, and I began walking.

My feet knew where I was going before I did. I headed into the woods, breathing deeply of the trees, the grasses, the layers of living things. The smell of my heart.

Deep in the forest, I rested my forehead against the bark of a tall oak and closed my eyes.

The wind came dancing through the trees, and I listened to the leaves rushing high above me. The noise of freedom, it swelled and vibrated inside me. I was home. I belonged here as sure as the leaves growing above me and the rich loamy soil turning beneath me. These colours ran with mine, we intermixed and beat together. My blood and bones were made of this place.

I knelt to pick up one of the acorns lying at the roots of the tree. Balancing it in my palm. Lovely though it was, satin smooth in its tiny cup, unless you knew, how could you possibly imagine all of the stretching curled within it? Could the seed itself even dream of its own towering possibilities?

On the way back to the cottage I stopped to wash my face in the stream. Watching the icy current run and gurgle over the pebbles on the creek-bed I suddenly found myself unbuttoning my dress. Rushing to pull the cloth free, I stepped into the stream. So cold, it was a roar in my ears. Gasping I knelt down into it and the water flowed over me. Washing away the mill, Wilks, the Mercers, all the blood. Clear and fast, and so cold. As the water rushed around me, it seemed even the scars across my back were being washed clean.

When I climbed back up onto the bank my skin was tingling and new.

All those times I'd dreamed of being home, clean and safe, and now here I was.

When Billy woke and came to find me later, I was in the shed milking the cow. Her milk steaming in the pail, her breathing grassy and warm.

'Want some blackberries today Billy?'

He grinned from ear to ear. 'Always!'

Rebecca was making hot oats when we got back in. We sat with Papa and Farris as she ladled the creamy porridge into our bowls. The men were discussing the carriage horses. The brown mare had a swollen knee and Papa was telling Farris it should be rested before journeying back to London. Farris didn't want to be away another day, but he was coming around to that view too. They were chuckling about how Farris could try his hand at some country chores. Papa wrapped his arm around my shoulders, hugging me to him, and told Farris that today was too much of a celebration for proper work anyway.

After breakfast Billy and I headed back into the woods. We took a cloth bag for mushrooms too. Yesterday's rain had brought

Penny Buns and plenty of field mushrooms. Billy was sharp-eyed and fast. He'd uncovered a late morel before I'd even spotted it, and was happily showing me what he'd learned since we used to go collecting together. It made me proud to watch him, nimble and sure as he darted ahead through the trees.

Billy was nearly nine, not quite as old as Harry had been, but already taller, his body fuller and stronger. I wondered how Harry would have grown if he'd not been taken to the mill. Would he have looked as healthy if he'd been given proper food? If he'd not spent all those years cramped under the machines, trying to make himself as small as possible?

The blackberries were sweet and warm with sunshine when we reached the brambles. Their vines rich with purple. We stood there eating for a good few minutes before either of us spoke.

'Mina, I wish you never left.'

'I thought of you every day Billy.'

'Every day?'

'Every day. I always will.'

He nodded, satisfied for the moment, chewing one of his berries. 'These are so good.'

I put another into my mouth, 'They're my favourite,'

'Me too.'

We grinned at each other. The moment perfect.

The only part of that day I would change would be that we could have another, similar day to follow. And another after that.

Walking back through the woods together, the sunshine filtering down through the leaves, blackbirds and thrushes singing, a pot of berries in one hand, a bag of mushrooms swung over my shoulder, I set this moment in amber inside my mind.

For I knew I could not stay.

Leaning out of the carriage window, looking back to see Billy standing against the shed, watching him get smaller for a second time, my veins filled with blood colder than the stream.

Billy wasn't crying now, he just waved forlornly as the carriage drove away.

This time he had Papa and Rebecca with him. Rebecca's arm around his shoulders. But this time the leaving was all of my choosing.

I was grateful Farris was riding up top, because when I couldn't see Billy any more, I started crying. And I couldn't stop for a long, long time.

EVERY

Tuesday, 4.26am

I'm so tired. No matter how late I stay up, here I am, wide awake and raw with exhaustion sometime around now. Staring at the ceiling, at my watch, out into the dark. Gritty-eyed. My head a roar of fear and stupid thoughts, I pad about the house. Creeping around, haunting the house like the ghost of my own childhood self. Waiting for the day to begin.

When there is enough light to read the sky, I can see rain is coming.

Dad doesn't come up for breakfast. Apparently he was up early too, but went directly from his bed to the studio downstairs. Joe is down there with him now. Kara and Janelle are sipping coffee in front of their laptops. Riz has sliced fruit and breads. No one is eating.

I pour myself a coffee. Thunder booms through the house, a few seconds later lightning hits the room like camera flashes. It's a raw, wet day and worse is on the way. Rain is coming down hard, lashing against the windows in heavy sprays. The balcony is dancing with water. Out on the sea, there's no line between water and sky. The world feels submerged and slippery.

Around noon Joe comes up from the studio. Janelle sees him out, the two of them speaking in hushed tones near the front door. I head to the stairs to go see if Dad wants some lunch brought down.

'Oh, I wouldn't, if I were you.' Kara's voice is arched and soft.

I know I'm too tired to think straight. Everything feels like an insult, but this woman seems bizarrely aggressive. Why does Dad even like her? She's everything Mum wasn't.

'Excuse me?'

'Well Aavaree,' she drags it out. 'You don't want to keep being in the way, do you?'

'In the way of what, Kara?'

'Oh sweetie, you *must* see time is limited.'

'Exactly. You think Dad should be spending this time in a dark room, staring at a screen?'

My voice sounds shrill and overemotional. Kara looks at me coolly, a cat playing with its prey. 'You don't know your father at all, do you?'

'Kara have I done something to offend you?'

'Look Aavaree, you can't just waltz back into his life and expect all his attention. You don't know what he's been going through. *Sweetie*, you haven't been here for years.'

I glare at her, my face blazing with indignant heat. Before I can think of something to reply, we're interrupted by a jazzy keyboard riff coming from Kara's phone. Kara brightens to see who's ringing, turning her back to me as she answers the call.

I pass Janelle in the hallway, she looks at me concerned. 'What was that all about?'

'Nothing. I'm going for a walk.'

'What? In this weather Evie?'

Down on the beach the wind is howling. It's dark and foul. By the time I reach the sand dunes, I'm wet to my skin. The beach is deserted. The waves are furious mountains, climbing and crashing high on the sandbank. I breathe in the briny air. Drawing it into the clench of my shoulders.

Janelle's right, it's ridiculous being out sulking in this weather, but I can't bring myself to turn around. There's nothing like being back in the house you grew up in to make you feel childish and powerless.

Kara is right too, hatefully right. I don't know my father.

It was Janelle who organised my leaving the house. After Mum died. It was Janelle who sat me down and explained how boarding school would be best. For me, for everyone. How it was going to be a big adventure. And only for a little while, just until everything had settled down a bit here.

It was Janelle who packed my bags and helped me choose which belongings to take. Showed me how to roll my clothes into neat rounds inside the suitcase so they wouldn't get creased. It was Janelle who told me I needed to stop crying and be a brave girl. And it was Janelle who drove me to the airport and saw me off into the care of the airline staff at the departure gates.

It had been raining hard that morning too. On the drive to the airport, the windscreen wipers swished angrily across the road ahead. I remember hoping the rain would be heavy enough to keep the plane from lifting into the sky, so Janelle would have to turn the car around and drive me home.

Leaving my sodden shoes next to a tangle of seaweed, I walk down to the edge of the waves. The rain is so wet, there's little difference on my skin between the feel of rain and the sea.

I start walking towards the rocks and the lighthouse. My bare feet sinking deep into the wet sand. The day is dark enough to see the long beam of light slicing through the rain and rotating out to sea. Beyond the sand dunes, the trees are bent low and whipping in the wind. Thunder growls through the sky. A wave slams into me, knocking me sideways, the sand underneath me loose and twirling. It sucks back down, hissing and foaming into the sea, leaving a thin layer of sand over my jeans.

Mum used to love the drama of weather like this. We'd rug up in raincoats and go out splashing. We would come down to see the waves crashing. Other times we'd drink sticky mugs of hot chocolate in the lounge, steaming up the glass doors watching the storms come in from the sea. Thrilled by the electricity and power of nature.

Nothing can be happy all the time she'd say. You need the sad times too. And you never know which times will turn out to be the most important.

I don't really know what happened to us. Dad and I.

After Mum died, we just drifted from each other. That morning there were people crawling over every inch of the house. Men in plastic suits collecting evidence. They set up a crime scene downstairs. Dad and his lawyers were interviewed into the night; Janelle sat with me while the police spoke to me. I didn't have much to tell them. When I went to bed Mum and Dad were in the lounge, on the sofas, talking and laughing. Mum looked up smiling when I came to say goodnight. She kissed me. I went to bed. I slept. I didn't hear anything.

Everything was normal until I found Mum lying on the floor.

Dad mostly stayed in his studio after that. I didn't see him much and when I did, he smelt unwashed and stale. He was red-eyed, and often drunk and unsteady. For the pigeons it was a feeding frenzy. Showbiz story of the decade. The perfect love affair, the perfect marriage, two of the world's biggest stars and now one of them was dead. Discovered in a pool of her own blood. She was only thirty-six, young to die – even for a celebrity. For days it was the lead story. On the TV were repeats of her films. She was on the cover of all the magazines. I remember standing in a newsagent, a wall of faces gazing back at me, and all of them were my mum. She was everywhere, but gone.

Leaving the house was difficult. Whenever we tried to go out, the pigeons would follow us. My school wasn't set up to withstand such a siege. There were long-range pictures published of me in the playground.

Within a month of Mum dying, I was on the other side of the world. An English boarding school that was well equipped for children who needed privacy. The grounds were extensive; paparazzi lenses couldn't get past the gate. Arriving in the heart of northern winter, it was so cold and grey – gloomy until nine in the morning and dark again by four – there wasn't much point going outside anyway.

I cried every night for the first few weeks. Stupid hot tears all over my pillow. I was being punished. I knew I deserved it. I knew I'd been sent away because I hadn't found Mum early enough to save her, but that didn't make my loneliness any less sharp. I rang begging to come home.

It was only for a little while Dad said, until things were quieter.

Weeks went to months, the British greyness lifted into spring, and by the time I saw Dad again when he came to visit three months later, school was fine. I'd made good friends. I liked the regularity of boarding school life. I liked knowing what to expect. There was a routine here with no nasty surprises. When we went on excursions, no pigeons leapt out with flashing cameras. When I got into arguments, the name-calling had nothing to do with my parents. I was just another girl in a school uniform and it was lovely. The next school break, when I flew out to visit Dad on his shoot in Sardinia, he said I was getting an English accent.

I missed the sun, I missed the sea. I missed my mother. I missed her so much. Her arms around me. Her complete, unconditional love. But thinking about Mum was like twisting metal inside my chest, and Dad and I seemed to have less and less to say to each other.

Over the next few years I came home less. He was filming back-to-back projects. There were always a lot of people around; other women. The house was refurnished. A different kitchen; the stairs were gone. New colours on the walls. New carpet in the bedrooms. None of Mum's stuff was in her cupboards. Her smell was gone. And being at the house made me think of her so much more.

I spent a Christmas with my best friend Soph and her family. Her parents were nice, she had a little sister and an older brother; a warm house in rural Sussex. We played board games. It snowed on Boxing Day. They made me feel really welcome. I knew this was the sort of life I wanted to have.

After our A Levels, some friends and I backpacked around Thailand. It didn't occur to me to apply to a university in Sydney, by that time I'd spent six years in England. A third of my life.

There wasn't a row. Not exactly. Just before I started university, I flew out for two weeks in Sydney with Dad. The plan was for us to spend some quality father-daughter time together. The first evening I asked him about the night Mum died. Where was he? I hadn't meant it to sound accusatory; I just wanted to know. Somehow this got into a discussion about his girlfriends and his life. We were both disappointed. Some post-production issue came up the next morning: he had to rush back to refilm a scene. I spent the two weeks swimming and reading. Holidaying on my own, in my own home, which didn't feel like home. It was perfectly pleasant; I didn't want for anything. But when my next break came up, I didn't want to go back.

Sometime into my degree I realised it had been six months since we'd spoken. When I got my first job, I didn't need his allowance anymore. It was bad of me, I should have called to let him know and thank him for the years of generously providing for me, but it seemed easier to simply close the account and email Janelle.

By dinnertime the rain's stopped. Looking down on the beach from the balcony, the sea's calm. I've showered out of my sandy wet clothes. Riz has made another excellent meal, although I'm the only one at the table to enjoy it. The studio door is closed, I'm not sure how many people are behind it.

Alone in the lounge I find myself standing next to Claudine's diaries. I pull out my great-great-great grandmother's very first one and decide to read.

In the slow, concentrating-carefully hand of a child, the diary begins with the explanation that it is a name-day gift, and that our narrator, Claudine Rigby-Williams, is eleven years old.

A few pages in, it's clear Claudine has a knack for storytelling. She describes her world in lively strokes. The joy of sliding down the dark wood of a well-polished banister, the smart of the scolding afterwards. The family dogs, riding her beloved pony, Pyke, in the countryside surrounding their home. Her entirely vexing younger brother, Alden. There's something in her descriptions, how brightly she sees the world around her that reminds me of Mum. I wonder what Claudine looked like, if she was petite and delicate like Mum. If she had a similar laugh. If she loved stormy weather; what other family similarities might have been passed down. I wish there were photos of her.

The diaries have been lined up along the bookshelf in the order they were written, so whoever needs to, can slide them out knowing roughly where Claudine was in her life. I'm pulling them out randomly, trying to get an overview.

About halfway along the shelf, Claudine describes teaching her daughter, Willow, to embroider little robins onto cushions. The same stitches she herself had been taught by the dearest friend who Willow is named for. It's not going well Claudine laughs: just like Mina, Willa is always far more interested in spending time outside.

The next diary I open is back at the beginning, fourth along the shelf. Claudine is fourteen. She and her brother are learning French in addition to their Latin and native English. Claudine despairs of French. She writes that *naturally* Alden is excelling, but Claudine can't imagine ever finding use for such a dreary language herself. Those tiresome hours of conjugating verbs would be far better spent with her pony Pyke or her water-colours. If she could spend even half the time at her easel that was wasted on French, she would finish several art pieces a week.

Claudine was an artist! It makes me smile to read how she describes painting: *a means to fashion thoughts and remembrances into colour.* I know exactly what she means. I can't believe I never knew about her or these diaries. There is such familiarity within these pages. She is so alive. I know the diaries were written a century-and-a-half before Mum was born, but somehow reading about my great-grandmother's life feels like being closer to my mother too.

There are no watercolours downstairs in my bedroom. But, before he dropped me off yesterday, Jake drove by an art supplies warehouse. We bought oil paints, pencils, charcoals, brushes and several good-sized canvases. Basically we went to town. Jake laughing and carrying a basket, then wheeling a trolley for me as we ran up the warehouse aisles. I even got an easel. I haven't used an easel since university.

So that I don't get paint on the carpet, I set up the easel on the balcony outside my bedroom. Bringing out the two bedside lamps, I tilt their shades up towards the canvas to see what I'm doing. Proper artists always talk about natural daylight, but I can see well enough. Most people don't view paintings outdoors anyway.

I carried a bottle of red down with me from the kitchen. I realise I've got the wine and corkscrew, but forgotten to bring a glass. I feel like some kind of wannabe popstar drinking straight from the bottle, but not badly enough to bother going back upstairs to the kitchen.

I change out of my new clothes and into my old AC/DC T-shirt. It still comes halfway to my knees so I don't bother with the jeans. It's late, no one can see.

I start, small at first, gradually spreading out across the canvas. Working with the charcoals, I sketch until my hand is sore from gripping the sticks. Scrawls, parts of faces and shapeless things. They're not great. I drink more wine and tell myself to loosen up and let my hands work without narration. After a couple of hours, I switch to oils. I haven't worked with them since university either.

The tutors said oil painting should be my thing. They wanted me to submit my canvases as graduation pieces. I didn't. The last thing I wanted then was to stand out. There was some fuss, so I just stopped painting. Not everyone needs to take over the world.

The sky can't all be stars.

I take another glug from the wine bottle. It feels good having a brush back in my hands, to be mixing greasy slicks of colour on the palette. Faces, eyes, mouths, people begin to emerge from the oil. I swap canvases and start again.

At some point I realise I'm painting Mum. Not Mum from her movies. Mum on the beach downstairs. Mum with long, dark wet hair. After we'd been swimming in the rain, on a cloudy day when the air felt colder than the water.

Fashioning thoughts and remembrances into colour.

It was just the two of us. Mum and me. It was not long before. Maybe a few months before she died. The waves were pummelling and dumping down hard. We were being thrown about and laughing. Enjoying the feeling of being small in the gracious mercy of a force far greater than ourselves. My mother is make-up-free and utterly beautiful.

What people don't realise is that without the darkness, it would just be a mess of light.

But it would have been hard for Mum to avoid being a star. Hers was a face destined for fifty-foot screens. Those people who can't take a bad photo. Whatever they do, it looks good? Mum was like that. She wasn't just lovely; her face was light.

First I pull out the delicate bone structure, the high cheekbones. For a long time I flesh out the background, the stormy greens and blues of the sea, the creamy foam-flecks of crashing breakers. The grey storm clouds. Her hair, twining and curling tendrils around her shoulders. Last of all, I come back to her eyes.

Stepping back to see the whole picture, I knock over the empty wine bottle. Picking up the broken pieces, I step down on a shard of glass. It doesn't hurt much, just the first sting cutting my skin, but it bleeds a lot.

When I come back from my bathroom with toilet paper wrapped around the cut, I see the bloodied footprints I've left on the concrete floor, ruby red on polished grey, and suddenly I'm crying. Crying so hard I fall to my knees.

I miss her. I still miss her so much.

Looking at the blood, I know I need to go back to the beach.

MINA

Return to London

Around eight o'clock we neared Berkeley Square. The journey back to the city felt longer than the same distance we'd covered two days before. The road away from my family was stretched and lonely. The horses were tired, Farris must have been too. I felt jangled and weary from the road and all I'd done was sit inside, staring out the carriage windows.

It was an outrageous imposition to be back on Lord Alden's doorstep. Already he had done more than I could thank him for, or hope to repay. And here I was, travelling back towards his generosity, intent on asking for more of it.

Walking through the woods with Billy, breathing in the sweet air and feeling the sun on my back, I'd remembered Harry lying cold on Mrs Hoyle's table.

I'd watched the sunlight play on the muscles of my brother's legs as he ran ahead, and known that I couldn't just slip back into my life. I couldn't pretend the mill's machines weren't still running unchecked. Or that my friends weren't still working in that stifling heat.

Somewhere in the city there had to be a way to make Mercer Mill safer.

I felt sure it would begin with finding the right laws. I was hoping Lord Alden would let me into his library to continue searching. We had looked through only a portion of what was there. With Lord Alden's permission, I would start from one side of the library, reading through the shelves thoroughly, as I had with Mr Coleman's ledgers.

Once we had the laws that proved Mercer Mill was unlawful, the challenge would be knowing who had the authority to ensure Mr Mercer heeded those laws. This was where I'd most need Lord Alden's help, because I knew that person would be a man. For right or wrong, it was men who made the rules. The men from my own village would hardly listen to a young woman on such matters; it was unlikely the important men of London had better ears.

As Farris drew the horses outside No.23, I looked up into the windows. The house's curtains were drawn and the glass panes revealed only the square's reflected lamplight and darkly silhouetted trees. Farris had parked in front of the house as if there was nothing unexpected about my visit: riding up in Lord Alden's own carriage to his door.

As Farris helped me down the carriage steps, the front door swung back. Mrs Peel was holding it wide open, behind her Lord Alden had just hurried into the hallway.

He looked surprised but perhaps not unhappily so. I hoped not unhappily so. There was a complicated set to his face and a slight unevenness to his step that made him hard to read. A whiff of liquor came to the door with him.

'You're back?'

'Is that alright?'

He steadied himself, bowing his head as he waved me inside, a gesture of clear welcome. 'Mrs Peel was just about to set for dinner.'

After breakfast the next morning we began reading through the library bookshelves. Lord Alden had listened to my plan over dinner. Not knowing Wilks, or the mill's cold efficiency, Lord Alden believed conditions at the mill would already be safer after the fuss my running away would have caused. Nonetheless he promised to help.

Starting in a corner of the first of two adjoining rooms, we read all that day, the following day, and the next. The two of us leafing through book after book.

Progress was slow: many of the parchment pages were handwritten. Spindly flourishes that were not always easy to decipher. My poor understanding of the legal language also meant that I often needed to check words with Lord Alden.

By the sixteenth day we had reached the shelves in the final corner of the second room. We'd not found anything that could have saved Harry. In all these hundreds of books; thousands of laws, there was not a single law that defended child workers.

The vast majority, and most vulnerable, of the mill's workforce were entirely unprotected.

We sat and looked at each other, the last of the books still in our hands.

'What can we do now?'

'There's nothing to do Mina. If no laws are being broken, we cannot push the matter further.'

'All these laws! Why do we even have them? What good are they?'

I had not meant offence, but Lord Alden bristled, 'Without laws, there would be no society. Laws are to govern and protect.'

'Who do they protect? Are they only for fine city families?'

'They are for everyone Willamina. In the eyes of the law, all must be equal.'

'How are we equal? Who wrote these laws? Powerful, rich men? Men who have never been to a mill. What would they know about our lives?'

I stopped, I knew I'd said too much. Lord Alden had been so kind, and in return I was showing him childish rudeness. I looked across the table nervously, expecting him to yell, rightfully demand I leave his house immediately. Through the doorway behind him was a gilt-edged painting that hung over much of the wall. It appeared to be three generations of family; their features sharing a stately uprightness as they stared down from the glossy canvas. There were two children in the painting and I realised the little boy was Lord Alden. The expression on his younger self matched the one he wore now: reserved and regal. If he was angry, he kept it well below his surface.

'Go on,' he said.

I took a deep breath, 'These laws, if they are truly for everyone, equally, does it seem right that there are none to protect the children at Mercer Mill?'

His face softened, and when he spoke again it was with a warmer tone, 'Mina, having laws solely for the children of one mill could not be practical. Laws don't work like that. I understand this has been frustrating. You want to help your friends, but you have done that already. Mercer will most certainly instruct his men to take better care with those looms in future,' he paused, trying and failing to hide a smile. 'If only to avoid other workers turning up, waving bits of dress at his windows.'

'...Besides, your friends will soon be finished with their apprenticeships and back with their families. Is it so bad working at the mill? Apart from what happened with the young boy, of course. They are learning a trade.'

'Learning a trade was not what any of us chose.'

'Yes, true, that's very true, but now that it's done, is it such a bad thing? Having a trade to fall back on? Especially for the boys? I don't imagine they all wished to be farmers?'

'Harry did, he loved his cow more than anything,' I could feel myself getting tearful, my voice faltering as I spoke. 'Harry would never have left his farm.'

'I know, and that is very sad. He meant a great deal to you Mina and to lose someone so young is terrible. But laws must be written for the many, not individuals. The fact there aren't relevant laws suggests this is an isolated case. What happened to your young friend was unfair, deeply unfair, but it was unusual.'

'What if it's not Lord Alden? What if it's not unusual? Harry wasn't the first to die. The mill is getting bigger. There will be more children under more machines...'

I stopped. This was my lacking; if I had better words to explain, Lord Alden might have a truer understanding of how dangerous it was. 'I'm sorry, if only you could see these machines for yourself.'

He looked at me for a moment. 'Visit a mill? Why not, I'm sure we can. Perhaps not the Mercer's one, I doubt either of us would be welcome there, but there must be other mills not far from here.'

Lord Alden made enquiries, and a day later we were in the carriage, Farris up front, travelling four hours' northeast to Gainsborough Mill.

As with Mercer Mill, we heard the hammering long before we saw the building. Gainsborough Mill seemed smaller, but perhaps it was just that I was bigger. No longer the terrified child I had been when we children first encountered a mill. Gainsborough was certainly no less ugly. Like the Mercer's mill, it hulked, squat and out-of-place on the surrounding landscape.

The pounding as we neared no less ominous.

Farris secured the horses and disappeared inside with Lord Alden's calling card. We had decided the simplest way to gain access to a running mill would be to let the manager believe Lord Alden was considering building a mill himself. Farris would tell him we were travelling past, and ahead of such an investment, wished to see the mechanical marvels in operation.

We didn't have to wait long for Farris to reappear with the manager. A short, stocky man, nervously tiding his hair as they approached. He was already speaking as Farris pulled open the carriage door for us to climb down.

'M'lord! M'lady. What a great honour! Mr Yorke at your service m'lord. You must forgive our lack of preparations. We've not received word from Mr Gainsborough to expect you.'

'No need for preparations,' Lord Alden answered. 'We happened to be passing and are most keen to witness Mr Gainsborough's fine manufactory in all its glory.'

'Oh of course m'lord, of course,' Mr Yorke's words tripped over themselves in his eagerness to get them out. 'I'm sure Mr Gainsborough would be delighted an acquaintance of his, especially one as esteemed as yourself m'lord… Well, it would be a privilege to show you whatever's of interest.'

Lord Alden breezed over the convenient assumption of friendship between himself and Mr Gainsborough. 'Greatly obliged Mr Yorke. We won't keep you long.'

'Not at all your lordship, not at all.'

Here Mr Yorke hesitated awkwardly, clearly debating something in his mind. He seemed about to speak to me, then changed tack and addressed Lord Alden instead, 'Your lordship, was the lady also thinking of coming inside? Only as a place of business, it may be somewhat strenuous to her feminine senses. It's warm inside m'lord, most warm. My wife won't come in, you see, not at all. Perhaps her ladyship would be more comfortable taking refreshments in our cottage, it's just thereways down the path?'

Lord Alden checked with me before replying, I shook my head firmly no. 'Most kind of you Mr Yorke. Miss Halewood is curious to see these modern wonders for herself.'

Mr Yorke looked doubtful, but directed us over to the mill's entrance nonetheless.

Stepping through the doorway the heat and smell hit us, as sudden and fierce as a firing oven. The familiarity of the place made my stomach clench. The thick dust coming up from the cotton. The roar and clatter of the reels, churning and racing beside us as we walked down the centre row. It wasn't Mercer Mill, but it could have been. The long lines of workers, sweaty and pale; their eyes never leaving the yarn that stretched and thinned a foot from their faces.

I looked to Lord Alden. Accustomed to crowded scenes as he was, living in the city, I could see it was still a struggle for him to keep the shock from showing. He only just maintained a look of detached curiosity as Mr Yorke proudly pointed out aspects of interest in the machines.

Mr Yorke kept leaning towards Lord Alden, yelling at his ear, but being a step behind them I couldn't hear what was being said.

As we made our way down the rows, I looked mainly to the workers. Thin, curved backs; each body rounding down towards the machines. Many of the workers here were children too. Their posture and bearing looked so familiar I found myself checking to see if there were any faces I knew.

As far as I could tell, the machines were the same as the ones at Mercer Mill. They were arranged in a similar formation. My stomach wound tighter as we climbed to the part of the machines where Harry and his friends had worked. The little scavengers, slipping under the fast-moving parts, tasked with collecting the stray bits of fallen cotton.

Sure enough, as Mr Yorke paused, his mouth wide in explanation, his arm expansively taking in the gleaming metal – the great pounding, dragging rotors that were faster, heavier, more lethal than a human body could possibly withstand – I saw a boy.

For a moment the child looked up, and in the gloom under the machine his eyes caught the light like a cat's. Then he shimmied further in and was gone.

I looked ahead to see if Lord Alden had seen the little boy too. His back was to me, but as he stepped forward, I saw his hand clenched white at his side.

Mr Yorke's tour finished in his office. As with Mr Coleman's, it had a thick, snug-fitted door that softened the pounding, making the machines as much a vibration under our feet as a noise to be heard. Tidier than Mr Coleman's, Mr Yorke's office had fewer books, although there were still plenty of ledgers. I wondered if one of them held a list of names that ended with single-number ages.

Mr Yorke offered us water. After just minutes in the heat, Lord Alden and I both drank deeply. Did the workers here have to wait until dinnertime to ease their thirsts as we had at Mercer Mill?

The men were talking. Lord Alden was telling Mr Yorke he'd never seen anything like the mill.

Mr Yorke beamed with pride, 'Thank you m'lord, we do believe we're on the brink of a new age at Gainsborough. The cotton we can process in an hour here is three times over what a village of weavers could do in a week.'

'And the quality of it?'

'The same your lordship, if not better. Many would argue better.'

'Most impressive.'

Mr Yorke affected a modest smile, as if he, himself, was responsible for all this fine cotton.

'And the workers? Do they require a higher payment to work with the machines? The noise and heat, does that put them off?'

The manager was shaken by the very suggestion, 'Not at all m'lord! They're only too happy to be part of such progress.'

The workers outside had given off an air of resigned misery. I didn't imagine anyone here was anymore thrilled to be part of the progress than we had been at Mercer Mill.

I didn't have Lord Alden's skill at containing thoughts and mine must have shown on my face, for again Mr Yorke looked at me uneasily, suggesting the matter of finances might be inappropriate for delicate company. I wondered if Mr Yorke ever worried for the delicacies of the women and girls facing the machines every day under his instruction downstairs.

Lord Alden waved off his concerns either way, 'Miss Halewood is contemporary enough in spirit to enjoy the study of progress sir, do continue.'

'Really? I see.' Mr Yorke raised a doubtful eyebrow. 'Well m'lord, a good share of our workers are apprentices. We provide them with bed and board and we're teaching them a trade. They're that grateful, is the truth of it, they don't require much else.'

'But do they provide efficient labour? Can young children get the task done?'

'Oh yes, very much so. The advancement of these machines, the beauty of them m'lord, is the scarce natural intelligence required to work them.'

'You don't say?'

Mr Yorke chuckled happily, 'M'lord, the work's so simple a dog could do it. If we could find a way of getting the beasts to pay attention, we'd have them up on their hind legs working along-side!'

'Indeed? And if the children don't pay attention, are there any hazards with the machines?'

There was another cautious glance towards my feminine sensibilities before Mr Yorke answered. 'As with anything m'lord, there have been a few spills. Only here and there. Unavoidable in any new venture I'd wager. But there's not been a day in six months we've missed quota. It's a sharp business you're going into m'lord, very sharp business.'

I looked for a whip as we made our way out. There wasn't one by the door, but I didn't doubt there would be one hanging somewhere at Gainsborough Mill.

As soon as we were back on the road, Lord Alden yanked the window down, breathing in the fresh air. 'Please tell me it wasn't like that where you worked.'

'Mercer Mill was much the same.'

'That heat and noise! The conditions are intolerable, and all those children!'

I nodded.

Lord Alden leaned back heavily into his seat. I watched him fretfully, anxious to guess what he might be thinking. Finally, he looked back over, his eyes locking with mine.

'You and I have a great deal of work ahead of us.'

'What are we going to do?'

'Something of no small matter. We're taking this to Parliament.'

EVERY

Wednesday, 4am

It's 4am. Down on the beach, the moon is low and translucent, a day or two shy of full. Ghosting over the now-calm sea. The sand is cool under my feet. The cut from the wine-bottle glass stings when I step into the salt water.

I wade up to my waist and dive under.

Surfacing, breathless from the cold, I look back to the shoreline. Beyond the sand, a sleepy line of street lights mark the road. The houses are shadowy, only the odd porch light still on. A few miles out to sea, the red lights on a container ship blink out across the dark water. The sea around me is smooth as black oil.

I swim overarm. All I can hear is my breathing and the lift and wash of my body pulling through the water. My arm bone-pale as it breaks the surface. I swim in a straight line outwards. Long past where the waves would be if there were any forming now. Until my arms and legs ache, and my chest is heaving for air, and I can't swim anymore.

Floating now, I look up at the sky, starless and murky. The moon has slipped behind clouds. Above and below me the darkness is alive. So impenetrable I could be floating in space.

I take a deep breath, close my eyes and slowly exhale. Emptying out my lungs, I let my body go limp, and sink down into the cool, soothing black. Its weight surrounding and taking me; letting me melt and dissolve into its salt. The same salts as human blood.

People worry about sharks feeding at night; that they can't tell you from a seal in the dark. It's the rips you should worry about. At night you can't see the currents.

When I was little, two teenagers died in this water. Other people must have drowned here before and since, but the death of these two kids became part of the local folklore. They were pupils at the local high school. Popular kids who, as far as anyone could see, had glorious Northern Suburbs lives ahead of them.

They were caught in a rip. If you grow up anywhere along the Australian coastline you know it's dangerous to fight a rip. As soon as you learn to swim, you're told it's better to float with it. Wait until it has pulled you out past the breakers and run out of steam, then swim back when you're not fighting against tonnes of water. But these boys panicked. Maybe they were drunk; they'd come down from a party in one of the houses across from the beach.

They were found washed up on the rocks the next morning, their bodies had been stung by jellyfish. I don't know if that came before or after, maybe that's why they panicked. I wonder if they knew they were dying. If they could feel their last moments.

I've spent a lot of time wondering about what goes through people's minds before they die. What they might be thinking as life bleeds out. In those seconds between death and knowing it is coming. Is it always a frantic scream for air?

The doctors told us that she didn't feel much pain. She hit her head. They think on the edge of the second step. There were three drops of blood there. Ruby red on polished grey. Apparently she picked herself up, made her way unsteadily downwards, felt dizzy and then sat on the third-to-last step.

It's unlikely Mum knew she was dying. They think she was already dead as she tumbled onto the concrete. They can't be certain. That's just their theory. Doctors don't know much. Like the ocean, the human body seems to baffle everyone. First we believed in krakens and sea monsters, then we didn't, and then we discovered forty-foot-long great squids.

She didn't look scared when I found her.

—

Drifting somewhere underneath the water's surface. The last of my oxygen hammering in my ears, I sink deeper down, until I feel seaweed reaching up, silkily wrapping my ankle.

I think only this: is this what dying feels like?

GREY

It usually *is* a frantic scream for air. A desperate fight for more.

Air. Life. These things which have been taken so very lightly suddenly become significant. When it comes to the end, I've not seen many let go lightly.

As much as life is about firsts, for everyone there will come a day when it will be about lasts. The last perfect cup of tea. The last time you sat with friends, laughing until you cried. The last time you closed your eyes as sunshine, sweet as honey, warmed your face. The last time you had wind rushing through your hair. The last time you felt truly *alive*.

What do they say, the devil's in the details? Life is too.

But existence wasn't built to understand its own end. So tell yourself what you need to: *yes, but not today. Not for me.* Tell yourself death is what happens to other people. That the frailty of the human scaffold does not apply: that you're different from all those who have come and gone before you.

Tell yourself whatever you like.

Chances are, you're right: it's probably not today.

MINA

A New Act of Parliament

At Lord Alden's dining table that night we began drafting a set of laws to protect working children. There was no precedent; they would be the first of their kind in Britain, most likely the entire empire.

We had raced to the library as soon as we got in from Gainsborough Mill, searching for everything that might guide our wording. Lord Alden had the dining-room table carried through and extended to its full size, so we could better spread out the books and begin writing our notes.

The process of creating a new law was complicated and involved two separate sets of gentlemen: those in a group called the House of Lords and those in another called the House of Commons (a curious name since neither group included anyone but gentry). Once both Houses approved, the petition would be called an Act of Parliament. Then, having been presented to His Royal Highness King George III, it would finally become new laws.

But before all of that, our petition would need to be approved to be considered by the Houses. This was what we were working on. Each word we used had to be the right one. Precise, and with clear reference. What we were drafting would be read by many great men, ultimately the King himself.

By flickering lamplight, we wrote and rewrote all through the night. Pages of parchment piling up on the floor as we shaped our draft. Lord Alden had patiently outlaid what could be reasonably attempted. I did not believe there should be any children working in mills. I had seen the blood and known the fear of being taken from our families. But Lord Alden explained that this proposal would be our starting point. Once we had something in place, it could then be updated, amendments added. Like taming a horse, he said, you had to start softly or you'd have no chance at all.

Mrs Peel brought us a tray of tea and breakfast muffins around 7 o'clock, just as Lord Alden was pressing his family seal into the glossy red wax binding our complete draft.

Our petition called for the working in a manufactory of any child aged less than nine years to be unlawful. Children aged nine to sixteen years to work no more than twelve hours a day and never at night. All mills and manufactories to be properly ventilated so as not to create ill health. We also called for basic requirements such as cleanliness to be met. Children employed in a live-in or apprenticeship capacity must be furnished with education, decent food and suitable clothing. There was so much more that I wanted to include but these simple measures alone would have saved Harry.

We were at the doors of Parliament quarter of an hour before they opened. I sat in the carriage while Lord Alden delivered our petition. It was a sunny morning and the street felt still and quiet, the occasional carriage rolling past.

A tall London plane tree was growing beside where Farris had secured the horses. Resting my head against the window I watched its leaves play in the wind. I was tired from working through the night but bright with happiness.

A little later Lord Alden emerged from the House of Lords' vast stone archway. His step brisk as he walked through the wrought-iron gates.

He opened the carriage door and we looked at each other. 'You did it? It's filed?'

He grinned in response, and I flung myself into his arms.

Dreadful manners but I couldn't help it. This was something so good. Thanks to Lord Alden, the lives of many children would be saved.

We waited for Lord Alden to be called to present the petition to the other lords. Our mood tapering from elation to uncertainty as we practised his arguments and any questions he might be asked. We paced the library. Went for walks in the park. Several times I tried to help Mrs Peel in the kitchen and was shooed away. Finally, twelve long days later, a messenger delivered word from Parliament.

Lord Alden tore open the envelope and we read the letter together.

The petition had been denied. *Regrettably Parliamentary time could not be spared to debate such a matter, at this time or in the near future.*

I sank down on the settee, hollow with disappointment.

Lord Alden reread the notice. 'I'm sorry Mina, I should have expected this. What we are proposing would have little advantage for anyone with a financial concern in a mill, and it's possible some of the Members have ties to the mills.'

'Is there anything we can do?'

'We can try again. Gather more evidence and submit another petition,' Lord Alden exhaled wearily. 'Unfortunately, right and wrong isn't always straightforward, not where profits are concerned. But we will persevere.'

I understood what he was saying. Even I could see the benefit in having children working in mills. At Mercer Mill we had done the work of adults. Indeed, unless it was a task of strength, we were faster. Yet if we were paid at all, it was a quarter of their wage. As apprentices, children were free labour at Mercer Mill.

Before the mill, before the city, I'd believed that those who were strong sheltered those who weren't. Like the seasons, I'd taken this for the natural order. Now I saw that protecting those smaller than you was a choice. And it seemed that the greater the number of people gathered in a place, the less often that choice was taken.

As Lord Alden promised, we persevered. But we would need more than perseverance.

Our battle wasn't just with the mill owners. It never had been.

Darker and far greater forces were against us.

EVERY

All I see is black. All I am is screaming lungs.

Tumbling in the water, disorientated, I can't tell which way is up or down.

I look to where I think is upwards, searching for a silvery sheen of surface, but the flat darkness I see there is as likely to be the sea floor.

My chest hammers, heavy as stone, pounding its panic. There is no time left.

Seaweed twines around my feet again. I kick. Either towards air or away from it, I don't know, but there is no more air inside me.

What I know is that if I'm kicking in the wrong direction I will die here.

In a few more seconds *I will be dying.*

Then, within the panic, comes calm. A sort of release. If this is my final decision, so be it. What should be, will be. If this is my last, I accept it. I see Mum's face. I feel her love. I think about things I haven't done. Things I want to do. I see the faces of the children at the refuge centre. I think about the children in boats. I see a little body in a red top washed up on a Mediterranean beach. There is a lot more I want to do. There are ways I can help.

I kick once more, hard.

Suddenly I'm light. Lighter than salt. The sea lifts me, pushes me upwards, faster and faster. Through the bubbles and layers of water, until I pop like a cork through the surface. Thrashing and gasping into the air.

Back in the world, night is softening into blue. It's a new day and everything is beautiful. Everything is swelling and light with beauty.

A wash of red along the horizon reflects across the water towards me. I can see the beach. The waves breaking against the shore in the distance. I'm out much further than I imagined.

I don't know if I have the strength left to swim back to shore, but I start, my arms aching lead. The colours changing, lightening around me as I slowly pull myself through the water.

By the time I've made it back to the sand, my legs are shaking so hard I can barely walk.

The sun is a line of gold at my back as I stagger up the path to home.

I fall onto the bed. Back down into cool, deep blackness.

MINA

The Petition

Too visionary. Impractical. Ludicrous. Again and again our petition was refused. Debating a Bill's merit in Parliament was usually where the challenge lay. For us, just getting it through the door was a battle. Working in Lord Alden's library, surrounded by the existing laws, it seemed incredible that something so plentiful could be so difficult to achieve.

Looking up at the walls of shelves I wondered if the people who had put forward proposals for the laws concerning stolen cabbages or driving carriage horses indoors had dealt with the opposition that our Cotton Mills petition was facing.

After breakfast we would begin. Reading and re-reading until the words swam and blurred in the evening lamplight. I kept track of the days on the last page of the ledger from Mercer Mill. Making a small black quill-mark for each day that passed. I knew that each mark meant twelve, maybe sixteen hours of hard labour for the children on the mill floor. And that every mark might have cost a child their life.

Still, the weeks ran to months, then a year. And another. Then a third.

My marks slowly blackening the page.

We persevered. It had now been almost three years since Lord Alden first promised we would. But how could he have possibly imagined the time he was promising?

Without him there would be no hope of getting safety to the mills, but I felt guilty for bringing him this unhappiness. I had stomped into his fine world and opened the door to things that could not be unseen. Unlike me, Lord Alden had no friends working at the mills. Whether we succeeded or not would make no difference to his life. Yet here he was, devoting most of his waking hours to something that would not have touched him otherwise.

It wasn't just the time it cost him, I worried too for the danger I had brought him. Even for a Member of Parliament there was considerable risk coming up against the powerful collective of mill owners. For the few, there was great wealth running off the mill floors, and those rich profits would be fiercely guarded.

It hadn't taken long before we were unwelcome at every mill door in the country. We'd been visiting as many as we could to gather supporting evidence: some mills were worse, some a little better than the Mercer's. All of them had children at the machines.

Then messengers were dispatched and we were banned on sight. The first time we were sent away felt a severe setback, then again when it happened a second time at a mill three days' ride north. But as we came to understand, this was just the beginning. Right and true though our petition was, we might have been standing in the way of progress itself.

Here in the city, far from the mill floor, most people celebrated this dawn of machines. Newspapers featured daily tributes to their wonderment. To those who had never been near one, machines were a good thing: innovative and bold. They would power Britain to her rightful destiny of all-conquering empire. Machines like those at the mill would deliver a glorious new era of industry and commerce, unlike anything history had witnessed, and England would be at the very hammering heart of it.

Mills with roaring machines were being built throughout the country, up as far as Scotland in the distant north. Already there were hundreds in operation; each one considered a manufactory of magnificent production, where one person at the reels could do the work of dozens at home.

As I updated the records of what we knew of the mills – their size and the quotas of cotton they produced – I thought of the children working inside them, and the grim ledgers that might be kept on each of their office shelves. But the newspapers never spoke of the blood spilt. The working conditions on the mill floors were not mentioned. It was dangerous to be seen standing in the way of this advancement. Anyone doing so was branded regressive, treasonous. Or worse, a Luddite sympathiser.

Working in the mill I'd not thought much about the work we were taking from others. How the mill might be taking livelihoods as well as lives. But, of course, it was.

It was in London that I learned of the country people who had stood against the first mills. How they had protested, rallied and fought, and how severely they had been dealt with. Their bodies hanging with murderers and traitors at the gallows.

The Luddites were ordinary people; they came from villages like mine. They represented the craftspeople whose trade had been eradicated by the machines. The families whose incomes, generation after generation, had been built on providing England with yarn and thread. Women like my mother whose perfect stitching drew down through hundreds of years' sewing and spinning by the light of kitchen lamps. Within a matter of months, the march of mills throughout the country had left a great swathe of families penniless and starving.

We children had no inkling of it then, but as we huddled in the cart bound for Mercer Mill, a hundred miles north there were people coming together in protest over the mills. Under the cover of darkness, farmers and weavers were desperately trying to learn how to defend themselves against the army of trained soldiers that would soon be sent to crush them. The British government had gone to war with its own people over the mills. Good, hard-working men – fathers and brothers – had been hung for the simple want of fair working conditions.

The same things I was asking Lord Alden to petition for now.

Here in London I could see the work of machines too. With more and more families unable to support themselves on the land, the city's population was swelling in a tearing rush. There were beautiful parts of the city, houses like palaces, squares like Berkeley. But, for most pulled into its rotation, London was a hard life. Its murky airs and dirty water offered precarious shelter.

It was said that a baby born in London was five times less likely to reach childhood than one raised outside of it. Entire families lived out of a single squalid room. No crops to harvest, no livestock to sustain them. Raw filth – animal and human – slopping down the streets. There was a grime of neglect in the poor areas of the city that I'd never seen in the country.

A woman my age locked eyes with me one morning. She carried her baby across her hip in a stained sling. Another child, maybe four years old, gripped tightly at her skirt. They looked hungry, their eyes too big, clothes too loose. I'd had that look, waiting outside the Mercer's house those first days in London, I knew I'd felt that hollow. But the expression of sheer hopelessness in this woman's eyes was something far worse than hunger. She'd got used to living with no expectation of hope or change. It was hard to see. Harder still from the comfort of a Lord's carriage knowing that there was little but luck separating us.

The woman's child ran over when I opened the carriage door. Her tiny hand left a dirty smudge on mine as I reached down to give her my purse.

I kept the smudge on my skin, holding it in my lap like a precious thing all the way back to Berkeley Square. Like the quill marks I made in the ledger every morning, I needed it to guard against my selfishness. Because even with the knowledge of such suffering around me and at the mills, behind the shield of Lord Alden's unfaltering generosity, there were wondrous distractions.

It wasn't just the food, the clothes or the accommodations. On the shelves at the far end of Lord Alden's library were the books written purely for the pleasure of reading. Rather than facts and laws, these books were collections of verses and tales that were wholly fictitious, which is to say they had never happened. Real though they might seem, Lord Alden assured me they had come entirely from the imagination of their writers.

What a thing to do, to make up a whole story. For all those thousands of words to come spirited and spiralling from someone's thoughts. And how entertaining the stories were. I often had to stop and remind myself that none of it was true.

In the evenings when Lord Alden was out canvassing for support and there was nothing else I should be doing, I would sit with a book on my lap, a dictionary on the table beside me to look up any words I didn't know. One of my favourite stories was about a man who travelled to faraway lands. A place where the inhabitants were just six inches tall; another land where they were towering giants. In a final kingdom the rulers were a noble race of talking horses. Try as he might to fit in and play a civic role in each of these foreign lands, the traveller was ultimately banished for his differences. Finally home in England, he became withdrawn and spent his last years trying to make conversation with his horses.

The next day, I found myself wondering if Trapper and Bonny, Lord Alden's carriage horses, could understand us. I laughed at myself for going mad like poor Gulliver, but looking into their eyes, there seemed such a depth of comprehension that I couldn't quite shake the feeling.

The poetry was not stories as such; more like snatches of dreams. Most were beyond my deciphering, although two twirled sweetly in memory. In the first, the poet wanders lonely as a cloud – an idea I liked very much – to see a field of daffodils fluttering in the breeze. Another that I kept returning to was about an animal called a tyger that burned brightly in the forests of the night. I knew I didn't understand this poem, but unlike the law books and ledgers, whether or not I fully understood didn't matter. My misinterpretation made the art of it no less.

Finding these shelves was like learning how to read all over again. These books brought new thoughts and ways of seeing things. With them I travelled to new, faraway worlds. To forests of fearful symmetry and kingdoms ruled by horses. How could I not return from such places changed?

Living in Berkeley Square had changed me on the outside too. To see me now, after three years of living in the city, it might be hard to tell me apart from any fine London lady. I wore several different dresses. My hair was styled like theirs. On my feet were shoes that had been made just for me. Mama's shoes I kept under my bed, safe under my head as I slept. Mrs Peel didn't want me to wear them anymore. They fit me well now; I hadn't needed to twist rags inside them for some time, but they did not suit these new dresses.

I had not wanted these new things, the city airs and graces. Mama's shoes were all I needed. The first blue dress was more than enough. You could only wear one dress at a time, and to see clothes hanging empty in my wardrobe felt a criminal waste of cotton. But Mrs Peel explained that it was unacceptable for a lady to wear the same dress every day. If I was to be seen out with Lord Rigby-Williams, I must present myself in a way that would not bring embarrassment to his good name. It was something to think about, that anyone would bother keeping track of such a thing as a woman's dress. Or that they might think less of someone making good use of one.

In such things I was glad to have read *Pride and Prejudice*. A book both entertaining and, for me at least, extremely instructive. The story described civilised behaviour in a most helpful way. If the woman in the book were real, not merely a gathering of words, I imagined we could have been dear friends. In Elizabeth Bennet's world, as with London, appearances were central. Indeed, it was the opinions of other people, those who did not know you, that mattered most. An upside-down approach that Mrs Peel agreed with wholeheartedly, describing it as proper decorum.

Decorum was a word I heard from Mrs Peel a lot, generally in the context of my lacking it. To improve this lack, she had insisted that dance and deportment classes be arranged for me.

'Mrs Peel, must I take these lessons? Couldn't I just help you in the kitchen?'

'Of course not! And you must stop wandering into the kitchen Mina, it's not appropriate.'

'It's my favourite part of the house.'

'That's maybe, but you're no longer a girl. You're a young lady living under Lord Rigby-Williams' roof, and you must behave as such.'

'Oh Mrs Peel, Lord Alden doesn't care how I sit.'

'That Miss Mina, is entirely beside the point. As Lord Alden's ward, everything you do is reflected on him. Now, after all he's done, do you want to be ungrateful?'

I did not. So I applied myself as well as I could to these lessons to spare Lord Alden's embarrassment. Eating, sitting and dancing as a civilised city woman should. These were not skills that would serve me at home on the farm, but it was a small price to pay to please Mrs Peel.

If Lord Alden noticed the improvement, he did not comment.

Aside from Lord Alden's bookshelves, my favourite part of London were the parks. Sunday afternoons at the mill had been a chance to get outside. Lord Alden insisted we also take a few hours from work each week. Berkeley Square was within short walking distance of London's three parks. Grounds that were once reserved for royal hunting. Having long since been run clear of deer and wild boar, they now provided city dwellers with the fleeting semblance of countryside. Regent's Park to the north was generally closed to the public. The pretty flowerbeds and paved paths of St James Park to the south were crowded with people taking the air. But Hyde Park to the west was a delight. A sweeping stretch of largely untended tall grasses and trees. Among the meandering trails with no one but ourselves in sight, I could sometimes imagine we were not in London at all.

It was in Hyde Park that I had planted an acorn from the woods at home. The acorn I had put into my pocket when I first went back to see my family, the morning I washed in the stream behind our farm. I hadn't meant to take it. Standing underneath the tall oak, lost in the music of the wind running through the leaves above me, I'd slipped it into my coat unthinkingly.

I had found the acorn, still in its tiny cup, inside my pocket on the ride back to London the next day. Playing with it in my hands, I'd known it should be thrown out of the carriage window to grow near where it belonged. I kept meaning to, telling myself I'd hold it just a little further. Turning it over in my palm, the seed seemed to represent something precious that I couldn't quite understand or bring myself to part with. Then I looked up out of the window and realised I'd left it too late.

For a week the little acorn had lain in the left toe of Mama's shoe. When Lord Alden took me to see Hyde Park, the first Sunday I spent in London, I'd planted it with a group of oaks on the edge of a glade. Sheltered by its elders, but in a small clearing for enough sun. Pushing the acorn into the soil, I'd closed my eyes and hoped life and strength for it, here so far away from home.

I missed home. I missed my family. With the great kindness I'd been shown by Lord Alden and Mrs Peel, it was ungrateful – appallingly ungrateful – to think it, but sometimes being far from home could feel as lonely here as it had at the mill. I missed my friends too. I wondered how I would seem to Ty now. He would be in the last year of his indentureship. Depending on how soon after their birthdays Wilks let them go, Ty and Cal could be home with their families within a few months.

Like Billy and the farm, I had tried to put Ty in the far corner of my thoughts while I worked on the petition. I'd been able to visit Billy regularly – Farris and I staying a few nights with my family each time before journeying back to London – but I could not go to Ty. As with Helen and Cal and all the other mill children, until Ty was twenty-one, he was lost. All I could do was work as hard as I could with what was in front of me. The future was an unreadable story.

Ty might not even want to see me. I had left them without goodbyes, sneaking away in the night. And even if he did, would he still recognise the girl he'd held by the river?

EVERY

Wednesday, 10am

I wake to howling sunshine. The sun high and blazing in through the open balcony doors. My head's blurry and there's an icing-sugar dusting of sea salt all over me, tight and stinging on my skin. My arms and legs are aching dead weight.

For a moment I don't remember why. Then the night comes gurgling back. The actions of someone else. Someone childish and irresponsibly selfish. I bury my head under the covers, not recognising the person who sulked off into the storm yesterday afternoon, much less the one who later swam out into unknowable darkness and currents after drinking a bottle of wine.

Sitting up, I see the bloodied footprints. A set of them leading away from the easel on the balcony. Then I remember the painting.

I'm shocked by this too. Standing in front of it before I realise I've even gotten out of bed.

She is beautiful. Of course, so beautiful, and it is unmistakably her, but there's also something wild and raw about the painting. It's hard to believe it has come from me.

Staring at my mother's face, I understand something about last night.

That moment of diving into water. The glistening wet second of submersion that washes away all thought. I was looking for that too.

I didn't just want to feel what she'd felt. I wanted to drown the memory of the morning I found her. To stop feeling so sad and guilty.

I stand in front of Mum for a long time. Looking into her eyes. Remembering the sensation of being lifted through the dark saltwater; the lightness of being lifted up into the air.

Then I wash the blood off the concrete floor and step into the shower.

As I make my way up the staircase, voices spill down. It's barely noon but it sounds like a party. A carefree summer's brunch. Lighter even. More surreal. A sunset cocktail party. There's laughter. The festive clink of glasses. I hear the merry pop of a cork.

I watch for a moment before joining them. Dad is holding court at the head of the table. A raised glass in one hand. Champagne bottle in the other.

'Here she is. The birthday girl!'

Janelle, Lenny, Nat and Nick, Joe, Chris, Kara, Kara's manager, even Nurse Sylvia and Riz are gathered around the table, lifting their glasses in a chorus of happy birthdays to me. There are presents, cards. Riz even brings out a cake he's baked specially. It's cute, the fuss they've made. With everything that's going on I wasn't expecting anyone to remember. I look around the table with a surge of affection at this unlikely collection of people. Everyone eating cake for brunch. It occurs to me that along with Dad, Janelle and Lenny are the people I've known longest. All my life. This is a family gathering.

Dad clinks his glass with a fork. 'It's a great day', he says, stretching out his arm to include the whole table. 'The sun is shining. And here we are together, raising our glasses to my darling daughter.' He pauses, a wider smile. 'Today we're also celebrating *Axlark*. The final cut is done and, in Every's honour, I'd like to screen it presently.'

There's a loud cheer and enthusiastic claps. Riz makes popcorn and everyone carries a bowl downstairs with their champagne flute. We pile into the cinema room and settle into the leather seats. Joe cues the film and Chris dims the lights. For a moment the screen's blank, then it flickers into life. The credits are still to be added so we're straight into the action.

The camera pans down across miles of snowy tundra. It's isolated and timeless. There are rocks and wizened bushes. For miles there is no sign of life, not even the startled retreat of an animal as the camera swoops low across the land. I can't place where in the world it is, or what time in history it is set. It could be now, or a hundred years ago.

Out of the bleak desolation comes a figure. Thin and dishevelled. Faltering, almost staggering. Like the setting, it's hard to place the person: the clothes and walk don't give much away. The clothes are dirty, nowhere near warm enough for the terrain; they're shivering, nursing what looks like a wound under their shirt. There's a sense of badness and violence in their recent past.

It's difficult to understand where this person has come from or where they could possibly be walking to, but they stagger onwards into the hopelessly barren landscape. It's only when the camera closes in, along the ground and then climbing up, from the boots, past the torn jeans, the ripped and blood-stained shirt and into their grime-flecked face that you see it's a woman. Kara.

There's a few whoops from the viewing room. Kara smiles and dips her head in acknowledgement from the seat in front of me. Kara on the screen stops walking. There's a faint brrr of a vibrating ringtone. We now know the action is set in relatively recent times. She answers the call but doesn't say anything.

The voice on the phone asks, 'Fields?'

'Yes,' says Kara/Fields.

'We'll send someone to your location', says the voice.

'No', says Kara/Fields, despite alternative options appearing perilously scarce. 'Tell Winslow it's over.'

She drops the phone on a rock, grinding its screen into bits with her boot heel.

The next two hours blaze across the screen as we sit in rapt silence. The lights come back on and everyone erupts in cheers and claps. It's a great film. One of Dad's best. I feel like I've genuinely been transported somewhere new and felt the experiences of someone else. Kara is in half the scenes and is annoyingly good. Really good.

'Oh Ford, it's got Oscar all over it!'

'For you too Kara.'

'Bravo! Bravo!'

We file back up the stairs to the lounge, blinking in the afternoon sunshine. There's more champagne and congratulations. Dad's looking tired. He's laughing and talking with the others but his movements are slower and heavy. I catch Janelle watching him from the other side of the room and the two of us exchange a worried look.

With the editing done, there's no reason for the team to be here and most of the group have places they need to be. Around 4pm everyone begins to disperse. Joe has to get *Axlark* to the studio. Lenny leaves with him, ruffling my hair on his way out.

'Happy 29 kiddo. Be seeing ya.'

Kara and her manager head for the airport not long afterwards. They're flying out to LA for a meeting they can't stall any further. Kara will be back Saturday morning. I hear her and Dad talking downstairs before he sees her off outside. Kara's voice is raised. For a second I think she's crying then I'm not so sure. Just before the car pulls away, she gets out again and they hold each other for a long time.

MINA

A Passage Abroad

In the early summer of 1819, one-thousand-and-sixty-two ledger marks since I left the mill, our Cotton Mills petition was finally accepted to be heard in Parliament.

Each time I'd watched Lord Alden walk through the stone archway to deliver the results of our latest round of research and drafting, I'd been convinced it would be the petition to be put through.

But this, our fifth attempt, had felt surest yet. I couldn't imagine a stronger argument for change than the one we'd submitted. The weight of its supporting documentation alone had been too heavy for one man. Farris had to leave the carriage to help Lord Alden carry it all in. Fifteen thick leather folders of meticulous notes – copies I'd made of every relevant piece of legislation in the library, careful to replicate the loops and falls of all the original handwriting as closely as I could.

Now that it was done, accepted at last, the next step would be for Lord Alden to present to his peers in the Lords Chamber. Parliament was now in recession and would not be sitting again during the heat of summer. We had eleven weeks to prepare.

It was hot and sticky in the city. We were restless and hemmed in as we waited. Anxious about what lay ahead when Parliament resumed. Even walking in the park felt close. I could see Lord Alden was tired. All day he worked in the library with me, head bowed over our sprawl of paperwork, and many of his nights had been out canvassing for letters of support.

Lord Alden came home one evening with blood on his shirt, his coat ripped. He dismissed it as nothing serious: just a couple of ruffians trying it on for some coin as he walked to the carriage. Purse-snatchings were not uncommon, but something about this robbery rang warning bells. As Mrs Peel saw to the cut above Lord Alden's eye, I went to find Farris in the kitchen.

'What happened out there?'

Farris was shaken, drinking his whisky and staring into the stove fire. He told me that three men had leapt from the shadows, setting on Lord Alden with deliberate intent. One of them armed with what looked like a constable's truncheon. They had been hiding, waiting. From across the square where Farris had been with the horses, it seemed very clear that they knew who they were after.

'His lordship held himself, but three of the brutes? Set to one man! We were lucky to get away as we did Miss.'

There were ten more weeks ahead of us before Parliament resumed. They could try again and be more coldblooded next time. Lying in bed that night, fears of the danger I'd put Lord Alden in wrapped around me. Encircling like wet cotton, drying tighter and tighter until I was startled awake, gasping for air. I had done this.

The next morning I watched Lord Alden eating his breakfast. The gash above his eyebrow was deep. An inch lower and it could have been his eye. I saw that Mrs Peel had also needed to bandage up his right hand.

'I think we should retract the petition.'

He looked up from his eggs, eyes twinkling in amusement, 'What, because of a bit of scuffle on the street?'

'Just for a few months.'

'We've worked too hard to falter now.' He paused, taking in my seriousness, 'Mina, you know it doesn't work like that. Our petition would not merely be postponed.'

'Yes, but what if something happened to you?'

He smiled, 'Nothing will happen. Besides, I was thinking of a trip out of London. Visiting my sister for the summer. The work we're doing now can be done just as well from there.'

'That's a fine idea Lord Alden, we can divide up the work and I'll sta—'

'Divide up the work? Nonsense. You know we need to work together.'

We hadn't spent much time together lately. Lord Alden was kind as ever, but outside of the library, where conversation focussed entirely on the work at hand, he'd seemed reluctant to be alone in my company. I didn't blame him, not with all the trouble I had brought to his door.

I'd always promised myself that as soon as I could, I would go back to the farm for good. I'd been trying to make myself as scarce as possible until the hearing. The last thing I wanted to do was intrude on Lord Alden's family time too. He had always insisted I think of Berkeley Square as much my home as the farm but, as with the petition, he could never have anticipated his generosity would still be burdened three years later.

I was a woman of twenty now, no longer the waif he'd first taken in.

Lord Alden was watching me, 'If you don't fancy it Mina, we'll work here.'

'But your sister must miss you dearly.'

'Excellent. It'll do us both the world of good. Only a few days' travel, nowadays perfectly safe.'

'Perfectly safe?'

'Oh yes, must be a good four years now since they signed the treaty.'

I knew Lord Alden hadn't seen his sister for several years. He had spoken of her living in the country. I hadn't realised it was French countryside or that one of the obstacles to their visits had been the aftermath of the Napoleonic Wars: relations between the two countries having only recently warmed enough to permit a safe crossing across the Channel.

'You're sure I won't be in the way?'

He looked at me, 'What a ridiculous thought! Claudine will adore you.'

Lord Alden arranged passage on a merchant vessel and two days later we set sail with the high tide.

From the moment we boarded, treading a narrow gangway up from the docks, it was clear a wonderful adventure lay ahead.

The anchor pulled up, its chain clanking into place, and the crew raced to catch the tide. As the clipper cleared the coastline, the wind picked up. The mainsail unfurled and flapped open above our heads, and the ship surged ahead like a galloping charger. Her timbers creaking as she bowed low and lifted high with each swell. There was surely technique far beyond my understanding in manning the ship – on the orders of the first mate, the crew scurried to-and-fro, tightening ropes, loosening others – but the effect was natural, graceful unity. Bound by wood and rope, we pulled through the waves together as one.

The setting sun threw fish scales of dazzling gold across the water. With the wind, clean and salty, whipping through my hair and seagulls wheeling and crying above, I could not think of a lighter or truer way to travel. Or a time I felt as free. Even breathing seemed fuller and freer out on the sea.

I made my way over to Lord Alden who was standing at the rails, watching the water break and froth up against the ship and fall away again in our wake.

He smiled as I stood next to him, 'Enjoying the journey Mina?'

'It's perfect!'

A spray of icy seawater flew up across our faces and we both laughed.

We took our supper with the captain in his quarters below. Later, while the men were enjoying after-dinner digestives, I excused myself and climbed back on deck.

The sea was calmer now and the sky was sparkling with stars. Brighter than I'd ever seen. Glowing down to where they met the water. They shone low enough that I imagined stretching out my fingers and gently pulling one from the sky. Would it feel cold, like snow in my hand? The moon herself was low and full, reflecting a long shimmering path across the water. The beauty of it all swelled inside me. I stood there in the dark, smiling to myself under such loveliness.

I leaned up against the railing at the ship's bow. The wind rushed in my face and caught at my dress, lifting my arms, almost releasing me from the tether of the deck as if I was a bird flying. There was such a sense of weightlessness. One day, I told myself, Billy must know this freedom.

My cabin was very cosy, wood panelling on the walls, floor and ceiling. There was room for my trunk, a small round window for peering out to the sea and a little bed built into the wall. I wanted to stay awake, to watch the water and listen to the curve of the ship wash against the waves all night. But the rocking could not be resisted.

I woke to voices yelling and the briny smell of harbour. The ship had berthed in a bustling port. Perhaps busier even than the one we'd left in England. Lord Alden was shaking hands with the captain as I stepped on deck blinking in the bright sun.

There were hundreds of ships anchored together, some three-deep from port. Towers of drums and casks were stacked along the dock's edge. Long lines of horse-drawn carts waited to be loaded or unloaded. Men lifting and carrying, scrubbing decks, scurrying down gangplanks, climbing up ropes. Such colour and movement, if I stood here all day I might not take it all in.

Seeing me, Lord Alden grinned and swept his arm wide across the panorama.

'Welcome to France, Willamina Halewood.'

EVERY

Wednesday, 8pm

By evening it's just the three of us. Sylvia's gone out for a few hours and Riz has the night off. Dad and Janelle are going through paperwork on the sofas. Dad's playing Nina Simone. I turn up the speakers in the kitchen and hum along as I make dinner, enjoying the sweet ordinariness of putting a meal together. Without all the industry and tapping laptops, the house feels like a home again.

'Congrats again on *Axlark*,' I say as we sit to eat. 'It's brilliant Dad.'

'It really is a triumph Ford,' agrees Janelle. 'Easily up there. And now it's safely with the studio you can take things a bit easier. All those hours in front of the screens can't have helped the pain.'

'Hmm,' he says, scooping pasta onto his plate. 'We've barely started the work I need to do.'

Janelle puts down her cutlery, her voice quiet, 'Ford, this next project, are you looking to see it through?'

'To finish? No. I don't imagine seeing it to shoot. But it needs to be outlined well enough for Joe to take it to the studio without me.' He pauses, 'Janelle, can you help set up those meetings?'

Janelle looks at Dad, measuring the weight of his question. 'If that's what you want.'

He nods, 'He'll need your help getting it through… Afterwards.'

The words hang in the air. The finality of what they mean.

'Dad, there must be something I can help you with. I've started reading Claudine's diaries: I could easily sketch locations or storyboards?'

'It's a good idea Ford,' says Janelle. 'You two have a similar sense of colour. Evie could work up palette and look and feel.'

Dad frowns, forking a cube of cucumber, then dropping it back on his plate with a dull splat, 'Ladies, thank you, both of you, but for the next few weeks Joe and I need to focus.' His voice sounds sharp, or maybe it's the word he uses next, 'We'll get it done faster without interruption.'

We eat in silence for the next few minutes.

By the time we've finished the meal, Dad's tone is easy again. He and Janelle are running through what has to be done tomorrow. Joe will be here by 8am. I start clearing the table, taking my time loading the dishwasher and tidying the kitchen. Dad's words echoing in my head. I know I'm being oversensitive: not sleeping properly for days, everything feels skinless and raw. But after Mum died, being around Dad as a kid, all I felt was an interruption.

Beside the recycling bin in the kitchen are a stack of today's newspapers. A woman in an AC/DC t-shirt like mine catches my eye. I lean down to look closer. In a sweaty rush of horror, I see the bare legs, the balcony. The fact she's swiping at an easel with one hand and swigging wine straight from the bottle with the other. The pictures are grainy, long-lens shots, but even with the pixellation it's obvious the woman, me, is crying.

I take one of the newspapers out to the lounge to show Dad and Janelle.

'Yes,' Janelle says, 'we saw that. I'll get that security company back to take another look at the balconies. It's obviously from the Careys' place. I spoke to them this morning. They've been hiring their house out. They'll talk to their agency, make sure it doesn't happen again.'

Satisfied with this solution Dad and Janelle turn back to their planning.

'I don't want anyone seeing me. It's private,' I blurt, my voice quivery and high.

They both look up at me with surprised eyes.

'I look deranged!'

Dad is watching me closely, 'Who cares?' he asks.

He flicks his thumb at the newspaper. 'These are just pictures of you Evie, they're not you. It's what you *looked* like in a fleeting moment, not how you *are*. If your friends see these photos, they'll get that. Anyone else, anyone you don't know, what does it matter what they think?'

He cocks his eyebrow, the signature Mitchell grin, 'It couldn't matter less.'

I flop into the chair beside him. The logic of what he's saying unarguable.

I wonder why it's taken me this long to understand such a ridiculously simple truth.

Dad walks over to the bookcase. Behind the framed photograph of Mum is a small red box.

'There's something I want you to have. Therese would've wanted you to have it ages ago.'

It's a jewellery box. Sitting on the satin inside it, is the necklace Mum always wore. A delicate five-pointed star on a thin chain, a diamond set in its centre.

Mum wore it every day. I can't believe I forgot about this necklace.

'She found it in an antique shop when we were in London doing promotion for *Port Wednesday*,' says Dad. 'We saw it there, glinting in the window of this poky little place down a lane off Covent Garden. It was the day we found out you were coming, we were walking back from the doctors.' He smiles, 'This piece of jewellery is the most precious thing I have.'

It's lovely. The chain is so thin, it coils almost invisibly in my palm. I can see where the metal has been worn from Mum's skin. I try it on and the star falls to the same spot it did on Mum, just inside the hollow at the beginning of her neck. I'll never take it off.

'I have something for you too Dad.'

I run downstairs to my bedroom balcony. Carrying the large canvas carefully back up the stairs, I prop it against a chair at the end of the table and angle it around towards Dad and Janelle. Watching Dad as he sees the painting. Complicated expressions running across his face.

'What do you think?'

He's just staring at it. Was this a bad idea? At this time?

Dad stands up and comes closer. He touches it; his fingers come away with brown paint from her hair. The canvas smells of oil and turpentine.

'It's still drying, sorry. I should put it out on the balcony so it doesn't stink up the room.'

Without taking his eyes off the painting, he shakes his head, 'No, it's fine. Leave it here.'

'Dad, is this okay?'

'Evie, this *is* Therese. The light, the expression. You've caught her exactly.'

He looks at me amazed. 'I didn't know you could paint like this.'

I laugh in agreement. 'Neither did I, really.'

'Well I did,' says Janelle. 'Evie, even as a teenager your paintings were worth framing.'

I'm surprised. 'Was that you Janelle? The ones downstairs?'

She winks at me, 'Might be worth a fortune someday.'

Later I carry the painting back downstairs. We hang it still sticky on Dad's bedroom wall. Directly in his eyeline opposite his bed as he requests.

I slide open Dad's balcony doors, 'You sure you don't want me to put it out here for a few hours? I can bring in my easel?

'Just leave the doors open.'

The two of us sit side-by-side on the end of his bed, admiring our hanging job. I ask him about the Alden project. If he's read Claudine's diaries. Like me, Dad's only flicked through a few pages so far. Nothing has been plotted or storyboarded yet, but Dad's researchers have uncovered an accident from Alden's childhood that Dad thinks could make an excellent opening scene.

'What happened?'

Dad reaches over to take a sip of his water. 'When your – I forget how many greats it is, let's just say *great*-granduncle – when your great-granduncle was a young boy, about twelve I think, he was almost killed by a coach and horses.'

'A coach and horses?'

'This was the 19th century, they didn't have car accidents. This wouldn't have been an uncommon death back then. Anyway, apparently Alden saw the coach charging towards him but was frozen on the spot, convinced he was about to die. His father was there. Dad froze too, also convinced his son was about to die. It was a busy London square, plenty of other people around, but no one moved.

'Picture it, in those seconds. Credits open on the coach. It's going fast, too fast. Camera tightens to the beating hooves. The cry of the coachman. Certain death rushing towards the child. Then, at the very last second, just before impact, a complete stranger steps into the road.'

'A stranger?'

Dad stretches his arm to an imaginary road beside the bed. 'They reach out, and yank our boy to safety.'

'Great opening scene Dad.'

'It all happened very fast of course, but this is a turning point. Apparently, it was this brush with death that led to everything else. His reforms, his work. It inspired him to help people; to change his world. It was pivotal.'

'Did they become friends? Alden and the person who saved him?'

'Not sure, don't know. I need to read through the diaries properly, I—'

'I can start doing that. I want to read them anyway. I'll make notes as I go. Dad, please let me help with this. Especially if it's for Mum. I won't get in the way of what you're doing with Joe.'

He smiles, putting his hands up in resignation, 'Alright, alright.'

'Great. What's the project's name?'

'Don't have a title yet. We're working with *The Cotton Mills Act*, but we'll have to see.'

MINA

France

A fine white carriage was waiting at the docks. The coachmen greeted us with such strange words that it took me a minute to realise the language they were speaking was my own. Their accents twisting each word into a musical new sound. Lord Alden replied in French. Whatever he said had the two men laughing appreciatively as they saw to our packing trunks.

Cushioned inside the carriage's rich expanse of velvet and gold panelling, we glided over the cobblestones. City streets soon gave way to fields, laced and creamy with yarrow. We wound down the windows and a hazy breeze blew in, warmed by rolling grasslands and wild flowers.

Two hours from the docks, the carriage slowed, and we turned into the cast-iron gates belonging to Lord Alden's sister and her husband. A wide gravel driveway curved up between two rows of poplars, tall, and neat as sentries.

After the calm of the ride, the crack of gravel under the wheels was an anxious rattle. I was nervous about how Lord Alden's sister would find me, and all of this finery was hardly easing my fears. I didn't know what Lord Alden had told them of me when he wrote of our intended visit, but with all the deportment lessons London could muster, it would still be clear I was from simple places. I could only hope my lacking would not be too awkward for everyone.

Up ahead the house came into view. Sloping dove-grey roof and turrets first, then the magnificent, buttery rectangle of Château de Maisons itself. With four floors of pillars and swirling stonework, the château took up the space of ten Berkeley Square townhouses. Its immaculate windows looking out across a perfect symmetry of fountains, lawn and flower beds.

Travelling through the French countryside Lord Alden had mentioned that the Parisian his sister had married was a Marquis. He'd said this was a notable title, but it hadn't prepared me to meet anyone who lived in such a building. We had arrived at a palace.

Lining up to greet us were the house staff. In black and white uniforms – the men suited, the women in crisp pinafores. I wondered how they were able to assemble so quickly at the sound of wheels on the drive. Hopefully we were on schedule and had not kept them waiting.

As the carriage came to a stop, a couple appeared. Gracefully stepping out from the front doorway, the lady's full red skirts blazed brightly against the grey. Lord Alden's sister and her husband: The Marchioness and Marquis de Saint-Aureville.

There was a family resemblance. Lord Alden and his sister shared the same clear-eyed gaze, the same full smile. But where he was tall and wide-shouldered, she was slim and delicate. Two years the elder, Lady Claudine would be thirty-six but she could pass for a decade younger. She flew down the steps, light as a ballerina, into her brother's arms.

It was a warm meeting between the men too, shoulder clasps and vigorous handshakes, before all three turned to me, 'Claudine, Marquis Ferrand, may I present Miss Willamina Halewood.'

I stepped forward, shy in such elegance, and dipped my head in the low curtsey Mrs Peel had taught me. 'Marchioness, Marquis de Saint-Aureville,' these new words felt clumsy in my mouth, I imagined Mrs Peel's disappointment.

Lord Alden's sister waved away my formality in either case. 'Look at you, how enchanting. Let's get inside and have you settled,' she said, taking my arm in hers. 'My dear, you must call me Claudine.

Shall I address you as Miss Willamina or do you prefer Mina?'

Looking over her shoulder she spoke to the men, now following us up the steps and into the château's enormous entranceway, 'Alden, are you tired from your journey? It's quite unfair how fresh you both look. And don't think I didn't notice that outrageous scrape above your eye.'

The Marchioness and Marquis were the warmest of hosts. Over the next week we read, walked in the gardens and ate ridiculous quantities of food. Each meal a banquet of overflowing dishes more incredible than the last. The richest of casseroles, the lightest of pastries: no one should die before trying food such as they served at Château de Maisons. And the chocolate! I'd tried chocolate before. A couple of times Lord Alden had brought home pretty tissue-wrapped boxes of it for me and Mrs Peel, but French chocolate was something more. Velvety, dark, almost warm in your mouth, it melted in a sweet rush that made you squeeze your eyes shut.

The château was daunting. Ballrooms led to grander ballrooms – even the corridors were extravagant spaces. My footsteps echoing off the gleaming floors like dropped spoons. By the second evening I'd given up trying to count the rooms: there were dozens on the first floor alone. Such grandeur would never seem natural to someone raised on dirt floors but I did my best to hide how intimidating the château was, and Lady Claudine did her best to make me feel welcome. Where it was my place to be grateful, she thanked me often.

'I'm so glad you made the journey with Alden, such a treat to share the same language with another woman… Oh Mina do show me that stitch again. I'm quite determined to master it.'

I knew our language wasn't entirely the same but Lady Claudine was so full-hearted, I could almost believe her. When she invited me to sit and needlepoint one evening I found myself proudly showing her some of my mother's stitches. Mama would have been amazed to see her craft travel to such a fine, faraway house. Lady Claudine was a quick study. Laughing and talking together it didn't take many evenings for the two of us to embroider flowers and robins across every one of the cushions lining her favourite window seat overlooking the garden.

In exchange, Lady Claudine said it was only fair she teach me a pastime. 'It's quite fashionable now of course, but archery's always been jolly good fun. I believe you'll like it Mina.'

I did. I liked it very much. Disloyal though it might be to Mama, I thought archery much more fun than needlepointing. Pulling the bow string taut, levelling the arrow against my cheek. Letting it fly, ripping through the air to the target. For a ladylike pursuit, archery was most satisfying.

There was also a library at Château de Maisons. Almost as many books as Lord Alden's own collection in editions of French, Latin and English. The majority of the English ones were fiction, and I was invited to read whichever I pleased. One that touched me deeply was the tale of an emaciated man who is found nearly perished and half maddened from cold in the Artic snow. He tells his rescuers a story of how years before as a young scientist he had dedicated himself to strange experiments, collecting parts of bodies together to fashion the freakish form of a man. But after reanimating the creature to life, the scientist abandons it. The wretched creature flees to the wilderness; teaching himself to read from a satchel of books he finds. Neither man nor beast, he is shunned for his monstrous appearance and becomes a murderer. The book ends with the scientist dead. His tragic creation drifting into the darkness on a raft of ice. An image that stayed with me for days afterwards. *Did I request thee, from darkness to promote me....?*

I asked Lady Claudine about this story, she told me it was written by a woman younger than me. Where did this woman draw such isolation from? Such haunting imagery? To write a story so unique and strange. It was such an exciting idea, I couldn't put it from my mind, playing with it like a shiny jewel. Could I do such a thing? Weave together words that might please others as this woman's story had enthralled me. After the petition was done, could I create a story? I'd seen Lady Claudine herself writing in a book.

When I asked her if she wrote stories, she laughed. 'In a sense, but they're all true. It's a diary Mina. An account of what happens. It's amusing sometimes to look back on things. Would you like to keep a diary? Shall we order one for you?'

'Oh no. Thank you Lady Claudine, I can't see anyone wanting to read my story.'

Lady Claudine smiled, 'Well, I shall have to put you in mine. And Mina *please*, just Claudine.'

The drapes in my bedroom had been pulled back each morning to reveal clear blue skies, and we spent much of our time in the gardens. The estate had vast vegetable plots, long rows of neatly pinned runners and well-tended squares of crawlers and growers. Beans, pumpkins and lettuces in such plentiful supply the château could feed itself several times over. Orchards, where plums, apricots, peaches and pears were being picked from the branches and carried off in wicker baskets to the kitchen. The estate's flowerbeds were beautiful with their swaying blooms and bustling bees, but there was something thrilling about being able to walk between plots of so much food.

I also loved the wild, unfarmed stretches of grassland and forest beyond the gardens that we could wander and ride through. The land was different here, there were plants and trees I didn't recognise, but the open feeling was similar to how it felt at home. A sense of belonging – of being in harmony with the life around me – drifted in the air.

It was on our sixth afternoon, as we sat taking tea in the rose garden, that Lady Claudine brought up the subject of a ball. So far I'd avoided such social occasions. As Lord Alden's ward, Mrs Peel had long threatened the possibility of me needing to attend one and had instructed in great detail what was required. Balls were the perfect opportunity for elegant ladies to display their dancing lessons and polite conversation. I couldn't imagine anything worse.

Everyone looking at me, asking difficult questions.

'It's a tiresome old thing really,' Lady Claudine was saying. 'A little fun too, I suppose. We must do it every year of course, it's quite expected now.'

'Of course it's expected *mon coeur*,' laughed her husband. 'My family have been holding a summer ball at the château for over a century.'

Lady Claudine laughed too, 'And every year we're surprised, and leave it almost too late to send for the dressmakers.'

The next morning a small army of tailors and seamstresses arrived in a convoy of carts overflowing with fabrics. Running my fingers over the rainbows of colour and pattern, I couldn't help but think of the mills where the bolts of cloth would have come from. But seeing Lady Claudine's delight as the tailors bustled about, ready to do war with their measuring tapes and pins, it would have been mean to spoil her excitement.

'Mina, let's select our cloth together. I prefer the bolder colours myself. So much more fun. Why should we women hide in shadows? What shades are you thinking?'

I'd never chosen the fabric for my dresses. It hadn't ever crossed my mind that I should do so. My mother had used whatever material she could find. At the mill, I'd worn the covering of a footstool, never once considering in all those years that I was dressed as furniture. Mrs Peel had taken care of my wardrobe since then. She knew far better than me what was suitable for my dresses. The only point I ever argued was whether I needed so many of them.

Here were fabrics in as many shades of colour as we might find in the gardens outside: soft pinks, blues as delicate as ice water. 'I don't know. Lady Claudine, please pick one for me.'

'Nonsense! What's your favourite colour Mina?'

I didn't have a clue. I'd never thought of such a question. In a world of so many colours, how could you pick one? Suddenly I realised I did have a favourite colour.

'Green. Green like the new leaves on an oak tree.'

'Perfect! What a vibrant choice. And wonderful with your eyes, I'd suspect.'

—

On the night of the ball, Lady Claudine came into my room before we were to go downstairs. I was dressed, and had been sitting by the window watching the carriages pull up along the driveway. Carriage after carriage opened to reveal guests of such gleaming finery it appeared a royal procession was making its way in across the lawn. How could I socialise with such grand people? What would I say? I might be wrapped in enough swirls of fabric to sheet half the bunkbeds at Mercer Mill, but my new ballgown wouldn't hide me entirely.

Lady Claudine stood in the doorway for a moment before coming to sit with me. 'Oh how lovely you look Mina. Not everyone can carry such a colour, on you it's positively radiant.'

She looked beautiful. Her own dress was a rich plum that suited her perfectly, making her eyes, the same deep-sea blue as Lord Alden's, dance and shine even more than usual. She had a handful of velvet boxes with her and laid them out on the cushions between us. Inside each one was a glittering necklace.

'With you both travelling so light, I don't imagine there was room for jewellery. I wondered if you might like to wear one of mine? Diamonds, I thought, would be most fun with your dress.'

'That's so kind of you, thank you Lady Claudine, but I couldn't possibly.'

'Why ever not?'

'What if I broke something?'

'Nonsense! These have been in the family for generations. They're positively unbreakable.'

In the end Lady Claudine insisted, and I chose the smallest, most modest-looking necklace. Three star-shaped diamonds that sparkled like sunshine on water against my skin.

Downstairs the guests had gathered and it was time for us to join them. At the top of the stairs Lady Claudine squeezed my hand before standing with her husband, as their names, then Lord Alden's, and then mine, were announced. My skirts rustling like dry leaves as we descended step-by-step into the view of hundreds of upturned faces.

At the foot of the stairs well-wishers crowded in. The Marquis and Marchioness were immediately spirited away. Three ladies had rushed to greet Lord Alden, they seemed most engaged with his conversation but as it was in French, I couldn't tell what was being said, or if the ladies knew him well. The throng of people thickened and Lord Alden was swallowed into it.

Standing there, alone in the crowd, it was only Mrs Peel's voice in my head that kept me from turning heel and running back up the stairs. Or better yet, out into the garden, where my green dress would best hide me.

A silver tray was offered: glasses of a golden bubbly liquid. For lack of anything else to do, I took one. It had an odd flavour, wetness that tasted dry in my mouth, but after a few sips I liked it more. The music being played by the orchestra began to swell and the lights from the chandeliers above glowed brighter. I reached to exchange my empty glass with a full one as the next silver tray came past.

'You enjoy drink the champagne?'

It was a man. His accent was silky like Marquis Ferrand's but perhaps thicker. It took me a moment to understand him.

'Yes, thank you. It is most agreeable.'

'Do you also enjoy the dancing?' He nodded to the adjoining ballroom. Over his shoulder I could see couples twirling around the floor in a pattern I recognised. Again I had Mrs Peel and her lessons to thank. I must show her more gratitude when we got back to London.

'I do.'

He bowed stylishly and offered his arm. 'I am Monsieur Louis de Rousseau at your disposal.'

I looked over to Lord Alden but he was still deep in conversation. He would be pleased I was making an effort to practise my lessons; meeting with the guests rather than hiding by the wall until it was acceptable to retreat back upstairs.

In the ballroom reserved for dancing, an orchestra was playing on a raised platform. Monsieur de Rousseau led me into the heart of the dancers and we fell into step, swirling with them in a great loop of the room. It was fun. The poor man tried to start a conversation several times but with the loudness of the orchestra, my lack of French and the thickness of his accent, we struggled to understand much more about each other beyond agreeing that we both enjoyed the dancing and the drinking of champagne. We had two more glasses to demonstrate the truth of this. We laughed about how peculiar it was that we both liked the same things, coming from such different countries. We agreed that we both liked to laugh. This was all very funny.

After a few dances another man came up and tapped Louis on the shoulder. I danced with him, and then another man, and another.

Concentrating on keeping to the correct steps, I lost track of their names. There was a Pierre, another Louis, a Jacques, and I think a third Louis... At some point the two of us – I think Louis Two – paused for more glasses of champagne. The dancing was making me thirsty so I drank it quickly and started on another glass before we stepped back into the whirl.

The men were gallant and some of them very pretty, but they only made me think of Ty. None of these men had the depth of his eyes. Close as they held me, their hands had no effect on the pace of my chest. Maybe it was that Ty and I had the advantage of history. When I had looked at Ty, I knew all that he was. We had come from the same air and earth. I could see in him where our lives had been and could go. And Ty knew my scars. The whip marks across my back had faded to pale white, only a slight ridge under my fingertips now, but to Ty I would not need to explain.

The orchestra seemed to have sped to a dizzying pitch as we spun around the floor. I was getting tired of dancing; my feet were sore in their tight new slippers and my face felt hot. The chandeliers now blazed too bright and despite the glasses of champagne, my mouth was dry and thirsty. I was trying to think of a Mrs Peel-prescribed way to excuse myself when we were interrupted.

The man I was dancing with immediately stepped back and Lord Alden held up his hand for me to take. An amused smile playing on his face.

'How are you enjoying your evening Miss Halewood?'

'It's been entirely diverting, thank you.'

He raised an eyebrow, 'Entirely diverting?'

'Yes, thank you Lord Alden, entirely. The orchestra are most skilful.'

'Indeed.'

I could smell the cognac on his breath, but he held me surely and his frame was confident. His steps anchoring us at a steadier pace that seemed to calm the music and let me catch my breath. After a length of the room, I looked up into his face again.

'You must be weary from all the dancing,' his smile was still one of amusement but his eyes were reading me carefully. 'You've had all the eligible men in quite a spin.'

'Oh no! Was that not civilised? I didn't think it would be good manners to say no when they asked so nicely. Mrs Peel's lessons never said anything about saying no.'

Lord Alden looked at me blankly for a moment, then roared with laughter. 'Manners? Manners be damned! Mina you can say no whenever, and to whoever you like.'

'Really?'

'My dear, men will always come to flutter in your light. Mrs Peel's lessons are useful, but the power you have is yours alone to wield. Be kind or let them burn.'

I wasn't quite sure what he meant, but I did know that my head was whirling from the dancing. 'Are you thirsty? The music is making me *so* thirsty. Shall we have more champagne? Those glasses are *so* small, we should probably take two each.'

Lord Alden smiled at me, clearly entertained.

'As you wish.'

The next morning I woke with an appalling sickness. I went to get up and dress for breakfast but any movement seemed to make the foulness grip worse. Thunder crashed against my temples, and my stomach lurched and rumbled like a storm was brewing there too. The sunlight streaming in seemed to aggravate everything. I begged to have the curtains drawn together again and crawled back under the covers, sending down my apologies.

Lady Claudine came to check on me a little later. She had brought some books for me to read and a cool compress for my forehead. I couldn't be sure of her expression in the darkened room, but she seemed amused to see me propped against the pillows.

'I'm sorry to miss breakfast Lady Claudine.'

'Oh, don't worry about that. How are you feeling?'

'A sickness has come over me as I slept. Treacherously fast, I was fine last night.'

Lady Claudine gently patted the compress into place across my forehead. She was plainly fighting back laughter. Perhaps a lingering joke from the breakfast table. 'This is the worst of it, rest up today. You'll be fine by sundown.'

'Lady Claudine, how can you tell?'

She smiled, 'I may have had this sickness myself once or twice. I'll have kitchen send up a pitcher with cucumber and mint, drink as much of it as you can. Do you think you could manage some broth? Perhaps a boiled egg and toast?'

I couldn't believe that such a depth of suffering would leave so simply, but I promised to do my best to drink the water. I spent most of the day feeling sorry for myself, lacking the strength to read more than a few pages, but by sunset I'd had a bowl of broth, finished the water and was feeling much better. Lady Claudine was right. A little tenderness lingered at my temples but otherwise I was quite recovered from the French sickness.

'Did you have a lovely time at the ball? It didn't seem right to ask you yesterday... With the sickness. But you did enjoy yourself, didn't you Mina? Alden says you spoke with lots of people?'

Lady Claudine and I were on the lawns beyond the rose gardens. Taking turns firing our arrows at coloured circles pinned to two boards a hundred and fifty feet away. Lady Claudine was an excellent shot, her arrows slicing through the air in a clean arc, each one hitting its target with a firm thwack. My own arrows wobbled nervously towards the board, slower and far less sure of themselves, deadly accuracy was still some way off.

The French sickness seemed to have addled my head. My memories of some parts of the evening were blurred, as if I was looking back on it now through heavy rain. I remembered my nerves almost getting the better of me, wanting to run back up the staircase. Then dancing, the relief of having something to do, a whirl of men. All of them generously making conversation in my language, when, as a visitor, it was me who should be speaking theirs. Beyond simple greetings, the only French I knew described food or were the names of flowers. Not very helpful words to exchange with men on the ballroom floor. I remembered being annoyed with myself for not learning more.

Then I remembered the steadiness of Lord Alden, his arm around my waist, how he calmed the rush of lights and music. The cool dark of the balcony, which we stepped out onto with our glasses of champagne. Looking out over the garden in the moonlight. Talking and laughing together about something I couldn't bring to mind now.

I remembered making him laugh a lot, and liking how that felt, how nice the sound of his laughter was, and how much younger he seemed when he was enjoying himself.

How together on the balcony the night had felt ours alone.

'I had a lovely time. Thank you very much Lady Claudine, your ball is wonderful.'

Another memory that lingered was being thirsty. I didn't quite see why champagne was so popular. It was a strangely ineffectual drink, the more you drank of it, the more parched you became. Just thinking about it prompted me to step back to the table, laid for us with glasses and a jug of cool elderflower pressé. I took a reassuring sip of the lacy-tasting water.

'I'm not sure champagne entirely agrees with me though Lady Claudine. I liked the bubbles very much but drinking them only seemed to make me thirstier.'

Lady Claudine smiled, her eyes twinkling, 'I know just what you mean.'

I wondered if life at Château de Maisons might be the perfect existence. Even to be an apprentice footman here would not be hardship. There was enough food for everyone. I had seen the dinners for the staff; they were not the luxury intended for our table but still a banquet that would have seemed unimaginable in our farm kitchen, much less along the apprentice hall benches.

As Lord Alden's ward, Mrs Peel had been very clear which side of the divide I belonged to. At Berkeley Square I was to stay upstairs. The staff were there to do their work, not for me to socialise with. It was ill-mannered towards everyone to pretend otherwise. I imagined it would be even worse manners to venture where I shouldn't in a residence as grand as Château de Maisons but I couldn't help myself. A couple of times I'd crept down towards the staff quarters. I couldn't understand what was being said, but the voices were light and there was plenty of laughter.

Upstairs, the summer days began to take on an idyllic calm. I knew we would have to leave soon for Lord Alden's parliamentary presentation. I knew there were still mill floors, and children in terrible danger. But in our garden chairs under the dappled shade of the hazel trees, each day was such a gentle passing of time, it was easy to imagine that this was the whole world and here we could stay forever. What a life it would be, such books to read, gardens to wander. The air fizzy with bees and butterflies, drowsy and sweet with honeysuckle and roses.

The four of us read, played cards, took walks and went riding. Claudine and I practised with our bows and arrows most afternoons. Claudine painted and wrote in her diary while I read beside her from one of the books from the library. We talked and laughed a lot.

Nothing altered day from day. But by the end of the summer, when Alden and I had to leave for London, something had changed, deeply and truly.

When I looked back to the beginning, things now felt very different between the two of us.

On the return journey back to London, we would travel via Paris. Alden had business to attend to there, but in any case Claudine told me, coming to France and not visiting Paris would be intolerable. It was the most beautiful city in the world, she said. Even ladies who preferred the countryside would be compelled to enjoy such elegance.

Ferrand kept a city apartment. Adequate enough accommodations for a couple of nights he said. The staff there had been notified of our arrival and would be expecting us for dinner. We set off mid-afternoon. Our trunks lashed securely to the back of the coach and everyone gathering outside to see us off. It was sad to see the staff lined up again, all neat as pins together to say goodbye.

I was especially heavyhearted to be farewelling Claudine. We were not particularly close in age, and far, far apart in upbringing, but she had become a sister to me. I could not imagine a dearer, truer friend than this wonderful woman. During the summer she had taught me so much. The grace and warmth she carried with her, and her lightness for life I would hold in my heart always.

Hugging each other tightly, we vowed to exchange letters detailing every scrap of our news until we could meet again in person. Claudine made me promise to visit again as soon as possible, I couldn't see how or when I might be able, but I most sincerely promised to do so.

It was a quiet ride to Paris, the countryside steadily rolling past. Alden and I watching out of our windows, travelling in our own thoughts as we rode through fields of wheat being harvested and bundled together. The air dusty and yellow with spiralling chaff. Alden must have been thinking similar thoughts. Even for him, Château de Maisons was some distance to return to.

A smudgy blot appeared on the horizon. It became a shadow, gradually taking shape until we were close enough for it to suddenly reach out and pull us within its walled valleys. Claudine was right: Paris was a beautiful city. Built up on both sides of the Seine, it was spiky and gothic as a fairy tale.

Taking up the two uppermost floors of a large block, the apartment was delightful. The floorboards throughout had been stained black, a simple idea that looked so charming. Did all Parisian homes have floors that made them seem like night sky? The windows stretched down from ceiling to floorboards and opened to little balconies: not quite deep enough to step out on, but affording wonderful views across the charcoal-dark steeples and rooftops.

After dinner, we threw the doors wide open and turned the lamps down low. Bringing our chairs to the balcony's edge so we could best see the twinkling lamps burning in attics and kitchens across the city's skyline. Fireflies in the forest of towers and spires.

Later when we stood for bed, we both reached forward to close the balcony doors. Alden's arm brushed mine, my skirts wrapping his legs.

I watched him pull the door close, securing the clasp tightly, then I turned towards him, reaching up to touch his cheek. We stood very close, neither of us stepping back to a respectable distance, as my fingertips traced his cheekbone. Slowly down to the line of his mouth.

He smiled softly, his eyes looking deep into mine, 'Do you know what you're doing?'

I tilted my face fully up to his, 'I think so.'

The next morning we rode down wide boulevards, far wider than London's streets. Alden had promised Claudine we would tour the city highlights before he saw to his business matters. I assured him I could see them by myself in the carriage, but Alden wouldn't be swayed. Laughing that his sister's wrath wasn't something either of us should risk.

Along the Champs-Élysées we came to an enormous white arch being assembled at the centre of twelve radiating avenues. Construction had paused but it was clear they were building something magnificent. The framework rose two hundred feet into the sky and was almost as wide across. The coachman explained this was the work of Emperor Bonaparte. Banished to one of the remotest islands in the world – a windswept rock off the west coast of Africa – Napoleon was somehow still supervising a monument dedicated to his own battle triumphs. A monument so large, it could be seen from every corner of Paris. I pictured the passionately worded letters the Emperor must be writing. Stirring enough to lift tonnes of stone, thousands of miles of land and sea from his desk.

We stopped the carriage to walk through some of the squares, the Place Vendôme, Place des Vosges… the Place de la Révolution where twenty-six years earlier the French people had dragged their young king and queen to the scaffold. Hundreds of other nobles had lost their heads in this square. Some of them Ferrand had known as a child.

'Alden was this about poor people wanting more?'

'It was more about power. The men driving the terror were not poor.'

We stood where the guillotine had loomed. I looked around, imagining the thousands of people crowded in to watch the spectacle of Marie-Antoinette's death. The biggest square in Paris was now empty but for flocks of pigeons, flapping and fussing across the flagstones. In the far corner an old woman was selling red apples from a tray strung around her neck. I was glad to move on.

At the very heart of Paris – the point from which all distances in France were measured – was the cathedral they called Our Lady. To me, Notre-Dame looked like a few different buildings wedged together. But built on her own tiny island, looped to the mainland by arched bridges, she was undeniably lovely. From there it was a short walk to the Musée du Louvre.

Alden had run out of time. The day was inching into afternoon and besides his own business engagements, he was seeing to a few errands for Ferrand. I would have been happy to go back to the apartments and read until dinnertime, but I knew Claudine would be disappointed if I'd missed the musée. A palace before the revolution, it was now the most-visited library of art in the known world. According to Claudine, the only thing more intolerable than coming to France and not seeing Paris, would be coming to Paris and not visiting the Louvre. It was said the Renaissance period alone required two full days of contemplation. Alden and I agreed that in this case, an afternoon would suffice. The carriage would be outside at sunset to drive me back to the apartment.

I liked the marble sculptures the best. The bodies were so flawlessly rendered, their muscles so perfectly captured in movement, that it was as though they had been dipped in cool milk. I came to a couple embracing. Her arms reaching up to him as he held her with such love, bending down towards her mouth. The tenderness between the couple was so true, it felt wrong to be witnessing such a private moment. The brass plaque read *Psyche Revived by Cupid's Kiss* by Antonio Canova, but I wanted to know more about them, what had happened; was their story a happy one?

The paintings were handsome. Some were large enough to depict scenes of life-size dimensions. Great, glossy scenes of battle: cannons firing, horses rearing up in pain. The ones that weren't of war were either fruit arrangements with jugs of wine, or stiff-backed, unsmiling portraits. As with the statues, the paintings were far greater than the sum of their parts – I had to keep reminding myself they were formed solely of stone, paint and canvas – but unlike the sculptures, the people in these paintings felt lifeless in their gilt frames. Indeed, judging from the dates on the plaques, most of them were decades gone.

I wandered the corridors, past the battles and brooding faces. The scenes were cheerless and the colours drab: blacks, browns, greys. More shades of brown than five fields of mud.

After a few hours the effect became gloomy. Outside it was nearing sunset, the sun low and golden through the windows. There would still be time before the coachman returned.

Creeping out past the musée gates, I followed a paved pathway along the riverbank.

Trees had been planted along the path and there were benches to sit on. I sat on the end of one and looked out. In front of me was the low, arched bridge that connected Île de la Cité and Notre-Dame to the rest of the city. Fast currents must flow beneath its surface, but the river appeared smooth and still as a mirror. Reflections of the bridge and island floated out across the water.

There was a powdery softness to the evening's light. The setting sun a blinking circle of blue-edged gold; it washed the skies in red, pink and orange and danced a golden path down the river towards me. This is what paintings should be of. The pinks and yellows of life. But maybe such colours were too alive to be framed?

The sun shone into my eyes so fully, it seemed the brown of them must surely melt to gold too; spilling gold from my eyes into my heart, which soared with happiness to be here in such a place. To see such things. How was I so fortunate to have witnessed so much beauty? To have such moments and memories inside me. To know Blake's words and the cool longing of Canova's marble. To have stood at the steps of St Paul's. To understand what it is to crest a wave from the bow of a ship, salt spray whipping my face. To have danced in a palace and eaten food that tasted so good, so complicated, you could cry. To know what it is to be alone in a forest or lost wandering in a book.

What joy I have had. Far more than my share. My life should have been simple. Like my mother before me, a life requiring but one pair of shoes. There was nothing of me to say that it should be otherwise, but here I was, sitting on the bank of a distant river. A coach fit for a princess waiting to take me to dinner with a great man. A man whose kindness would save many lives. The wonder I have had in twenty years has been enough for many lifetimes.

I watched the sun lower into the far rooftops, wrapping the buildings in shades of drying lavender. For the first time, I noticed how the sun's pace seemed to quicken in the last moments of its arc.

What precious time that remained of the day could only be understood when it was almost gone.

Our passage back to Berkeley Square was lovely and uneventful. We arrived at Calais in good time and set sail with the evening's tide. I wished there was more sea in the channel that we might cross it. Peering into the depths of blue as we sailed across its surface, I wondered at the other world that lived beneath us. Were there really monsters and mermaids down there where we could not breathe and dared not venture? I'd seen drawings of fearsome beasts, krakens large enough to wrap their tentacles around whole ships and drag them under the waves. But it all seemed peaceful. The slap and chop of the waves against the sides of the ship, the clean salty winds. The only creatures I saw were fish swimming together, turning and diving as one, their scales catching the light as they moved in such agreement it reminded me of swallows in the dusk skies.

Farris was waiting for us with the carriage at the docks. His smiling face standing clear from the bustle of the port. We'd been gone nine weeks, but it felt longer, and when we pulled up outside No.23, I felt a warm sense of returning.

I'd only just resisted the urge to hug Farris. Mrs Peel wasn't so lucky. She stood stiffly as I threw my arms around her, then patted me awkwardly and tried to look inconvenienced by the lack of good manners. But it was clear she was pleased to see us safely back, and not just because of the French chocolates we brought her.

As we were unpacking my trunk later, I noticed a corner of red velvet tucked into a side pocket. I pulled out one of Claudine's jewellery boxes, a satin ribbon tying it to a creamy parchment envelope. Mrs Peel and I looked at each other and I read the letter.

> *My dearest Mina*
>
> *Now don't make a fuss, I want you to have this. It is the slightest of trinkets but it looked so lovely on you. Think of me when you wear it, as I shall think of you often, and always when we drink champagne.*
>
> *Always, your loving friend and sister,*
> *Claudine*

I lifted the necklace out to show Mrs Peel. I'd first taken it to be a single necklace, but in truth it was a set of three delicate chains, each with a single star set with a flash of diamond. Once Claudine had fastened it, the three stars hung in perfect formation, the centre star in the soft hollow at my throat, the other two on either side.

I took the necklace down to Alden, asking if we could send it back. I could not keep such a valuable thing. But he already knew about the stowaway box and had been expecting me. The necklace had originally belonged to Alden and Claudine's mother, and the siblings had discussed the gift together before we left the château.

'Alden the necklace must stay in your family.'

'I agree! You know Claudine sees you as a sister. Now, I'm sending over some watercolour paints and tea this week, perhaps you would like to enclose a note for Claudine?'

Climbing into bed that night I realised how familiar it was here. How much it now felt like home.

Like weather changing or the tide coming in, suddenly I'd looked up and seen that the world around me had transformed.

At the mill, and here in the city, I'd never doubted that my true home was the place I came from. The North Star of farm and family had always guided me faithfully. It was my true life that I would return to as soon as I could.

But what if that had changed?

It had never troubled me that I didn't fit in here in the city. This was not where I belonged. But after so long away, could I really match and blend with the village either? Did I even understand how far from it I had ventured?

Maybe it was the travel tangling my bearings: the dust of a foreign land and the salt of the sea still on my skin. But the farm now shimmered with distance.

And what would a life without Alden feel like now?

GREY

The necklace? No, that wasn't me. There would have been no point to it. No plot incentive, if you will. But it's a nice touch. If you push your finger down into that spot where your collarbones come together – that little hollow at the base of your throat – you'll feel your blood pumping like a galloping horse. Draped in a thin drum of skin, that's where you'll find the arterial intersection which feeds directly to your heart. Thum, thum. Thum, thum…

The necklace should have been passed down, woman to woman, through generations of family to arrive at the same pulse, more or less at the same time.

But life isn't always shaped the way it should be. Something happened, something that shouldn't have happened. The necklace was broken, spilling unnoticed on a road. Two of its chains beyond repair. One of the stars skittered towards the gutter, down the dark mouth of a drain, eventually lost to the sea. Another star somersaulted, point over point, in the rainwater that would fall heavily later that night, until it was caught in a crack, where I believe it lies still, cocooned in centuries of tar and cement.

The third, centre star, landed determinedly on its back, glinting up at the sky until its shine caught the eye of a flower-girl passing on her weekly deliveries of peonies.

It was sold for a life-changing price, and for the next couple of centuries it sat mainly in the dark of velvet boxes. Worn by very few until it was polished up and put on display in the window of a small shop down a laneway off Covent Garden.

Just like people, objects often find themselves in the right place. Washing up on the right beaches. It's the order of things.

Like water searching for the lowest ground.

The sea flowing with the same salts that fill your veins.

Look closely. Stand back. There are few coincidences.

No star falls unseen.

EVERY

Thursday, 6.15am

Framed by Norfolk pines, a bloodshot line of sunrise ripples towards me across the sea. Out on the balcony I watch the sky change: shepherd's warning red to white-blue. What does it say about me that this house is the one I feel most connected to? The house where my mother died. Where right now, downstairs in his bedroom, my father is dying?

Once the sun has cleared the line of water I come back inside, brew a large pot of coffee, gather together notepads and pens, and begin reading Claudine's diaries.

By 9am I've made plenty of notes and earmarked dozens of pages referencing Alden. Claudine might have grumbled about Alden in her first diaries but it's clear the siblings were close. When Alden's in trouble: a scuffle with two older bullies; reprimands from their parents, it's Claudine who stands up for him.

Dad hasn't come upstairs yet. Riz has brought out breakfast and Janelle is working on her laptop. Joe has been here an hour, waiting, scrolling through his phone. I check the studio, no sign of Dad there. Nurse Sylvia says he had a bad night and shouldn't be woken.

Janelle and I look at each other worried, well aware that Dad would never have chosen to stay in bed. But Sylvia is clear that we should let him sleep, so Janelle keeps typing, I keep reading.

The next diary I slide out is towards the end of the shelf. Claudine is in her late sixties. She writes about a man called Rowland Hill. At first I skip those pages, but it seems Claudine's been exchanging letters with him since he was a young man, so I flick back in case there's anything relevant to Alden. Rowland knows her friend Mina too.

I google the name Rowland Hill on the off-chance anything comes up, and the search engine whirls happily into life. There are nine-and-a-half-million results. Like her brother, it turns out Claudine's pen-pal was also a notable reformer. According to some websites, nothing less than a history-altering visionary. One link leads to another, and I get a bit side-tracked following Rowland's story.

He was quite a bit younger. When Alden was petitioning for the Cotton Mills Act, Rowland would have only been about eleven or twelve, but he was already working with his father who was a teacher, coaching students with their handwriting. By the time Rowland was twenty-five, he was running a highly regarded school and looking at a wider picture. As he saw it, society was built on the labours of the poor, with little reward offered and the harshest of consequences should they step from the narrow confines prescribed to them. There were 150 crimes punishable by death: the comfortable classes living their lives generally untroubled by the law, yet Rowland read of an eight-year-old pauper sent to the gallows for pocketing a teaspoon, two young sisters hung for the taking of a loaf of bread.

At the time, fewer than half of England's population could read or write even a few words. In many quarters, literacy was considered the preserve of the wealthy. But Rowland saw the difference education could make. He believed any hope of fair society would depend on it. He spent years mulling over the problem, finally reaching a solution of simple motivation. Learning to read had to be considered a basic right, and for that to happen, it had to be incentivised.

Rowland knew it would be a long time before anyone of ordinary means could afford books. Postage was also prohibitively expensive; back then it had to be paid by the recipient on delivery.

With the cost of receiving a letter being so far beyond the budget of most people, learning how to read or write one of them wasn't of much use. Without communication there was a vacuum of silence: Family members who moved away were never heard from again. During wartimes, letters coming from soldiers at the front were too costly to be read by the sweethearts they were intended for.

What Rowland also saw was that the businesses flourishing were generally those who could afford to maintain communication with their suppliers. In the zenith of the Industrial Revolution, trade and commerce was being held back for all but the wealthiest enterprises.

In 1837, Rowland put forward a proposal for a postal service for all. Low and uniform rates charged according to weight, rather than distance, and to be prepaid by the sender. In 1839 he was granted a two-year trial to run the pioneering system, and in May 1840 the world's first stamps were distributed. Featuring a simple silhouette of Queen Victoria (whose twenty-first birthday had been celebrated that month), the Penny Black stamp revolutionised communication around the world, helping to equalise the playing field between rich and poor, and making commerce more efficient almost overnight. By 1870, over eighty per cent of the British population could read and write fluently.

I'd never thought about how or why the postage system had been invented, much less associated it with literacy. It's a lot to think about. How much had this egalitarian system of communication shaped the world. Without it, would telegraphs and telephones have happened? Would the internet exist?

Rowland and Alden share something else besides their civic works. As a boy, Rowland was also involved in a carriage accident. It feels an odd coincidence. Just how dangerous were London's coach drivers? It seems Rowland's brush with death became a pivotal moment for him too.

On Google maps, I zoom in to a statue of Rowland in London. It's near Postman's Park, just down from St Paul's. On a red granite plinth, Rowland holds a pen in one hand, a notepad in the other.

How did Rowland's story fit with Claudine and Alden?

Was Claudine's friend, Mina, the link? If so, how?

MINA

A Visitor

Now that we were back in London, our window to prepare was narrowing fast. We had just four days before Parliament, and the doorknocker rang repeatedly with requests from the Members. Demanding to see further proof of something, or a precedent for something else. Unable to dismiss the petition outright, they were now doing their best to make the process as difficult as possible.

We had to work fast. Each time the knocker went meant hours of further research, and the dread that the Members had finally found something that could throw out our whole petition.

When we heard the door for the second time that hour, Alden and I exchanged looks of dismay. We sat back from the piles of papers strewn across the table, listening as Mrs Peel's footsteps clipped neatly across the hallway.

There was muted discussion, the front door closed again and Mrs Peel came to the library. Not with a letter or handful of files as expected, but a curious expression.

'Miss Mina, there's a visitor. A Mr Swanson wanting to speak with you. Shall I send him away or do you wish to see him?'

I stared at her in astonishment.

Lightheaded, I stood and followed her to the front door. The man standing in the street was dressed in simple farmer's clothes. His horse's reins looped unceremoniously around the nearest lamppost. He had his back to us as he looked out across the square.

He had changed too: from this angle there was little sign of the boy he had been. Tall, broader across the shoulders. His hair was darker now and cut shorter. But it was unmistakably him.

I stepped down towards him, 'Ty?'

He turned around, a polite smile at first, then a flash of shock as he recognised me.

'Well look at you.'

We grinned at each other. Neither of us knowing what to do, for a long moment just staring. Trying to see the years and what they had brought to our faces. The lives we had lived since we last saw each other. He had little crinkles around his eyes now when he smiled.

He reached to pull me into a hug. I felt my arms wrap around his body as I breathed in the smell of him. The warmth of summer grass and racing heartbeats swirled around me.

A terse cough interrupted us. Mrs Peel clearing her throat from the doorway.

'Miss Mina, will your visitor be coming inside?'

Standing behind Mrs Peel's stern expression was an even less happy one belonging to Alden.

But when I asked Alden if that would be alright, if Ty could come into his home, he nodded, and I invited Ty inside for tea. For what else could I do?

The three of us sat at the dining table watching Mrs Peel set the tea service. I could see Ty's eyes widening at the surroundings, the furniture, the plate of biscuits and the fine China cups we sipped from. He was taking in all the luxury and trying not to appear too overawed. Just as I had three years ago when Alden welcomed me in from the streets and the prospect of Bedlam.

I looked at what Ty saw and realised how much I took for granted.

'So, the two of you were childhood friends?' Alden was asking as he reached for the biscuits, offering the plate to Ty.

Ty shook his head as he took one, 'We were together at the mill.'

'I see.'

'We're from the same village, but didn't know much of each other until then.'

Alden's expression was hard to read. 'No? Well, it's kind of you to check on our Miss Mina now.'

Ty looked over to me, 'It was on my mind to do so, as soon as I could.'

'I see.'

We sat and drank our tea.

Ty explained that he had been allowed to leave the mill a few weeks after his twenty-first birthday. Catching a ride most of the way home with one of the supply carts. As the oldest of the five of us in the cart all those years ago, it was always Ty who was meant to leave the mill first. Not me. Not Harry.

Ty had ridden around to see Papa as soon as he got back. There had been talk at the mill; that I had died, lost in the forest. An idea that seemed farfetched to my friends, but Ty was relieved all the same to learn I was living well. My father passed on the directions Farris and I had left with my family for how they could find Alden's home, and here he was.

Alden was watching us carefully. He drained his cup and pushed back his chair.

'If you'll excuse me, there are errands I must attend to.'

I stood too, 'I should get back to our notes.'

Alden waved the idea away, 'Course not. Stay with your guest Mina, the books can wait a few hours.'

I nodded, trying to think what errands needed doing this afternoon. Alden hadn't said anything earlier about going out. He turned to Ty.

'Mr Swanson, I trust you'll be staying for supper?'

Ty looked at me before answering, 'I'd be grateful if there's spare. I'll head back after that.'

'Nonsense. We can't be sending you and your horse back out on a dark road.'

'Would there be room to put my head down in the stables?'

Alden smiled politely, 'There would be, there's also plenty of room upstairs. We will be glad of your company Mr Swanson. Mina has missed her people very much.'

After Alden left, Ty looked at me, one eyebrow raised over a thin smile. 'Is that true? Have you missed us Mina? Or is this your life now? In your fancy dress.'

My face flushed, 'Did you expect to find me in the same dress?'

'Maybe not. But your hair, how you talk, the way you're sitting. Have *you* changed Mina, or is it just the outside that's new?'

I had no answer for that. I watched him look around the room.

'It's quite something all of this. You've come a long way since the mill.'

'I'm sorry Ty.'

'For what?'

'For leaving, for not saying goodbye. For not coming back.'

He snorted, 'I was very glad you didn't come back. Wilks would have killed you.'

I didn't know how to answer that either. We looked at each other, not knowing what to say, then Ty changed the subject and we talked about our friends and families.

I'd not been back to the farm for some months and asked after Billy and Papa and Rebecca. They sent their love. It had been a good summer on the farms; crops had harvested well. Papa worried for me in the city. They thanked me for the packages Alden and I sent back each month; jams and biscuits. Warm coats and blankets in winter, strong boots. Ty told me Helen was missing me at the mill too. Cal was sweet on Clary now and they were planning to be together after the mill.

I told Ty about what Alden and I had been working on all this time. That in just a few days, Alden would be presenting our petition to Parliament. I tried to explain how our proposal could make it against the law for children like Harry to work in a mill. How it would be the first of its kind in the world.

Saying it aloud reminded me how important it was. Harry's life wouldn't be forgotten, his time could reach much further than all of our lives. Having this law would never answer to the pain and loss, but it could ensure no more children died in such a way.

Ty seemed unconvinced. I hadn't explained it properly. Perhaps he was just tired. He had been up since before dawn, riding all day. Seeing a city for the first time.

Not long after dinner Ty excused himself and went up to his room.

Alden and I worked for a couple of hours, then I excused myself too. Alden had come back from his errands brooding and distracted, and agreed an early night would suit us all.

As I walked past Ty's door, I saw it was ajar, and knocked to check he had everything he needed. Ty looked relieved to see me when he came to the door.

'Can you come in for a bit?'

I hesitated: it felt disrespectful in Alden's house.

As I wavered, Ty reached out and pulled me to him. I found myself stepping through the doorway and into his arms. Closing my eyes as I had on the street outside earlier, inhaling deeply.

'Do you still wear my name Mina?' Ty asked, his eyes bright with feeling. 'That night down by the river? Remember?'

He brought my hand up to his chest, over his heart, 'It's still your name here.'

Ty had come to bring me back to the village. He talked about the life we could have together. Working in the fields, dirt under my feet. In rhythm with the colours and seasons of the land. The life I had been born to live. His words wound around me, heady as wine. I thought about riding away with him. Leaving the city behind. Ty would be a good, loving husband. We would have children, together we would raise them into their own lives. We would live near Papa and their uncle Billy. It was a good, true life that stretched out in front of us.

But I knew it wasn't that easy. Even if it were possible to take Alden from the equation, would I be a good wife to Ty? Would a woman who longed for city libraries be the wife he deserved? The farm girl I had been, the mill worker after that. Those girls were gone. Like cicada husks left gripped to a shed wall, I couldn't step back into their skins again, however I might want to.

Did I want to?

I stayed until the night sky began to lighten. Creeping back to my own bed when I realised Ty's breathing had deepened to sleep. We had laid side-by-side in our clothes on the top of the bed. Talking and watching the candle slowly burn to a glowing puddle, and puff out in a trail of smoke.

'Lord Alden? What is he to you?' Ty had asked before he drifted off.

'Without Alden, there would be no petition; none of it would be possible. If it wasn't for him, I might be locked in the madhouse.'

'That doesn't answer my question Mina.'

As I lay awake in my own bed later, watching the sky turn to day, I realised how truly I hadn't answered Ty's question.

After breakfast, Ty made his goodbyes. Thanking Mrs Peel especially for the fine meals until she blushed prettily. Something neither Alden nor I could remember ever seeing Mrs Peel do.

Before he swung up into the saddle, Ty hugged me, stepping back just enough that we could see each other's face.

'I didn't hear you leave.'

'You needed to sleep.'

'I don't like the feeling of waking up to have you gone.' He searched my eyes, 'Mina, I've no right to ask you to leave all of this. You know the life I can give you and it's nothing like this. But I'm asking. Come home to us Mina. When this thing is done, come home.'

I watched Ty ride up and out of the square. I stood there long after he had disappeared around the corner, then I wiped my eyes and walked back up the stairs, inside the house and into the library.

Alden looked up from his work, 'Mr Swanson has left?'

'Yes.'

Alden watched me sit and gather together the ledgers and papers. I opened the ledger to the page I'd left last night, not meeting his eyes.

With three days before Parliament, time raced. Each time I looked up at the clock, it was hours later than I'd expected. Mrs Peel brought in trays of tea and food, then carried them out again when we'd let it go cold.

We rehearsed Alden's speech. We re-read hundreds of previous petitions that had been successful, studying the notes, looking for the patterns. We practised possible questions and objections. Alden stood for hours as I quizzed him with every difficult objection I could think of. Stopping and correcting him when he strayed from precise wordings.

Getting our petition to Parliamentary debate had felt a great victory, but we knew the real battle lay inside the Lord's Chamber. There were three hundred sitting lords and Alden could be cross-examined by any of them for as long as they liked. They would be within their rights to question Alden on any distantly related clause or law they saw fit. Debates were generally settled in a matter of minutes but there was no rule to say they couldn't run for hours.

The afternoon before Parliament, we were sitting at opposite ends of the library, looking through the shelves for any last bit of helpful legislation. Alden snapped shut his book.

'We need to get out of this damn room.'

'Alden, there are at least fifteen more shelves I need to check.'

'Mina you know these laws better than any city lawyer, if there's something we need, we've already included it. Let's go for a walk.'

It was the first time I'd left the house since we got back from France. Falling into step as we talked, we set out absent-mindedly in the direction of our usual Sunday walk. Down the centre of the square, between the two lines of plane trees, along Charles Street, Queen Street, then Curzon and into the calm green of Hyde Park.

Still going over possible objections and rebuttals, we followed the path inwards, winding our way through the tall grass and past the ponds.

As always, we found ourselves beside the little oak tree. The tree that had grown from the acorn I'd carried back in my pocket from the farm. I'd worried that squirrels would find it, then later, that one of the park gardeners might pull it up. But the acorn had taken, and its sapling had thrived. Rising clear from the grass in its first year. Dear little rounded leaves, a bright, strong green. It was now almost four foot tall.

Oaks grow slowly. Neither Alden nor I would be around to see the tree reach anywhere near its full height, but it was pleasing to think we had helped to provide shade for generations to come. Well aware of how ridiculous a notion it was, we considered the tree ours. Noting its growth, bringing bottles of water on dry weeks. With summer in France, it had been several months since we had last come to see it.

Alden smiled proudly, 'Our little tree is doing fine.'

'So fine! Look at all these leaves.' I bent down to feel one of them, 'It will always be here now, won't it Alden? It's safely taken root?'

He nodded, 'I think so, yes.'

'Just think, if we wrote our names on its bark, we could live right here with it.'

Alden laughed, 'At least for the next few hundred years.'

We stood there smiling at the sapling.

'Would you want to live here Mina?'

I looked around at the trees, the tall grasses shifting with the wind, like waves on the ocean. 'It's beautiful.'

'In London? Are you still of a mind to return to the farm once the petition is done?'

'Going home was always the plan.'

'You have a home here too. More than that Mina. You have a life here...'

Alden turned to face me, his eyes clear, his face so dear and precious. 'That night in Paris, it doesn't have to change what we are, I'm not saying that. If friendship is our fate, I take that. I gladly take that. Working together, living under the same roof, it has been the greatest adventure. You have been a gift to me.'

He paused, collecting his thoughts. 'Maybe I should have spoken of this before, but I never wanted you to feel compromised, and I know there are differences between us... What I'm saying, what I am *trying* to say, is that for me, what we share, the common ground we stand on together, goes far beyond friendship.'

He took a deep breath, 'My heart is yours Mina, it has been yours for some time. Completely yours.'

I looked up into his eyes, the colour of deepest sea. As Ty had days before, what Alden asked to know was fair. He was right: there was a night sky of stars beyond friendship between us. And France *had* changed what we were. How could it not? Laughing together, his skin warm against mine. His mouth and hands. The way he looked at me that night with the twinkling skyline of Paris in the window behind him. *Everything* was different.

But my head could not untangle such precious things now.

Too much, too many lives depended on our course staying true.

I reached to touch his face. 'You have been a gift to me too...'

As though he could see my thoughts, Alden smiled, 'Now's not the time. Tomorrow we will make changes enough. I just wanted you to know that you have a home here too Mina.'

EVERY

Thursday, 11.30am

It's now 11.30am and there's still no sign of Dad. Joe has driven back to his office. The sense of unease is creeping like a vine, curling and constricting through the house.

I sneak down to check on Dad. The curtains are drawn and he is deep asleep. His monitors glowing faintly beside him. Neither Janelle nor I can ever remember a time when he slept so late. Are we doing the right thing not waking him up?

Back upstairs Janelle asks how I'm getting on with the diaries. I tell her about Rowland.

'Goodness, he sounds like a film all by himself. How does he know your great-uncle?'

'Not sure. Rowland was a bit younger. I'm not even sure how he knows Claudine yet. He might be connected to one of her friends. All I know for sure is that they wrote to each other for years.'

Janelle's eyes widen, 'There were some letters. A bundle of them Claudine kept inside her diaries. I had them photocopied too, just in case. Think they might have been signed from an R.'

'Ooh. Can I see them?'

'I'll get them couriered over from the office this afternoon.'

To work out how it's all connected, I decide to go back and read the diaries in the order Claudine wrote them, from start to finish so I don't miss anything important.

For the next few hours I read solidly, watching out for Dad and checking the time every half hour or so. There's some great stuff about Alden's progress with the infamous Bethlem 'Bedlam' hospital. High-minded and recklessly anti-establishment, Alden's shaping up to be an excellent hero. I've been expecting to read about his near-miss with the carriage, but well into Claudine's twenties there's no mention of her brother's childhood accident. Perhaps Dad's team pulled it from their independent research: Claudine might have felt uneasy committing such a traumatic event to paper.

It's cute to read how handy those tedious French lessons turned out to be: Claudine has fallen in love with Ferrand. A young Marquis sent to England ahead of the bloodshed of an escalating revolution. In 1815, at the end of the Napoleon wars, the couple immigrate to France to live in Ferrand's ancestral chateau – what sounds like a sweet country home an hour or so outside Paris – and the two are very happy there together. Claudine still writes about her brother in her diaries, but mainly that she misses him; most of the key updates about what Alden's up to come via snatches of his letters to her and newspaper clippings.

I skim through the next couple of diaries, without needing to make many notes. I'm halfway across the shelf to the year 1819, when Claudine writes that her brother is coming. A date has finally been set for the Parliamentary hearing of the petition that Alden has spent the past few years working on. There have been difficult setbacks but Alden is optimistic. He and Miss Willamina Halewood, his partner in the enterprise, will be docking in Calais on the morning of July 15. *Partner in the enterprise?*

We know this petition will become the historic Cotton Mills Act of 1819, but I don't think Dad's aware of anyone else working on it with Alden, much less there being a partner.

Willamina Halewood. Writing up my notes, I circle the name. She might not be helpful for Dad's one-man-against-the-establishment storyline but if this is the same Mina who knows Rowland, and becomes dear enough friends with Alden's sister that Claudine names her only child after her, Mina could be an interesting enough link to get Rowland into the script.

I also find something that's a piece of luck for Dad's casting director: Lord Alden Rigby-Williams must have been a bit of a dish. A detail cruelly left off the History of Britain websites I've been referencing. At this point Alden is thirty-four and one of London's most eligible bachelors. A man who has been fending off concerted and numerous marriage advances for over a decade.

Claudine is most intrigued to meet the woman he's bringing to visit.

4pm and no Dad. Janelle and I are both jittery, anxiously watching the stairs as the day crawls onwards.

I tiptoe down to check on him again. He's still asleep. Sylvia says it's to be expected at this stage. Janelle and I call the hospital. They agree. Patients at this stage generally sleep more. They can't give us any more information about what this stage actually is.

Dad has now been asleep for over fifteen hours. Neither Janelle nor I can remember a time when he slept more than six hours.

'Is it possible he might not wake up?' I ask, scared to hear the answer.

'That's unlikely,' comes the matter-of-fact reply down the line. 'But of course, it is a possibility. All we can advise is that you wait and see.'

MINA

Parliament

It was still dark when I woke up. I lay watching the sky shift and lighten over the rooftops. For good luck I fastened Claudine's beautiful stars around my neck, feeling the cool metal under the high collar of my coat.

Downstairs neither Alden nor I felt hungry. Mrs Peel insisted we eat something for the day ahead anyway. We went over everything one last time in the library. Checking and double-checking Alden's notes until it was time to leave. In the carriage we spoke little. Sitting side-by-side as we had so many times. I held Alden's hand, warm and steady on the seat between us, as Farris steered us through the morning streets.

When we arrived at Parliament's black spiked-iron gates, Alden offered his arm to help me down from the carriage. I looked up at what lay behind the railings.

These were the greatest buildings in the British Empire. The high seat of its power.

The lives of not just every single person I had ever seen, but thousands more, in new worlds as far-flung as India and Australia. Even the smallest decisions made within these walls were winds that roared across continents.

Alden had arranged for me to be shown to a whispering gallery above the Lords Chamber. Rather than sit in the carriage, waiting blindly and not knowing what was happening, I would be able to watch and listen to the proceedings below.

Many times I had watched Alden disappear under this archway and into the gloom of the Houses of Parliament. To be walking under these arches myself felt very strange.

As the heavily guarded iron gates swung open, I looked up at the buildings we were about to enter – the cloud-piercing towers and turrets, the long rows of metal-edged windows – and tried not to think of all that depended on what would happen in the next few hours.

Once the sentries let us pass, a rabbit warren unfolded in front of us, a miniature city of interweaving corridors and hallways. Alden walked decisively, nodding occasionally to the men we passed. Following a half step behind, I looked for other women, but we walked through room after room without seeing another. Dozens of men, not a single woman. Alden had assured me it would be fine for me to be here. As long as I stayed in the whispering galley, I'd not be troubled. But from the angry glares I was getting, my presence wasn't welcome.

A long passageway opened up and I found myself inside the soaring walls of Westminster Hall. I looked up to the hammer-beams stretched across the colossal medieval hall. Each of the domed windows running along its sides was the size of a townhouse. This was the hall where kings and queens had held court for more than four hundred years. I was standing in history. It took us a full minute just to cross its vast floor.

At the foot of a flight of stairs, through another set of arched corridors, a grumpy-looking man in formal evening dress was waiting for us. He would show me to the gallery.

Alden smiled, bowing slightly. 'See you on the other side my dear.'

I watched Alden run up the stairs, turning to wave reassuringly before stepping out of sight.

The usher scowled, and set off down a long corridor, through a maze of dark wood and medieval stonework. Down stairs, up more stairs and along near-countless turns and twists. Finally, we climbed a tight corkscrew staircase to a small, wood-panelled room, where he left me with a last frown.

Through a lattice section I saw I was looking down from what must be the ceiling of a large room.

I was dizzyingly high.

Far, far below, rows of leather-embossed benches circled inwards to a centre desk. Gold filigree decorated the walls. At the head of the room, on a raised platform was what looked to be a lavishly detailed throne.

It was the most imposing room I'd ever seen. Even from the safety of a hidden panel, it felt intimidating.

Down on the ground men were beginning to gather, gradually taking up the rows. Hundreds of them, loudly greeting each other. There was a lot of raucous crowing, slapping one another on the back. Most were dressed in black. From where I sat, looking down over the rows, I had an image of a horde of crows picking over meat. Jostling and squawking against each other, their long-coats flapping.

Alden entered the room, shoulders straight, head high. He showed no sign of the pressure resting on him as he strode to the centre desk. He had training for this, speaking to a crowd did not send terrors through him. But still, one man against so many. I held my breath, so nervous for him that the bones in my hands ached. Surrounded on all sides, what he was about to do took bravery I could not imagine commanding.

A sharp gavel called the session to order and the Members crowded into position along the rows.

There seemed too many Members for the bench space provided: the men were packed in so tight they must have been sitting on the edges of each other.

From his throne on the raised platform, the Lord Speaker introduced Alden and his Bill. Then, noting it was an unusually full house, the Lord Speaker suggested proceedings begin in earnest.

Alden had promised to speak loudly so I could hear at least his arguments. True to his word, his voice reached me clear and assured. He thanked the Members for their consideration of the petition, then outlined the points we had practised together.

Listening to his words, I couldn't see how any reasonable person would dispute them.

Then debate began.

We didn't need to worry about any of the discussion being too quiet for me to hear. The objections ringing out were furious and loud. On all sides the Members were openly hostile, as though each of them had been personally slighted by what we had prepared. United in their disbelief of everything Alden said, they disregarded the sense he made and were unwilling to consider any change whatsoever to current mill practices.

Each time a Member stood to ask a question, or made another belittling comment, they were supported with a hearty chorus of, 'Here, here!' from both sides of the benches.

It stretched to an hour. Then two. On and on the cross-examination dragged.

Above the ceiling I watched horrified, my hands cramping from gripping the bars.

If our petition wasn't passed today, it could be years before the Members accepted another one. How many lives would be lost in that time?

But the Members did not see the problem with young children working under machines. Despite the reams of paperwork we had provided – the terrible facts and figures – they refused to accept these dangers warranted new laws. Indeed, they said, it was Alden and his perilously incendiary views that should be feared. Was the man a revolutionary?

Again and again Alden patiently, tirelessly stood to counter their questions.

Gripping the wooden bars in front of my face, I willed him strength.

After five hours, it seemed hopeless.

Then something began to change, something slowly twisting through the air. I saw Alden's answers were starting to land. The room had quietened, Alden's words were gradually gaining weight and being heard.

The 'Here, heres!' were becoming less convinced.

One, then two Members admitted there might be room to compromise.

Finally, it came down to a matter of source. If it was to be believed that mill conditions were a blot on the conscience of modern society, where was the proof? How could Alden's sole account be trusted? He was neither a mill owner nor a cotton merchant.

'As a gentleman with no ties to the manufactory industry, how could our honourable friend have the faintest clue of the inner workings of a mill?' one lord demanded.

'I have been to these mills,' Alden replied. 'I have seen the inhumanity of the conditions. It is unconscionable that in these advanced times our children work in such fear.'

'Yes, so you say, but what proof?'

'Besides the notes and research submitted, I have the ledger from Mercer Mill, a mill less than a day's travel from here. This ledger bears proof of the deaths resulting from present conditions.'

'That's all very well, but what witness do you have to the book's validity?'

Alden stopped, and looked down at his papers. There was a long moment before he answered. 'Are you saying that if I were able to produce a witness to this ledger, its validity and all the evidence contained within it, it will be admitted as fact?'

There was a delay, some murmurings. 'Why yes. A witness to swear its legitimacy.'

'Is that the consensus of my fellow lords?'

There was a reluctant rumble of assent.

Alden addressed the Lord Speaker. 'Sir, I call for a brief recess.'

'Granted. A fifteen-minute recess is called.'

The members fell out of their rows, expectant crows, hawking and jeering among themselves. An icy wash of dread swept over me as I stared, dazed, at the door Alden had just hurried out of.

A few minutes later the usher swung open the door, I was needed downstairs.

Numbly I followed him back down the spiral staircase and along the corridors to where Alden was waiting. My vision was as spangled with fear as it had been when I'd followed Wilks to the whipping fence.

I could not do this. I was nowhere near equal to the task. The weight of so many lives could not rest in my hands. Every bone in my body knew it had no place even being inside this building.

I looked at Alden panic-struck.

'I'm sorry Mina, I could not think of another way.'

'Alden, I cannot do this. How could I even stand in that room?'

'You can. You know this petition inside and out – far better than me.'

'Those men won't listen to me. I'll ruin everything you've worked for.'

'Mina without your testimony we may lose.'

From above, the room had been intimidating. Walking into the bowels of it was raw, white terror.

I stood at the desk in the centre of the room. Behind, and on both sides of me were rows of great lords. All three hundred of them frowning down at me. I could not speak to these men. These were the most powerful men in Britain. How could I possibly speak to them? What words could I say that would be enough? How could I form sentences that would make even a shred of Alden's sense?

My heart hammered in my chest. Blood rushed, pounding in my ears. I looked down and saw my hands were shaking. The weight of six hundred eyes was too heavy for me to hold against.

The Lord Speaker was peering down disapprovingly, 'A woman? This is most irregular.'

Alden dipped his head respectfully, 'Lord Speaker, I request the tolerance of the chambers. Miss Halewood has first-hand experience of the ledger.'

'Very well.' The Lord Speaker turned to me, 'Miss Halewood, is it?'

All thought had gone: my head was a screaming hollow. I could not remember a single legal term.

'Yes my lord.'

'Speak up girl!'

'Yes, my lord.' I pushed against the desk to stop my whole body from shaking.

'Can you verify this is indeed a legitimate ledger from the Mercer Mill?'

'I can my lord.'

He rolled his eyes, 'Miss Halewood, you'll have to speak louder if you intend anyone in this room to hear you.'

'I'm-I'm sorry my lord. I can. I can verify the ledger is legitimate.'

'And how is that?'

'I took it from the mill myself my lord.'

There were gasps. Several angry cries of thief.

I picked up the ledger. Feeling its familiar weight and edges in my hands, I pictured Harry's name in Mr Coleman's neat handwriting on its fifth page.

I remembered how far we had come together, Harry's name and I.

Together we had walked dark roads, through country fields and city sprawl. We had slept on a park bench. We had withstood years of doubt and harsh disappointments. Now we stood together in one of the highest rooms in England, maybe in the known world. We had the attention of those who could make all of this matter.

I looked over at Alden. He nodded encouragingly. I remembered that he was a great man too. Powerful and high-standing like these men. Alden had listened to me. Many times he had asked my opinion, often heeding it. Yes, he was compassionate and kind, generous beyond comparison, but he was not indulgent. He did not suffer fools.

I raised my voice.

'My lord, I had to take the ledger. I did not know of this room when I brought it to London. But I knew this book was something great men like you must see.'

'And why is that?'

'Because the men in this room have the power of life.'

The Lord Speaker laughed, 'Miss Halewood, we write laws, we are not gods.'

'This law we are asking for would save the lives of thousands of children. You would be like gods to them.'

I looked at the ledger, trembling in my hands. 'Lord Speaker, may I present the pages inside this ledger for you to see?

He stared at me incredulously.

There was now complete silence in the room.

Finally he indicated I could approach. Respectfully as I could, I opened the book in front of him. 'My lord these are the names of the children who died at the mill. These are their ages at the time of their deaths.'

I ran my finger down the column of single figures, stopping at Harry's name. 'This boy, Henry Deason, was a good, cheerful boy. He was brave and loyal. A hard worker who always made the best of things. He would have made a decent, honest life. He died when he was ten years old. A twelve-foot engine dragged his body through its barrels. By the time they were able to pull this little boy, Harry, free, both of his legs, his arm and shoulder were broken. His insides had been twisted and ripped open.'

There were whispers and mutterings. I stepped back to stand beside the desk, leaving the ledger and Harry's name in the Lord Speaker's hands. Several of the lords asked me questions. I answered as well as I could. I swore all of this and more was true. I testified that the manner of these deaths were beyond what a decent mind could fabricate.

Lastly, I pleaded to the Members to employ their power and pass this petition. That many good children would owe the great men here today their lives.

The ledger was handed around, and I was excused as witness and asked to leave the room.

For some time I sat on a dark wood bench, down the hallway from the Lords Chamber, waiting for the door to open. I could hear waves of loud voices rise and fall inside the chamber but I couldn't make out what was being said. The usher who had shown me to the whispering gallery had not come back. Other gentlemen, similarly dressed, had hurried past but to a man they had looked at me so critically, I'd not dared stop them. It had taken a good half hour for my hands to stop shaking.

Finally the door opened. The Members pouring out much like we children had rushed from the mill each night. I stood up, searching the sea of faces for Alden. When I saw him, his eyes were shining.

As he got closer his smile widened into a huge grin.

'It passed! They voted yes!'

I cried out with relief, flinging myself into his arms. 'You did it! Alden you did it!'

'Mina *we* did it. I shall always be proud of what you did in there.'

We stood laughing in the corridor as the lords streamed past us. Hugging each other again and grinning like fools, oblivious to everything except our own vast, joyous relief.

There was paperwork to attend to before Alden could leave, his signature was required across today's documentation. I wanted to wait for him, but this could take some time and my presence in the hallway had already raised enough eyebrows. It was simplest for me to go on ahead and send the carriage back.

I gave Alden a last hug, both of us laughing again.

'We did it!'

'I'll get this done as quickly as I can. See you back at the house to celebrate.'

'See you at home Alden.'

Trusty as always, Farris was waiting outside with the carriage. But stepping out into the warm early evening my happiness felt too big to fit inside a carriage. It was too lovely an evening to be cooped up, even for a ten-minute carriage ride.

We did it. Tingling inside me were these words. Over and over. They were a million joyful pieces spiralling inside. *We did it.* Nothing would ever be dark again. *We did it. We did it.* Today we bettered our world.

'We did it,' I told Farris. 'The petition will go through!'

'Oh congratulations Miss Mina,' he beamed. 'That's grand news, grand news indeed.'

'If it's alright Farris I'll walk? Lord Alden will be along soon and he'll need the carriage.'

'I can drop you off Miss, and come straight back?'

'Be good to stretch my legs, I'll cut through the park and be home just as quick. See you in a bit Farris.'

I walked up Great George St and into St James Park. The late summer sun hazy and sleepy. *We did it. We did it.* I thought about everyone. Alden, Billy, Ty, Papa, Cal and Helen. Dear Claudine and Ferrand. Mrs Peel and Farris. Little Harry. My heart so full of gratefulness, it felt as though it could lift me clear from the footpath. Everything we had worked for was finally happening. *We did it.*

It was a beautiful evening. The setting sun sweet and low, dancing through the trees. As I walked, a tightness that had been gripping me for so long seemed to unpeel itself and float away. Light as a feather I turned into Berkeley Street, walking up towards the square. My shadow bobbing and stretching merrily ahead of me.

As the square came into view, I had a clear, shining certainty of coming home. Home to Alden.

Alden.

However we worked it out, wherever we lived, I knew it was with him that I belonged. I thought of how proud I was of him. I thought of his smile. The sound of his laugh. How he looked when he was worried.

My life was with his.

In the fast sureness of this thought, I realised it always had been.

Up ahead of me, through the line of trees, a young boy ran across the square.

It was Harry. His golden hair flying.

For a moment it was Harry. Alive, running and giggling in the sunshine.

I knew it was ridiculous, a trick of the light. But the way this boy ran was so much like Harry. How he held his head, the way the sun caught his curls.

I needed to see his face. I walked faster.

The boy was chasing a piece of paper that the wind tossed and gusted just out of his grasp. Now I was close enough, I could see his clothes were finer. He was taller, and as he neared, I saw he wasn't laughing at all. As he ran after the paper, his face was set in an anxious frown.

He was a nice-looking boy, with a bright, intelligent face. Probably a few years older than Harry had been. Maybe eleven or twelve. I smiled at him as he passed. For whatever weight my wish might carry, I hoped a wonderful life lay ahead for him.

I looked back over my shoulder a moment later to see if he'd caught his piece of paper, and saw the boy run out into the street, into the path of a horse and coach.

In the blur of movement, everything slowed down.

I saw the coach was going too fast, and realised the driver would not stop in time.

I saw the boy's face. That he was frozen where he stood, staring at the coach, the piece of paper clutched in his hand.

A man, the boy's father most likely, cried out in alarm beside me.

I saw it all very clearly, as I stepped off the footpath and grabbed the boy.

EVERY

Thursday, 6pm

By 6pm we were scared.

Is this it? Is Dad just not going to wake up?

Janelle and I had taken turns creeping down to his bedroom through the afternoon. He was still asleep. Instruction from both the hospital and Sylvia is clear: we are not to wake him. His body needs this sleep. Pulling him from it now could be dangerous.

But none of our questions have been answered. For all their tests and monitors, no one can tell us what is actually happening inside his head during all this sleep. So Janelle and I sit here, shoulders tight as wire coat-hangers, hoping we are doing the right thing following their advice.

Trying not to think that downstairs, in a room directly underneath us, the tentacles of tumour could be dragging Dad out to dark sea forever.

When the gate intercom buzzes we both jump. It's just a courier with the letters from Claudine's diaries. But then, as Janelle's signing the courier's electronic pad, we hear a shuffle on the stairs.

The top of Dad's head comes into view, and Janelle and I rush to help him. Our hands fluttering with relief, reaching to touch him, reassuring ourselves we still have him.

'Dad! How are you feeling?'

He looks okay. Groggy and puffy from sleep and he's moving slowly, his hand gripping the banister to support himself, but we can see he's himself. It's still Dad in there behind his eyes.

He leans heavily as he sits down at the table, 'Like I just slept eighteen hours.'

'Are you in pain? Can we get you anything?'

Dad shakes his head, dismissing the question, 'What's been going on up here?'

Janelle updates him on the emails. Everyone's loving *Axlark* – both here and in LA. The London office wants a video conference as soon as possible to discuss *The Cotton Mills Act*.

'Joe and I need to lock down the storyline first,' says Dad. 'When's he getting here?'

While Janelle tries Joe's numbers, Dad reaches over for one of Claudine's diaries that I've piled up to read next. He opens it, looks at the page, winces and closes it again.

I watch him quietly. Sylvia had warned us that neurological tasks like reading and writing could become difficult as the tumour advanced. She said this was especially likely towards the final stages. I can see he's agitated, from pain or loss of time, most likely both.

'We've made good progress with the diaries Dad. What's the best way to write up my notes for you and Joe?'

He looks over, rubbing his eyes, 'Found anything interesting?'

'The accident you told me about, with the coach and horses when Alden was little? Where did your team find out about that?

'Think the guys lifted that scene from the diaries. Claudine writes about it, doesn't she?'

'Not so far, the only carriage accident I've found was Rowland's.

'Who the hell's Rowland?'

'Rowland Hill. He's a friend of Claudine's. He goes on to invent the postage system.'

I pull my laptop round to show Dad some of my Rowland screengrabs, 'I was wondering if he might be interesting to include?'

'Interesting yes. Not sure how relevant he is to our story though.'

The next bit I say more cautiously, 'Dad, there's something else. Claudine says Alden had someone working with him on the Cotton Mills Act.'

Dad frowns deeper, 'That can't be right. I've seen the records myself, there was huge opposition to the law: he was the only lord who steered it through Parliament.'

'That's probably true. The person who worked on it with him was a woman. Were women even allowed in Parliament then?'

Dad sits back, taking in the information, 'How far into the diaries are you?'

'A good chunk. Alden's in France with Claudine.'

'Keep reading. Not sure about these new characters of yours, it might start getting too complicated, but we'll see. Be great to shape a loose storyline tonight.'

'Okay Dad.'

I take a stack of diaries back to the sofa and I open up the next one. It's the summer of 1819. Claudine is writing from the library at Château de Maisons. It's after supper. Ferrand and Alden are playing cards, Willamina is reading beside her in a shared circle of lamplight. The guests have been at the Château for three weeks. Claudine writes warmly of Willamina. She calls her Mina and describes her as spirited and dear company. It seems Mina is a partner to Alden romantically as well as professionally: Claudine is thrilled to see her brother 'completely smitten, at last!'

Over the next few pages Mina comes up a lot. Claudine writes of how wonderful it is that Alden has found a companion so perfectly suited. Watching them work together, she says it's clear Mina is as dedicated, if not more so, to the advancement of others as Alden is.

Claudine doesn't go into detail about the petition itself that they're working on, but from what she writes, it is clear that it was Mina who introduced Alden to the dangers children faced at the mills.

Wow.

The Cotton Mills Act that Alden puts through Parliament a few weeks later ends the practice of children younger than nine working in mills and factories. How many young lives the Act saved was never officially estimated, but it would have been thousands, perhaps hundreds of thousands.

It's hard to understand just how much these people, Mina, Alden and Rowland shaped the world.

For the men, there were professional entry points: Rowland was a prominent teacher and Alden a Member of Parliament. But Mina must have been incredibly brave. Women didn't even get the vote for another hundred years. Yet her handwriting is across history. The Cotton Mills Act made children persons of law with human rights like adults. It laid the foundation for future child protection legislation. Even now, in a modern, connected world, it's hard to see how one person can make a difference. Here was a young woman who had courage to speak out in a time when women didn't have a voice.

I skim the following pages, making few notes. Alden and Mina leave for London, and life goes back to its regular routine at the Château. There are updates from the gardens. A trip to Paris for Ferrand. Then Claudine discovers she is pregnant – most longed-for and unexpected news. She hopes Alden and Mina will be able to return the following summer to meet the family's newest addition.

'Evie, do you want to see if these letters are from your Rowland?'

Janelle calls me back to the table where she and Dad are sitting. Dad's looking a little brighter. He's sipping coffee, going over plans for tomorrow with Janelle. Joe has been held up at the studio, but will be back here for 8am tomorrow morning.

On the table in front of them is the brown envelope the courier brought from Dad's office.

Inside there is a manila folder that's been tied together with string, across and lengthways like an old-fashioned parcel. I pull the string undone and lift out a bundle of pages.

The handwriting on the first letter is even enough to be a typeface. Graceful, forward-slanting loops and arches. It's addressed to Marchioness Claudine de Saint-Aureville and the signature on the last page almost definitely says Rowland Hill. The letter is dated August 23, 1828. Rowland begins with a sincere hope that this letter is not too upsetting an intrusion. He understands he's taking a great liberty writing in such a way and admits that he has previously tried to contact her brother, Lord Rigby-Williams, but has had no reply.

Rowland writes that not a day goes by without him thinking about the accident in Berkeley Square. He says it happened nine years before, which would have been around the time, or maybe just after, Claudine wrote the diary I've just put down.

Rowland was twelve years old he says, visiting London for the first time and very much looking forward to seeing the modern metropolis. He explains that he and his father were attending an educators' symposium. He was in charge of his father's notes and eager to prove himself responsible. The accident was entirely his fault: if he'd had better grip on the papers none of it would have happened. He writes how Miss Halewood stepped out into the road and saved his life.

> *Like an angel she smiled at me although she must have been in pain. I wanted you to know. Dear lady, I wanted your family to know. Scarce comfort though it may offer, not a day has passed since that in some way, large or small, has not honoured the courage and selflessness of your beloved friend.*
> *Her example will be a guiding light in everything I do.*
> *Yours most humbly,*
> *Rowland Hill*

I'm starting to get a bad feeling. I google Berkeley Square, London W1. It's a pretty oval in the heart of Mayfair, just down from Oxford Street, a short walk from Hyde Park. I've walked through it often, never thinking about its history, all the life that's happened there.

From what I can see it hasn't changed too much since it was first laid out as a town square in the eighteenth century. Many of its original buildings still stand, elegantly stoic against the modern architectural jostle. An address of desirability from the start, according to Wikipedia it's been home to the founder of Selfridges, the co-founder of Rolls-Royce, William Waldorf Astor, and no less than six Prime Ministers – including Winston Churchill. The London plane trees in the green space at its heart are some of the oldest living in London.

I switch to maps and zoom in, wondering where it was exactly that Rowland nearly died. It's not something you think of much, but London has been so well lived, for so long, there probably aren't many of its streets and squares that haven't witnessed human drama. I drop the pin into the centre of Berkeley Square and arrow key around. The picture used is from summer and it all looks leafy and bright.

Also in the folder, with Rowland's letters is a photocopy of an old newspaper clipping dated September 30, 1819. At first, I can't see the relevance. The clipping has come from one of the paper's back pages. Its antique typeface is dense and uninviting, all one uniform size, and the ink print was smudged, collecting in blurry shadows across the page. From the copy in my hands, it's clear the original newspaper page had been folded and refolded many times. I scan the columns looking for something on Alden or Rowland.

It's not until the fifth and final column that my stomach sinks.

A memorial service will be held for Miss Willamina Halewood, daughter of Thomas and Margaret Halewood, elder sister to William. Perished at the age of twenty from injuries sustained in an incident involving a horse and carriage. Any enquiries should be directed to Lord Alden Rigby-Williams of No.23 Berkeley Sq, London. At the time of her death Miss Halewood was engaged in the betterment of others. Two hundred oak trees will be planted forthwith throughout London in her memory.

I sit stunned. She died. Mina died. The loss hits me in a rush of sadness. All that life and goodness. Everything she might have gone on to do. The life she and Alden could have had together.

I know Mina is not related by blood, but as Claudine wrote so lovingly of her, as a sister, I feel connected to her somehow too.

There's a sense of being part of a long line of women going back in history, a little part of each woman, their strengths and light, helping guide the next. It's a feeling of family. A linking of arms through time.

The enormity of her impact and courage has been so moving. There's no way Mina's not being included in the script about Mum's family.

'Dad, the carriage. That accident, it wasn't Alden, it was Rowland.'

'Alden never had an accident?'

'No. It was Rowland. He wrote letters to Claudine describing the accident and that's what your guys must have seen. But it's all connected, part of the same story. The stranger who saved Rowland's life was a woman. The same woman who worked on the Cotton Mills Act with Alden. When she pulled Rowland out of the way, the carriage hit her. Dad she died.'

He leans back, trying to process all the information.

'I think she and Alden were together too. Claudine calls her family. And look at her funeral notice. *Engaged in the betterment of others.* Dad she was only twenty and she helped shape history. Not just the stuff with Alden, if it wasn't for her, we might never have had the post. She needs to be in the film.'

Dad thinks about this for a minute. 'What was her name?'

'Willamina Halewood. Mina.'

Dad and I spend the next few hours going through the diaries. Drafting up the arc of the story.

I read out pages to him. We highlight passages. He dictates notes. Casting suggestions. Lists of locations. Dad's bright with excitement. Almost manic as he scrawls directions. His handwriting looks different: childish in its messiness, as though he's struggling to remember each letter's shape. His instructions are still clear and coherent, but he's misspelt many of the words.

I try not to think about what these changes mean.

When we have the basic storyline down, I run to get my pad and felt-tip pens from my room and start sketching out storyboards for each scene. I lay them out over the sofas. We tweak the order until Dad's happy with it, then I number each page.

Riz makes dinner and we sit down together with Janelle and Sylvia.

Dad hardly touches his plate. It's unlike him not to have a hearty appetite. I look to Sylvia to see if this is another warning sign, but she avoids my eye. Dad wants to get back to the work straightaway. He won't have the carrot juice. I have to remind him to drink some water.

I keep asking Dad if he'd like to take a break. He wants to carry on until we've finished. In the flurry of productivity, he seems to be enjoying himself.

Riz leaves for the day. An hour or so later Janelle and Sylvia go to bed. Janelle hesitates before going downstairs.

'Shall I start typing up these notes Ford? Very happy to?'

He looks over, 'Can you read this writing?'

Janelle picks up one of the pages from the sofa. There's a flicker of alarm as she sees the handwriting but she keeps her voice steady, 'I've had enough practice deciphering your scrawl.'

Dad smiles, 'Tomorrow will be great. Get some sleep.'

As she turns to leave, he calls after her, 'Thanks Janelle.'

'For the typing?'

'For everything. You're a true friend Janelle. The best.'

Janelle tries to brush off her delighted flush, 'Don't stay up too late you two.'

Dad and I carry on. The hours fly by as the story comes together around us.

He's driving it, pushing us to finish it tonight. I keep suggesting that he rest, but he won't hear of it. There are sketches of scenes propped against the table and chair legs, spread across the length of the floor. All over the sofas. Some of them we've re-numbered a dozen times.

In the end, I tape all of the drawings to the glass balcony doors. Four lines of scenes down the length of the inside of the house. We walk down the lines, swapping them around until Dad's satisfied with the running order. I number them a final time.

Just after 4am we have a full outline for Joe's screenwriter to work on. Dad dictates who this should be. And, if not her, then a second choice. I tidy up our notes.

Across one page I write Berkeley Square in thick black marker. I'd just meant to flag up some of the key scenes with Alden and Mina, but Dad sees it and asks me to hold up the page. He repeats the words a few times, then tells me to tape it to the doors with the drawings.

'I think we have our title,' he says.

'Berkeley Square?'

He smiles, *'Berkeley Square.'*

I nod to where I've taped the last page, 'You happy with this Dad?'

He sits back on the sofa. Considering all the sketches across the balcony doors. 'Hmm? Yes. Yes, I think I am. Thank you Evie.'

Dad's movements have slowed. I notice his hands are shaking. He tries to stand and staggers slightly, gripping the back of the sofa to steady himself.

I rush to help him. 'Dad what do you want? I'll get it.'

'Scotch. We have something to celebrate.'

'You sure?'

He smiles, an eyebrow raised. 'If not now...'

I get two tumblers and open the drinks cabinet. There are seven different bottles of scotch.

'Which one?'

'At the back. There's a thin silver flask. Should be right at the back. Let's take it out on the balcony.'

The sketches flutter against the glass as we slide open one of the doors. I bring out the throws from the sofa and we both take a lounger. Even in the dark Dad looks pale and gripped with pain. He's shaking so I wrap both throws around him. Rubbing his legs to get some circulation back in them.

'It's fine Evie, I'm not cold.'

'Do you want me to get Sylvia, I think I should.'

'No, I don't want any more morphine. Let's just you and I sit here and have a drink.'

I pass him the flask. Dawn is on the way. There's a line forming on the horizon and the sky is lifting to deep blue. Enough of the night remains for us to be sitting in darkness, but Dad knows the flask by feel.

'This is the one, pass me your glass.'

I draw up my chair so it's near his. We clink our glasses and lean back into the cushions. The smell of fires and smoke from the scotch fills the air. I wince at the taste and look over to see he's smiling widely.

'What Dad?'

'It still tastes tinny.'

'Do you want another one? Shall I bring the other bottles out?'

He shakes his head, still smiling. 'You remind me so much of your mother.'

'I look nothing like her.'

'You do, sweetheart. You were always your mother's daughter. Take another look at that painting downstairs: they're your eyes too. She loved you so much. You were everything to her. Literally. You know that's what she wanted to call you. *Everything*. I had to convince her that wasn't a name.'

I laugh, 'Thank fuck Dad. I've had trouble enough with Every. It's not exactly a name either.'

'It's a great name! It suits you.'

We sip our scotch for a minute.

'Dad what happened that night?'

He turns to look at me, measuring the question, knowing exactly which night I mean. I don't think he's going to answer when he finally does.

'It was my fault. How she died. The whole thing. It was my fault.'

I sit upright, 'What do you mean?'

He takes a long sip from his glass, 'I didn't want her taking any more of those pills.'

'What pills?'

'She never wanted you to know, never wanted you to worry about things like that Evie. You were already so protective of her. But you must remember how high, how bright she'd get? Dancing in the rain. Running down to the beach in the middle of the night. All that stuff.'

'I thought that was just Mum. She was animated and fun.'

'She was. So much fun. It was her, it was beautiful, but it was hard for her when she was working, she couldn't always control it. And the downs were very low, she couldn't look at herself, didn't like mirrors in the house, she'd freak out at the paparazzi. She wouldn't eat, all she needed was air she'd say, like that damn song. I'd come home and the only thing you two had had all day were mugs of hot chocolate. She'd get so skinny, with these big sad eyes. So the studio got her on these pills...'

'But the pills really flattened her out. They locked her to a flat keel. She wasn't herself. Like an idiot, not knowing anything about anything, I talked her out of taking them. I *thought* I had.

'That night we were drinking red wine. I'd flown in from New York that afternoon, I'd had a couple of Valium on the plane. I was pretty buzzed. We were watching a film, I noticed she was a bit wobbly, but I figured it was the wine. We'd had two bottles. I knew she wasn't allowed to drink when she was on the medication, but I thought that was behind us. I should have been watching her, paying closer attention but I was knackered, we were celebrating. We hadn't seen each other for a week.

'What I didn't know is that Therese had taken four of those pills. She'd been off them and absolutely fine for months, but apparently there'd been some bad days while I was away. The dose was one every 24hrs, and *not* with alcohol. She was so bright and alive that night Evie, I didn't even suspect. She was a brilliant actor, but if I'd had my shit together just a fraction, she'd still be alive. The pills made her trip, but she would never have fallen if I'd been paying attention.

'We both fell asleep watching the film. Or I did, she must have gone up to the kitchen for something. I didn't wake until I heard... you.'

My head swirls. The pieces fall together. The police investiga-
tion. Dad's behaviour.

'I thought it was my fault.'

He looks confused. 'What do you mean?'

'When you sent me away.'

'Janelle argued with me about that. She didn't think you should
go. That you were too young to be that far away. But I wanted you to
be free of it all. Away from the blood, what you saw… Sweetheart,
you should never have been the one to find her; your father passed
out in the screening room. Jesus, those screams. No child should
ever scream like that.'

'Were there no boarding schools in Australia?'

'I was a mess. I couldn't look after myself, much less a child.
Yes, you were a miniature Therese, same mannerisms, same
expressions, and I was ruined with guilt. But I also wanted you
as far from the sadness as possible. Paparazzi were crawling
everywhere. You needed to get on with your life – be a kid and
have fun. It was only going to be for a while. A few school terms.
But when you came back you had a proper little English accent,
you'd grown up so much. So self-assured. I knew it'd been the
right thing.'

'I missed everything Dad, I felt so alone and so far away.
England was miserable, all cold and grey. When I saw you had a
new girlfriend, I thought you'd replaced Mum.'

He finishes his scotch, 'I could never replace your mother.
Therese was a one-off, you know that Evie.'

I refill our glasses. 'Dad, it wasn't your fault. Mum would never
have blamed you.'

He smiles, 'I know, but your mother was a saint.'

'I miss her.'

'Me too.'

We sit quietly, listening to the bird calls of the dawn. 'Look,
here's the sun.'

I turn and he's right. The line of orange along the horizon
has thickened into a molten ball rising from the sea. Behind us

the sketches that will be Dad's film are fluttering softly. I see Mina walking towards Berkeley Square.

'Do you remember when you were little, just a squeak of a thing, and you would lie on your back watching the sky? You'd lie there for hours, just staring up at the sky.'

I nod, 'I used to ask you what happened after the sky.'

Dad smiles, 'That's right, exactly right, and I'd tell you, "More blue."'

'Then you'd ask, "After that?"'

'"The stars," I'd say.'

'"Stars like Mummy's necklace?" you'd ask and I'd say, "Yep."'

'"And after that?" you'd ask, and I'd always tell you, "An infinity of blue and the rest of your life."'

'I do remember that Dad.'

We smile at each other. I can see he's very pale. I tuck the throw in tighter around him. 'Dad, are you scared?'

'Yes. No.'

'What do you think it's going to be like?'

'Sleep, nothingness. An infinity of blue. I doubt it's anything like any heaven scene I've seen in a movie. I don't know. Sometimes I feel her here. Other times I think we die and that's it. We don't know anything really, do we? Maybe we're not meant to.'

'Dad is there anything I can get you? Is there anything you want to see? We can go anywhere.'

'I'm right where I want to be. This is what I want to be looking at.'

The sky is now awash in gold.

'It's so beautiful here. I love this view. Thanks for getting us this view Dad.'

He smiles weakly. 'It's your home Evie.'

When I look over again his eyes are closed. For a moment I think he's asleep. Then I realise something is different. His chest is very still. There's a quiet, where before there was great noise.

It's lighter now. I can see the flask is still in his hands. I read the inscription engraved on it. *A lion is not concerned by the opinions of sheep.*

Later, after I've sat with him. Holding him. Crying, wetting the throw across his shoulders. After Janelle comes and finds us, and she cries and we stand there hugging each other. After all of that, I see the sky has softened into a forget-me-not blue. It's a beautiful, cloudless sky.

An infinity of blue.

I watch the sky for what feels like a long time, and then I ask Janelle to start making the calls.

I pick myself up and walk to the door. As the front gate slides back, the cameras start flashing. There are dozens of pigeons and TV crews. Vans parked all up the street. They run towards me, scrambling to point their lenses and microphones at me.

I take a deep breath and start talking.

GREY

Birth and death. They're not for the fainthearted.

Yet we've all been birthed. In some fashion or another, we've all been pulled to this world.

And who among us was not born to die? We're made from the bodies of dying stars: all we can ever be is borrowed time.

But we do not rise and fall alone. Those before you. Those who will come after you. Wherever you are, whoever you are, you are also part of their story.

We are all in this together.

Dust to dust, ashes to ashes? Nothing so dry. Nothing so desolate.

From the very start, life has always been wet.

How do I know? I've watched the whole great tapestry being strung.

First there was water. Great, roaring oceans: a rolling tempest of unformed possibility.

Then, from the sea – from the salt and tides – came blood.

Blue and green ran to red, and then there was me.

I am the memory of everything. The one who must keep score and remember it all.

I am the memory of all the blood.

—

But I promised you a story and I've been a little obscure. I apologise, I'm not used to being the one observed. Let me try to explain.

There is a beginning. Then there is what matters. And it is this:

Do you remember when I said there were pivotal points in time? Moments that pull shift, turning everything in a different direction. Perhaps I should have explained that these points in time are people.

For every generation a number of them are born. Weighty with star dust. A fixed number must always be alive, and for a period of time – some for minutes, others for decades – they are tested. It is their thoughts and deeds; their light on which everything perilously spins. They are the few upon which everything depends. Nothing matters more.

I don't use words like good and bad. After a while, these words are too simple. But there is a balance that must be kept. Light versus dark. It has always been this way.

If the light fails, all of us will fall.

These people, these pinpoints of light, they do not know what they are. They do not know when their test begins. It could be in a wooden cart. It could be in a mill's small, dusty infirmary. It could be down a lonely night-time road. It could be while waiting to order lunch at the sandwich bar around the corner. It could be you, reading this now, who is about to step into the light. Does that sound farfetched? Stranger than other facts you know to be true?

I don't have favourites. Each one of them has been extraordinary.

Literally one in a million. Rarer, in fact.

But Mina. *Mina.*

I sat with her there under the tree, long after her body had been carried away. I felt her light. I found her memories in the bloodied grass and held them tightly to me. Her taste for blackberries and fairness. All those shining thoughts and dreams. Her grace, and her talent for gratitude. The sensation of sailing at full wind. Her mother's neat black stitches. Her love of words. The dome of St Paul's. The smell of Billy's hair. Harry. The heat of Alden's hand on the arch of her back. The sound of rustling oak leaves.

Mina was one of the brightest lights. Her brilliance shone way beyond Berkeley Square. Her thoughts and deeds set off a great many things. That they weren't realised in her time makes them no less immense. Let me assure you again, no star goes unseen. The tree that falls in the forest *is* heard.

And Mina made a very great sound. She shone so very bright.

Because she lived, many other people did too. Not because of her death, because of her life: an important distinction. Had Mina lived longer, as she was meant to, we would have been richer still. But her influence continues.

Even the trees planted in her memory created ripples, stories of life.

Mina's own oak, grown from an acorn brought from the woods behind the cottage where she was born. Later etched with her name, now stands, greatest of the great oaks in Hyde Park.

From the children saved by Mina and Alden's law, to the people Rowland educated and elevated, many have flourished; helped light the way. Some of them went on to do interesting things, to have children who did interesting things. Claudine's daughter, Willa, product of a fond summer, and named for Mina, went on to do interesting things.

Two centuries later, on the other side of the world, I find myself watching a descendant of Willa's. And I have a feeling Every is about to do some *very. interesting* things.

MINA

Berkeley Square

At first it hurts. A blanket of panic and pain. Confusion. There are people around me. A circle of worried faces above me. I see the boy. Safe and unharmed, a halo of gold curls peering down. I try to smile to reassure him. It's okay: this is the right way around.

In my head I tell him to be good, to live great things.

There is a lot of yelling, directions. Someone carries me to the grass and lays me down. But I am past this. I am somewhere else. Another warm summer's evening. I hear Alden laughing. I am filled with so much love, so much gratitude for all that I have been given. My life has been such a good one.

There is blood. I know it's mine. It smells warm and earthy, and I know I am where I should be. My body softens and I let the movement go. I let the crosses and dashes on an old dress bring me home.

Deep, familiar as sleep, a wave of darkness comes over me.

Like a dreamy black sea.

Then I hear wind, wind through leaves. The sound of freedom. I think of everyone I love and I wrap them in my love for their lives ahead, and all that they are.

I open my eyes. I open my eyes one last time and I see that I'm lying under a tree and I look up at the leaves.

For a moment there are just leaves. Dancing and rustling green above me. Then one leaf loosens and floats up with the wind into the blue sky, and then there's nothing but blue.

THANK YOU

A book's journey into the world is as magical as any story's journey. People have been important characters along the way in this story. I have so much love and gratitude in my heart for all of them. But especially these ones.

Thank you Stephen Cheliotis, for being my person through thick and thin, including a global pandemic, a foot op and both our families, and for letting me have the living room to write in way more than my fair share. You're family, honey. Sorry about that.

I was very shy about who read early drafts. I'll be better next time.

Thank you Elaine Gowran, for your beautiful and generous heart.

Thank you Susanna Dinnage, my pineapple sister, for being such a kind early reader that you made me cry.

Thank you Jacq Carroll, for being insightful, entirely irreplaceable you.

Thank you Tracey Collins, for the champagne moments.

Thank you Rachel Jones, for reading and re-reading and being such a super-cutie all the times.

Thank you Charley Stone, for the neighbourly excellence and exquisite punctuation.

Thank you Anna Smith, Ben Robards and Jane Dunford for the crucial support wine and tequila evenings.

Thank you Mick 'BoC' Hollands for the consults and laughs.

Thank you Rob for Parliament, and thank you Jen, Will, Rob and Bryony for reading TMofB when it was just scraps of paper (and a less-than-ideal wordcount). You let me think those scraps could be a book. So much love to you for that. Let's always be Keeping On…

Thank you to the readers. You people rock. Thank you Donna Swajeski, Natalia Weissfeld and Brit Hayes. You three were the first and your feedback blew me away. I'll never forget reading your emails.

Thank you Ann and Derek Bird, for being so generous in spirit and time.

Thank you Vicki Heath Silk for making TMofB look so beautiful. You brought my cover dreams to life.

And to anyone who cares for Mina and Evie and Alden and Harry and Ty and Claudine and Janelle and Ford and Grey and the others so much that you're still reading now. Thank you. I see you. You are amazing, and you're one of us now.

Come find the rest of us at **www.ponylouder.com**

OCTOPUS IS COMING

Saylor Starling wants to be normal. Her family have other ideas.
And there's the issue with what her father does for a living.
He may work covertly for the government; he might just be
smuggling cocaine.

Against a backdrop of seventies counter-culture and eighties
excess, their journey takes them from hedonistic hippy communes
in Goa and devout ashrams in the mountains northeast of
Bangalore, to luxury penthouses in Europe and guns and madness
in one of Australia's most historic houses.

Finally, in an abandoned cattle farm in the outback wilderness of
Queensland, they come to the end of the road. Saylor must choose
between her family and herself.

A story based on real events.

For a sneak preview of Octopus and the first pages,
go to **www.ponylouder.com**